Ralph dropped the horse's reins so that he could use both hands to take the shawl and drape it around her shoulders.

'Thank you. There are rain clouds on the horizon. I am glad we are back in time to avoid a soaking.'

She was laughing, completely unaware of how pretty she looked with her windswept curls rioting around her bare head and her skin glowing from the fresh air.

Kiss her.

She was knotting the ends of her shawl, oblivious of his hands hovering over her shoulders. He snatched his hands away as she turned her head to address him.

'What say you, my lord? Will it last? Shall we be confined indoors by the inclement weather?'

She was peeping up at him through her lashes and he felt his blood stirring. It was unconsciously done, he would swear to it, but by God that look was inviting! With a silent oath he tore his eyes away from her. She was here for a purpose and he would not allow himself to be distract

AUTHOR NOTE

Some books start with a person—this one started with a title. THE SCARLET GOWN was always the premise for this romance: the idea of a man insisting a woman wear a specific gown. Why is it so important? Why would any woman do it? If you gave the same title and questions to twenty different authors I have no doubt you would get twenty very different stories: this is mine—a Regency romance.

As soon as I began weaving the story Lucy Halbrook came along, a spirited, independent young lady in need of employment. She travels far away from London to the country seat of Ralph, Lord Adversane, a man as hard and rugged as the Yorkshire moors that surround his house.

Ralph has his reasons for bringing Lucy to Adversane Hall and dictating the clothes she shall wear, but he is not used to sharing his thoughts with anyone. He is a man with secrets—a man who has forgotten how to laugh until Lucy comes into his life.

Ralph is interested in logic and science; Lucy is artistic and outspoken. It is inevitable that sparks will fly when they get together, and I hope you enjoy the fireworks!

THE SCARLET GOWN

Sarah Mallory

Published in Great Britain 2014
by Mills & Boon, an imprint of Harlequin (UK) Limited,
Eton House, 18-24 Paradise Road, Richmond, Surrey, TW9 1SR

© 2014 Sarah Mallory

ISBN: 978 0 263 90968 5

Harlequin (UK) Limited's policy is to use papers that are natural,
renewable and recyclable products and made from wood grown in
sustainable forests. The logging and manufacturing processes conform
to the legal environmental regulations of the country of origin.

Printed and bound in Spain
by Blackprint CPI, Barcelona

Sarah Mallory was born in Bristol, and now lives in an old farmhouse on the edge of the Pennines with her husband and family. She left grammar school at sixteen to work in companies as varied as stockbrokers, marine engineers, insurance brokers, biscuit manufacturers and even a quarrying company. Her first book was published shortly after the birth of her daughter. She has published more than a dozen books under the pen-name of Melinda Hammond, winning the Reviewers' Choice Award from singletitles.com for *Dance for a Diamond* and the Historical Novel Society's Editors' Choice for *Gentlemen in Question*. Sarah Mallory has also twice won the Romantic Novelists' Association's RONA Rose® Award for 2012 and 2013 for *The Dangerous Lord Darrington* and *Beneath the Major's Scars*.

Previous novels by the same author:

THE WICKED BARON
MORE THAN A GOVERNESS
  (part of *On Mothering Sunday*)
WICKED CAPTAIN, WAYWARD WIFE
THE EARL'S RUNAWAY BRIDE
DISGRACE AND DESIRE
TO CATCH A HUSBAND…
SNOWBOUND WITH THE NOTORIOUS RAKE
  (part of *An Improper Regency Christmas*)
THE DANGEROUS LORD DARRINGTON
BENEATH THE MAJOR'S SCARS*
BEHIND THE RAKE'S WICKED WAGER*
BOUGHT FOR REVENGE
LADY BENEATH THE VEIL**
AT THE HIGHWAYMAN'S PLEASURE **

The Notorious Coale Brothers
**Linked by character

And in Mills & Boon® *Undone!* eBooks:

THE TANTALISING MISS COALE*

And in M&B:

THE ILLEGITIMATE MONTAGUE
  (part of *Castonbury Park* Regency mini-series)

**Did you know that some of these novels
are also available as eBooks?
Visit www.millsandboon.co.uk**

DEDICATION

To Cecilia and David.

Thank you for preserving the moor
that inspired a large part of this story!

Chapter One

Mrs Killinghurst's register office was well known as the saviour of many a gently bred young lady who had fallen upon hard times and needed to earn a living. Mrs Killinghurst specialised in finding employment for such young ladies as companions, governesses or even seamstresses, depending upon their accomplishments. Her offices occupied a suite of rooms above a hatter's shop in Bond Street, and young ladies wishful of finding employment could slip along the narrow alley beside the shop and through the freshly painted doorway with its discreet brass plate.

Miss Lucy Halbrook had already made one visit to Mrs Killinghurst's establishment and now, a fortnight later, she was returning to the office, as instructed by the proprietress herself, with high hopes of obtaining the gainful employment she so desperately needed. When her father

had died twelve months ago Lucy had been prepared for life to change for herself and Mama,
but it was only after the funeral that Lucy discovered just how poor they really were. They
had been taken in by Mrs Halbrook's invalid sister, but Lucy soon realised that although Mama
had found a niche as nurse-companion to Mrs
Edgeworth, she herself was constantly harassed
by Mr Edgeworth. Lucy had always thought it a
little odd that the female servants in her aunt's
house were all rather mature, but within days of
moving in she knew the reason for it. She had
so far managed to evade her uncle's lascivious
attentions but she must find somewhere else to
live, and soon. If she was honest with herself,
she also wanted a little more independence. Her
father's death had been painful, but her mother's sudden revelation that they were penniless
had been even harder to bear. They had never
been rich, and it was not just their poverty, but
the knowledge that Mama had kept the situation from her. And what of her father, a man she
had adored? To find that he was not the hero she
had thought him was a severe blow. If only they
had told her. After all, it was not as if she was
a child. Surely they could have trusted her with
the truth when she reached her majority, three
years ago? She might even have been able to
help. By finding employment, for example, as
she was doing now.

Lucy hurried along New Bond Street, dodging between the crowds of fashionable ladies and gentlemen who were taking advantage of the mild spring weather to stroll along, giving more attention to the shop windows than to where they were going. At last she reached the hatter's and stepped quickly into the alley. It was darker than she had expected and it took her a moment to realise this was because someone was standing at the far end, blocking the light.

Her step faltered, but she pressed on. After all, Mrs Killinghurst was expecting her and she was not to be put off. She might wish she had worn a veil, but since there was no help for it, Lucy continued towards the door. The man— for it was undoubtedly a man—had apparently just emerged from Mrs Killinghurst's door, so he was either looking for work or for someone to employ. The latter, she thought as her eyes grew accustomed to the shadows and she took in at a glance his coat of blue superfine, buckskin breeches and black boots. In fact, he might well have purchased his coat from Mr Weston's hallowed portals in nearby Old Bond Street, for it fitted him perfectly with never a wrinkle to mar its elegance. His boots, too, shone with a smooth, highly polished gloss. The buckskins may well have been similarly free of creases, but Lucy had felt a frisson of something she did not quite understand when she had first observed the man and now she dared not let her eyes dwell on those muscular limbs.

Instead, she kept her head up, chin defiantly raised. She would not stare at the ground like some humble, subservient creature. Consequently she could not avoid at least one quick glance at the man's face. It was rugged rather than handsome, black-browed and with a deep cleft in his chin. There was a latent strength about him that sat oddly with his fashionable dress—clearly he was no Bond Street Beau. Whatever his status, Lucy's main concern was that he was blocking her way. His curly-brimmed hat almost brushed the roof of the alley and his broad shoulders filled the narrow space.

She observed all this in the time it took her to cover the short distance between them, and it struck her in the same instant that he was the most solid and immovable object she had ever encountered. She stopped, but refused to be intimidated and returned his direct gaze with a steady look. His grey eyes were curiously compelling and again she felt that tremor run through her. An odd, unfamiliar mixture of excitement and attraction that had her wanting to know more about this man and at the same time to turn around and run for her life.

Lucy quelled such feelings immediately. She was not the sort to run away from a problem— not that there had ever been many problems in her life until now. She realised a little sadly that her parents had protected her from the harsher realities of life. Perhaps a little too much. But all that was at an end. She must now stand up for herself and that meant not being intimidated by this solid wall of man standing in her way. She wondered if she was going to have to ask him to move, but at that moment he stepped back, pushing the door open with one hand.

Silently, Lucy sailed past him and up the stairs. She had the uncomfortable sensation that he was watching her ascent, for her spine tingled uncomfortably, but when she reached the landing and looked back there was no one below and the door was firmly shut.

An iron-haired woman was guarding the small reception room at the top of the stairs. She showed Lucy into Mrs Killinghurst's office, invited her to remove her cloak and bonnet and sit down, then she shut the door upon her. Left alone, Lucy folded her cloak neatly and laid it on a chair then carefully placed her bonnet on top. There was no mirror in the room, so she could only put her hands up to make sure her soft brown hair was still neatly confined in a knot at the back of her head. She had put on the same high-necked gown she had worn for her first interview, a plain closed robe of pewter-coloured wool, and hoped she portrayed the modest, unassuming character that an employer would be looking for.

After a few moments alone, Lucy became prey to uncertainty. She thought over her previous visit, wondering if she had perhaps mistaken the day.

No, she had been sitting on this very chair, facing Mrs Killinghurst across the desk, exactly two weeks ago. Lucy had been encouraged by the lady's businesslike air, and once she had explained her circumstances and answered a number of searching questions, the lady had risen and disappeared through a door at the back of the room. Some personal inner sanctum, thought Lucy, for she had glimpsed the carved and gilded edge of a picture frame. This had surprised her a little, for the walls of the office and the reception room were singularly bare of ornament, and Lucy had been puzzling over this when Mrs Killinghurst had returned, saying that, yes, she did think there was a suitable position for Lucy.

'It is rather an unusual position but perfectly respectable, I assure you, and the remuneration is extremely generous, considering that it is only a temporary position. You will only be required for a short period—part of May and the whole of June. However, I need to ascertain from my client—that is—you will need to come back. Shall we say two weeks from today, at eleven o'clock?'

Lucy had agreed immediately. Another two

weeks in her uncle's house would be a trial, but she would manage, somehow. The date and time of the next meeting had been repeated and confirmed, Lucy remembered, with Mrs Killinghurst promising that she would then be in a position to explain the post in detail. Lucy had thanked her and prepared to leave, but now she recalled that at that point the proprietress had shown a diffidence that had not been apparent throughout the rest of their meeting.

'Good day to you, Miss Halbrook and—my dear, should you find another post in the meantime I hope you will feel free to take it. A little note to me explaining the situation will suffice...'

Lucy had looked at her in surprise.

'I assure you, Mrs Killinghurst, I am more than content to wait two weeks, unless perhaps you think there is some doubt about my suitability for the post you have in mind?'

'Oh, no, no, I think you are eminently suitable.' Thinking back, Lucy remembered the slightly anxious timbre of the lady's voice, as if she regretted the circumstance. She had looked a little uncomfortable as she continued, 'Of course, this post is by no means guaranteed, and if something else should come up I would be failing you if I did not advise you to accept it.'

'But you do not have anything else to offer me?'

'Well, no, not at present.'

Lucy had thought it an odd way to go about business, suggesting that she should look elsewhere for employment, but she guessed it was some sort of a test of her loyalty, and she had been quick to reassure Mrs Killinghurst that she would return in two weeks' time at the agreed hour.

'And here I am,' she announced to the empty room. 'Ready and waiting to know my fate.'

The rattle of the doorknob made her jump, and she wondered if someone had been listening, for at that moment the door to the inner sanctum opened, and Mrs Killinghurst came in, smiling and apologising for keeping Lucy waiting. She went to her desk and in her haste left the door slightly ajar.

'Now then, Miss Halbrook, where were we?' She sat down, pulling a sheaf of papers towards her. 'Ah, yes. The character references I have received for you are excellent. As I mentioned when we last met, this is an unusual post. My client is looking for an accomplished young lady of gentle birth to spend some time at his house in the north.'

A movement from Lucy caused the lady to pause.

'Excuse me, ma'am, but your client is a married gentleman, I assume?'

Mrs Killinghurst shook her head.

'He is a widower, but quite respectable,' she added quickly, a little too hastily perhaps.

Lucy felt her heart sinking. She decided she must speak frankly.

'Mrs Killinghurst, is—is there anything, ah, *questionable* about this particular post?'

'Oh, no, no, nothing like that! My client assures me that a chaperone will be provided, and you will be treated with the utmost respect during your stay. You are to live at the house, as his guest. And the remuneration is extremely generous.'

She mentioned a sum that made Lucy's eyebrows fly up.

'But I do not understand. Your, ah, client wishes to *pay* me to be a guest in his house?'

'Yes.'

'But, why?'

Mrs Killinghurst began to straighten the papers on her desk.

'I believe he wishes you to be there as his hostess.'

Lucy's disappointment was searing. For the past two weeks she had been looking forward to this meeting, speculating about the 'lucrative post' that Mrs Killinghurst had in mind. A governess, perhaps, or companion to some elderly and infirm lady, or even a gentleman. The temporary nature of the post had indicated that perhaps she was being engaged to make someone's last months on this earth as comfortable as possible. Now she realised that her daydreams and speculation had been wildly inaccurate and naive. An unmarried man—even a widower— would not hire a hostess for any respectable purpose. Thoughts of Uncle Edgeworth and his wandering hands came to her mind.

She rose, saying coldly, 'I am very sorry, Mrs Killinghurst, but this is not the kind of employment I envisaged. If you had only told me a little more about this post two weeks ago we might have saved ourselves a great deal of inconvenience.'

She had already turned to leave when she was halted by the sound of a deep, male voice behind her.

'Perhaps, Mrs Killinghurst, you would allow me to explain to the young lady?'

Lucy whipped around. Standing in the doorway to the inner sanctum was the man she had seen below.

His solid form had filled the alleyway, but here in this small office he looked even more imposing. Mrs Killinghurst rose from her seat, but she barely reached his shoulder and only emphasised the man's size. He had removed his hat to display his black hair, cut ruthlessly short, and his impassive countenance did nothing to dispel Lucy's first impression of a stern, unyielding character.

She was aware of the latent power of the man. It was apparent in every line of his body, from the rough-hewn countenance, through those broad shoulders to his feet, planted firmly, slightly apart, as if he was ready to take on the world.

Ready to pounce on her. This man was dangerous, she was convinced of it, but some tiny, treacherous part of her found that danger very attractive.

Alarmed by her own reaction Lucy stepped back, one hand behind her feeling for the door handle.

'I really do not think there is any need—'

'Oh, but there is,' he said. 'You've waited two weeks to learn about this position; it would be a pity if you were to leave now without knowing just what it entailed, don't you think?' He spoke quietly, but with a natural authority that brooked no argument and when he invited her to return to her seat, Lucy found herself complying.

He indicated to Mrs Killinghurst that she should sit down and while the lady was settling herself Lucy made a mental note that if this stranger should try to get between her and the door to the reception area she would flee, however foolish and cowardly that might appear. Thankfully, though, the gentleman contented himself with moving to one side of the room where both ladies could see him. He nodded to Mrs Killinghurst.

'Perhaps, ma'am, you would be good enough to introduce me.'

'Yes, yes, of course. Miss Halbrook, this is Lord Adversane, my client.'

He bowed to Lucy, who was surprised at the elegance with which he performed this courtesy. For such a large man he had the lithe grace of a natural athlete. She inclined her head in acknowledgement, but remained silent, waiting to hear what he had to say.

'Mrs Killinghurst has told you that I am in need of your services for my house in Yorkshire,' he began. 'Adversane is the largest estate and the most prominent house in the area. Since the death of my wife, I have lived there very quietly, but you will appreciate that this has had an adverse effect upon the neighbourhood since I am not employing so many staff, nor is the housekeeper ordering so much from the local tradesmen. I think it is time to open up the house again and invite guests—family and friends—to join me there. However, I require a hostess.'

Lucy nodded. 'I understand that, my lord, but surely there is some lady within your family who would be more than willing to fulfil that role.'

A sardonic gleam lit his eyes.

'Oh, yes, dozens of 'em!'

'Then I do not see—'

'The thing is,' he interrupted her ruthlessly, 'I have been a widower for nigh on two years now and my family and friends are all determined I should be much happier if I were to marry again. To this end they are constantly badgering me to find a wife.' He paused for a moment. 'What I am looking for, Miss Halbrook, is not only a hostess, but a fiancée.'

Lucy knew she was staring at him. She also knew that her mouth was open, but it was some moments before she could command her muscles to work so that she could close it. Lord Adversane continued as if he had said nothing out of the ordinary.

'I have invited a number of guests to stay at Adversane for the summer and I need a young woman to pose as my future wife. She must have all the accomplishments of a young lady of good family and her reputation must be above reproach. From everything Mrs Killinghurst has told me, you are perfectly suited to fulfil this role.'

'Thank you,' Lucy responded with a touch of asperity. 'Let me make sure I understand you. You wish to enact this…this charade to stop everyone, er, *badgering* you?'

'Exactly.'

'If you will forgive me for saying so, my lord,

from the little I have seen of you I cannot believe
that you would allow *anyone* to badger you!'

Ralph regarded the little figure before him and
felt a stir of appreciation. The chit was dressed
in a dowdy grey gown, demure as a nun, yet she
was not afraid to voice her opinion or to meet his
eyes with a challenging sparkle in her own. A
smile tugged at the corners of his mouth.

'Ah, but then, you do not know my family.'
This was unanswerable, but clearly did not reassure the girl. He could tell she was seeking the
words to decline gracefully and take her leave,
so he added, 'I realise this is not the post you
were expecting to be offered, Miss Halbrook,
but I have considered my dilemma and conclude
that hiring a hostess is the best solution.' How
much more to tell her? He added, a shade of impatience in his voice, 'I am an educated man. I
have never yet found a problem that could not be
solved by logic. Believe me, there is not the least
risk to your person or your good name. Indeed, it
is imperative that your stay at Adversane is perfectly respectable if we are to convince everyone that the engagement is genuine. When the
time comes to part I shall make sure it is understood that the decision was yours—you may be
assured that those who know me will not find
that at all surprising—and you will walk away
with enough money to allow you to live in comfort and style for at least the next year. A hand-

some remuneration for less than two months' work.' He paused. 'So, Miss Halbrook, what do you say?'

Preposterous. Outrageous. Not to be considered.

These were the first words that came to Lucy's mind, but she did not utter them. Her situation, living in her uncle's house, was not comfortable. To spend six weeks as the guest of Lord Adversane, no doubt living very luxuriously, would not be a hardship, and with the money she earned she would not need to rush into another post for some time. In fact, she might even be able to invest the money—in a shop, say, or a little school—and provide herself with an income. She might even be able to travel. She forced her gaze away from those compelling grey eyes and addressed Mrs Killinghurst.

'You can assure me there is nothing untoward in this?'

'Nothing at all, Miss Halbrook. It is unusual, but you may be sure I looked into the matter thoroughly before I accepted Lord Adversane's commission. After all, I have my own reputation and that of my business to consider.' Mrs Killinghurst tapped the paper on the desk in front of her. 'The contract is drawn up, which will make everything legally binding. All that is required is your signature.'

Lucy hesitated. The offer was very tempting, and neither Mrs Killinghurst nor the advertisements she had scanned in the newspaper could offer anything else. And what choice did she have? Her uncle's attentions were becoming more persistent and it could only be a matter of time before her aunt and her mother became aware of a situation which Lucy knew would distress them greatly.

'Very well,' she said. 'I will do it.'

Ralph watched in silence as she came to the desk to sign the contract. A slight doubt shook him. Perhaps it would have been better to hire an actress to play the role he had envisaged, but the danger of being found out would be that much greater, and the matter was too important to take that risk. He would not put it past his family to investigate his supposed fiancée's background.

No, overall Mrs Killinghurst had succeeded very well. Miss Lucy Halbrook was everything he required and her breeding was impeccable, his family would find no fault there. She was not quite as tall as he had hoped, and her hair was not guinea-gold but a soft honey-brown. She also had rather more spirit than he had expected and he found himself wanting to tease her, to bring that sparkle to her eyes. He would have to be careful about that. He had been brought up to believe a gentleman should not flirt with a lady under his protection. However, he needed someone who could fulfil the role he had in mind convincingly, so she needed to be at least moderately attractive, and beneath that dowdy gown Miss Halbrook's figure looked to be good. His eyes dwelled on the rounded bottom displayed beneath the grey folds as she bent over the desk to sign her name. It might even be very good.

He quickly suppressed that line of thought. The woman was being hired for a specific purpose and that did not include dalliance, however enjoyable that might be. No, his reasons for taking her to Adversane were much more serious than that. Deadly serious.

Chapter Two

Lord Adversane insisted upon sending his luxurious carriage to carry Lucy to the north country. She had never travelled in such style, and as the elegant equipage bowled out of London she was forced to admit that there was something to be said for being betrothed to a rich man.

Two weeks had passed since that second visit to Mrs Killinghurst's registry office. Lucy had signed her contract and stepped back into New Bond Street with a thick roll of banknotes in her reticule, her new employer requesting her to buy whatever was necessary for her journey to Adversane. He had also given her the name of a very exclusive modiste and told her she might order anything she wished and have it charged to his account.

Lucy had felt compelled to question this.

'Forgive me, but if your wife is—that is, if you

have been a widower for two years, will you still *have* an account?'

'Oh, my wife never bought anything from Celeste.'

Lucy had blushed hotly at the implication of his careless response, and had immediately given him back his card. He had grinned at that, giving Lucy the unsettling feeling that he was teasing her.

'Don't worry,' he said. 'There is a very good dressmaker near Adversane who will provide you with everything you need for the duration of your stay. I shall arrange for her to call on you once you are settled in.'

Recalling the incident, she wondered again if she had been wise to accept employment with a stranger and in a house so far away from everyone and everything she knew. She had looked out her uncle's copy of *The New Peerage* and learned that Ralph Adversane was the fifth baron, that he owned several properties, his principal seat being Adversane Hall, in Yorkshire. There was no mention of a wife, but she knew this edition of the Peerage was at least five years old, so presumably the marriage had taken place after that date.

Discreet enquiries of her family had brought forth very little information. Her aunt, who was an avid reader of the Court and Society pages, admitted she had *heard* of Lord Adversane, but it appeared he was an infrequent visitor to London, or at least, thought Lucy, to those circles that warranted a mention in the newspapers, even if he was well known in less respectable circles, whose ladies patronised a certain expensive modiste. She must therefore trust to Mrs Killinghurst's assurance that she made thorough enquiries into the veracity of every client who came to her.

However, just as a precaution, Lucy had kept back some of the money Lord Adversane had given her and stitched it into the hem of her cloak. It was not a lot, but sufficient to pay for her journey back to London, and knowing that she had a means of escape should she need it, she now settled back against the comfortable squabs of the travelling carriage and prepared to enjoy herself.

Lord Adversane was waiting for her when she arrived at his country seat. He was dressed very much as she had last seen him, in blue coat and buckskins, and as the coach drew up on the sweeping drive he strode across to open the door and hand her down.

'Welcome, Miss Halbrook. How was your journey?'

'Extremely entertaining.' Lucy gave a little gurgle of laughter at his look of surprise, her head still buzzing with the excitement of all the new sights and sounds she had experienced. 'I have never before been farther north than Hertfordshire, you see, so it was an adventure. Of course, I doubt I would have enjoyed it so much if it had not been undertaken in a fast and comfortable vehicle, with your servants to take care of everything for me, and overnight stops arranged at the very best coaching inns. I am very grateful to you for your solicitude, my lord.'

'I could do nothing less for my future wife.'

Lucy blushed, but quickly realised that his words were for the benefit of the servants, as was the kiss he bestowed upon her fingers. After all, if this charade was to work then everyone must believe it.

Collecting her thoughts, she stood for a moment looking up at the house. It was a very large building in the Jacobean style with stone transom and mullion windows set between diapered red brickwork. Her first impression was that it had a frowning aspect, but she put this down to the overcast day and the fact that they were standing on the drive and the house appeared to tower over them. Her eyes moved to the stone pediment above the entrance, which framed an intricately carved cartouche.

'The Adversane coat of arms,' he said, following her glance. 'The house was built for the first Baron Adversane at the time of the Restoration.'

Still buzzing with the excitement of the jour-

ney, Lucy could not resist giving voice to a mischievous thought.

'And will the shades of your illustrious ances-
tors approve of me?'

'I have no idea. Shall we go in?'

Chastened by his stony retort, Lucy allowed
him to escort her into the house. The butler was
waiting for them in the entrance passage with a
line of servants, all of whom bowed or curtseyed
as Lord Adversane led her past them.

'Byrne will not introduce them to you today,'
he said as he took her into the Great Hall. 'You
are here ostensibly as a guest, but of course they
all know we are betrothed because I mentioned it
to my cousin in front of the housekeeper. Come
along and meet her. She is waiting in the drawing room.'

'The housekeeper?' asked Lucy, suddenly
quite daunted by the grandeur of her surroundings.

'My cousin, Mrs Dean.'

There was no mistaking the impatience in his
voice, and Lucy gave herself a mental shake. It
was too late now for second thoughts. She must
concentrate upon her new role.

Ralph swore silently, ashamed of his own ill
humour. Perhaps it was understandable that he
should be on edge, knowing how important it
was that the girl fulfil her role to perfection, but

surely he did not need to be quite so serious? He gave an inward sigh. How long had it been since anyone had teased him? Even his sisters rarely did so now. Since Helene's death they had treated him with more sympathy than he deserved. After all it was not as if he had loved his wife. He had cared for her, yes, but the strain of living with such a nervous, timid creature, of watching his every utterance, curbing every impatient remark, had taken its toll. He had forgotten what it was like to laugh…

He escorted Miss Halbrook into the drawing room where his cousin was busy filling a teapot from a spirit kettle.

'Ah, there you are, Ralph. And this must be our guest.' Ariadne carefully set down the teapot and came forwards to greet them. As she approached she fixed her rather myopic gaze upon Lucy, frowned a little then turned a puzzled look upon him. He spoke quickly, before she could voice her thoughts.

'It is indeed, Cousin.' He added quietly, 'I thought it best to tell Mrs Dean the truth, Miss Halbrook. She will introduce you to everyone as a young friend who is spending a few weeks with her, but in reality everyone will believe that you are my fiancée, is that not so, Cousin?'

He was relieved to see Ariadne's frown clear as she took Miss Halbrook's hands.

Lucy. He must get used to calling her Lucy.

'Oh, indeed. You know how quickly gossip spreads in the country, my dear. Now, before we go any further I should tell you that I am so pleased my cousin has asked me to help him with this.'

He smiled. 'I persuaded Ariadne to leave her comfortable little house in Bath and join me for the summer.'

'There is very little persuasion needed to bring me to Adversane, Cousin, and you know it.' Mrs Dean chuckled. She pulled Lucy close and kissed her cheek. 'Welcome, my dear. Ralph has indeed told me all about it, although I really do not see—but there, it will be a pleasure to have this house filled with people again.'

Lucy relaxed in the face of such a friendly welcome. Mrs Dean led her over to a sofa and gently pushed her down onto the seat, chattering all the time.

'Now, my dear, I have prepared some tea, if you would like it. I find it very restorative after a long journey. You have come all the way from London, Ralph tells me—more than two hundred miles! You must be exhausted.'

'In which case brandy might be more appropriate,' put in Lord Adversane.

Lucy ignored him. He had snubbed her once already, so she would not risk responding to his remark.

'Tea would be very welcome, Mrs Dean, thank you.'

'Oh, do call me Ariadne, my dear. And I shall address you as Lucy, if you will allow me.'

'Gladly.' She glanced around to make sure they were alone. 'Is it safe to talk in here?'

'Perfectly, as long as we do not raise our voices.' Lord Adversane poured himself a glass of brandy from the decanter on the sideboard and took a seat opposite the sofa. He said conversationally, 'What do you want to talk about?'

'I should have thought that was obvious,' she retorted. 'We have not had the opportunity to discuss my story. We will need to agree on the particulars, if I am to be at all convincing.'

He sat back in his chair and stretched out his legs, crossing one booted foot over the other.

'It would be sensible to keep as close to the truth as possible. There is no need for false names or imaginary families. We met in London, but our betrothal has not yet been made public because you have been in mourning for your father—'

'How do you know that?'

'Mrs Killinghurst apprised me of all your details, naturally.'

'Naturally.' She eyed him with growing resentment. 'You appear to know everything about me, my lord.'

'Not *everything*, Miss Halbrook.' There was

a sardonic gleam in his hard, grey eyes as they rested upon her. So he was amusing himself at her expense, yet her light-hearted comments had met with a chilly rebuff. She put up her chin.

'I know no more of you than I have been able to discover from *The Peerage*,' she told him. 'I am ill prepared for this role.'

He waved a dismissive hand. 'We have three weeks before the first house guests arrive. Time enough to get to know one another. It will be my pleasure to tell you anything you wish to know.'

His very reasonable response made Lucy grind her teeth, but she swallowed her irritation and tried to match his cool tone.

'Perhaps the first thing we need to ascertain is why my mother did not accompany me on this visit.'

'If we are keeping to the truth, then you have not told her about me. She thinks you have been employed as companion to some elderly invalid, is that not correct?'

'Well, well, yes, that is what we agreed I would tell her—'

'And it gave you the excuse to remove yourself from your uncle's unwelcome attentions.'

'I never told Mrs Killinghurst *that*,' Lucy retorted, her face flaming.

Mrs Dean gave a little tut and busied herself with the tea tray, but Lord Adversane merely shrugged.

'It is the truth, is it not? I made a few enquiries of my own before engaging you, Miss Halbrook, and what I learned of Silas Edgeworth did not lead me to think he would be able to keep his hands off a pretty young girl living beneath his roof.'

'Ralph, you are putting Miss Halbrook to the blush,' Mrs Dean reprimanded him in her gentle way. She handed Lucy a cup of tea. 'You may be sure there will be nothing like *that* going on at Adversane, my dear. My cousin may have hired you to prevent his family from importuning him, but his reasons for inviting me to act as your chaperone are to make sure that your stay here is not marred by any impropriety.' She rose. 'Now, if you will excuse me for a moment, I must go and check that your trunks have been carried upstairs and everything is as it should be.'

With a vague smile she bustled off, leaving Lucy alone with Lord Adversane. There was an uneasy silence as the door closed behind her. Lucy's glance slid to her host.

'I know,' he said, a measure of understanding softening his hard eyes. 'She tells you there will be no indecorum here, then promptly leaves us alone. I'm afraid you will have to accustom yourself to it. We are supposed to be engaged, you know.'

'Yes, of course.'

'If I have made you uncomfortable then I am sorry for it.'

His blunt apology surprised her. She put down her cup and, to cover her agitation, she raised her eyes to the fireplace. 'The overmantel is very finely carved. Grinling Gibbons?'

'Yes. My ancestor paid him the princely sum of forty pounds for it. Heaven knows what it would cost today.'

'If you could find someone skilled enough to do it,' she replied. 'My father was an artist, but of course Mrs Killinghurst will have told you. He was a great admirer of the old masters like Gibbons.'

'I am aware of that. And I knew your father.' Her brows went up and he explained. 'At Somerset House. It is the home of the Royal Society as well as the Royal Academy. We met there once or twice when I was attending lectures. My condolences for your loss.'

The words were spoken in a matter-of-fact tone, but Lucy felt the tears prickle at the back of her eyes. Rather than show any weakness she rose and went across to the window, where she stood looking out at the fine prospect, although she saw little of it, her thoughts going back to happier times.

'Papa used to take me to his studio sometimes, and encourage me to try my hand at painting.'

'There are many fine views at Adversane for you to capture.'

'I brought my sketchbook with the intention of doing just that, but as for painting—I enjoy working in oils and watercolours but I do not have Papa's gift. When I was a child I loved best to curl up in a chair and watch him at work. He had a passion for the picturesque. Vast, dramatic landscapes.' She thought of the hills and valleys she had seen on her journey. How her father would have loved them. She gave a little shrug. 'But everyone wanted portraits.'

'From the work of your father's I have seen he was very good and in demand.'

'You wonder, then, why it is I need to earn a living.' Lucy bit her lip. She had never spoken of this to anyone, but now felt a need to explain. 'He drank to excess. And gambled. I only discovered the truth after his death. With his talent, the money he earned might have paid for one or other of those vices and still allowed him to provide for his family, but together...'

'Disastrous,' he said bluntly. 'And your mother, did she—was it an arranged marriage?'

'Yes. She had a large dowry. He was a younger son, you see, and needed to marry well. Unfortunately the settlements were badly drawn up and very little was secured upon her. The money was all spent years ago.'

The room seemed to grow a little darker. The

cloud outside the window had thickened and a blustery wind agitated the trees, threatening rain. She turned and came back to the sofa, throwing off her melancholy to say brightly, 'For all that they were very much in love.'

So much so that they united to keep me in ignorance of our poverty.

The swift, unbidden thought twisted like a knife in her ribs.

Ralph saw the sudden crease in her brow and the way she folded her arms across her stomach, as if to defend herself. But from what? Her parents' happiness? Not all arranged marriages ended in love, as he knew to his cost. Bitterness made him reply more curtly than he intended.

'They were very fortunate, then.' Her eyes were upon him, questioning, but he did not wish to explain himself. He looked up with relief as the door opened. 'And here is Ariadne returned. I take it the rooms are in readiness for our guest, Cousin?' He rose, glad of the opportunity to get away. This young woman unsettled him. 'If you will excuse me, I have business that requires my attention. Until dinnertime, Miss Halbrook.'

Mrs Dean escorted Lucy to her room, talking all the way. She was very knowledgeable about the house and by the time they reached the upper floor Lucy knew its history, including the im-

provements made by the fourth baron, Ralph's
father. Lucy let the lady's chatter flow over her
while she tried to take in the stunning beauty of
the interior. Baroque carvings and plasterwork
vied for her attention with dozens of magnificent paintings.

'And here we are in the Long Gallery,' said
Mrs Dean, puffing slightly from having talked
all the way up the stairs. 'The principal bedchambers lead off the corridor just along here
and at the end of the gallery is the passage to
the east wing, where all the guests will be ac-
commodated.'

'I have never seen such splendid interiors,' remarked Lucy. She stopped to watch two servants
carefully hanging a large painting upon the far
wall, while a third stood back and directed them
as to the correct alignment. 'Has Lord Adversane made a new purchase?'

'No, no, it is not new. I suppose my cousin
thought it would look better here.'

Lucy regarded the painting with some surprise. It was a dark and rather nondescript view
of some classical ruins, and looked out of place
amongst the portraits of past barons and their
wives. Mrs Dean touched her arm.

'Shall we go on?' She led the way into a dim
corridor running parallel to the gallery and
threw open a door at one end. 'The two main

bedrooms are here. You will be occupying the mistress's bedchamber—'

'Oh, but I do not think I should!'

Lucy stopped in the doorway, but Mrs Dean urged her to enter.

'Lord Adversane thought it necessary,' she said, closing the door behind them. 'If my cousin truly intended to make you his wife then this is the apartment he would choose for you.'

Lucy's reluctance must have shown clearly on her face, for Mrs Dean smiled and patted her arm.

'You need have no fear of impropriety, my dear. Believe me, Adversane was not at all happy about putting you in his wife's room, but he knows it must be so, if his family are to believe he is serious about marrying you. There is a dressing room through that door where your maid will sleep—he has appointed one for you, of course. She has already unpacked your trunk, you see, and has probably gone off to fetch your hot water.'

Lucy made no further protest, and when Mrs Dean left her she wandered around the room, taking in her surroundings. The furniture was dark and heavy, the huge tester bed hung with faded brocade and while the walls were covered in a pretty Chinese wallpaper it was of no very recent date. In fact, there was nothing new in the room at all, and nothing to give any clue to the character of the last occupant. The brushes resting on the dressing table were Lucy's and the linen press held only the meagre supply of clothes she had brought with her. All the other drawers and cupboards were quite empty. One part of her was relieved, for she would have felt even more of an impostor if the chamber had been redolent of the late Lady Adversane. As it was, there was nothing to say this was not a guest room, albeit a very grand one.

Knowing it would be sensible to rest before the dinner hour, Lucy stretched herself on the bed, determined to go over all the questions she wished to put to her host when they met again, but within a very few minutes she was sound asleep.

She awoke when the door to her room opened and a shy, breathless voice said, 'Ooh, ma'am, I'm didn't mean to disturb you, but Mrs Green says its time I brought up your hot water and made you ready to go down to dinner—'

'That is quite all right.' Lucy sat up, stretching. 'You are to be my maid, I take it?'

'Aye, ma'am—miss.'

'And who is Mrs Green?'

'The housekeeper, miss. She sent me up.' The young girl put down the heavy jug on the wash stand and bobbed a curtsey. 'And I am Ruthie, miss, if you please.'

'Well, Ruthie, perhaps you would help me out

of this gown.' Lucy slid off the bed. 'I am afraid it is sadly crumpled and not a little grubby. I have been travelling in it for days.'

'I know, miss. From London,' said Ruthie triumphantly as she unfastened Lucy's travelling dress and laid it over a chair. 'Everyone's that pleased to see you. Mrs Green says the house has been too long without a mistress.'

'Oh, but I am not—'

Lucy's involuntary exclamation had the effect of making the maid jump back, her hands clasped nervously in front of her.

'Ooh, miss, I'm that sorry, I forgot we wasn't meant to say anything!'

Lucy gazed in some dismay at the maid's woebegone face. So word had spread, just as Adversane had planned. She nodded and said gently, 'Well, do not mention it again. Now, I think I saw my green gown in the press, perhaps you will lay that out for me.'

It was her only evening gown, a plain robe of French cambric with puff sleeves and a modest neckline. Lucy thought it would look very dull against the splendid interiors of the house, but it was all she had and it would have to do.

Lucy found her new maid very willing and eager to help. Ruthie carried away Lucy's travelling gown and half-boots, promising to clean them up as good as new, then came hurrying back, determined to help Lucy to dress for dinner. Her enthusiasm was endearing, but Lucy was a little reluctant to let her do more than brush out her hair.

'Oh, but I can do it, miss,' said Ruthie, as Lucy sat before the looking glass. 'Lady Adversane's maid showed me how to dress hair in several styles. O'course that were a couple of years ago now, but I'm sure I can remember.'

Lucy glanced at the little clock. There was plenty of time to brush it all out and start again, if necessary.

'Very well, let us see what you can do,' she said, smiling. 'All I wish this evening is for you to put it up in a simple knot.'

Ruthie's face fell. 'No ringlets, miss?'

'No ringlets.'

The young maid looked a little disappointed, but she set about her task with a will.

'You were training to be a lady's maid?' asked Lucy as Ruthie concentrated on unpinning and brushing out each shining lock.

'Oh, aye, miss, I was. Lady Adversane's maid broke her arm, you see, so Mrs Green sent me up to help her.' She gave a gusty sigh. 'Oh, my lady was *so* pretty, with her golden curls and blue, blue eyes, like the china doll they keep in the nursery! It was such a pleasure to dress her. I learned such a lot from Miss Crimplesham, too—that was my lady's maid, you see—she was a tough old stick, and all the servants was a bit in awe of her, even Mrs Green, but she wasn't so bad when you got to know her, and so devoted to my lady.'

She paused to look at the honey-brown curls that cascaded over Lucy's shoulders. Lucy knew she should reprimand the maid for chattering, but she was amused by her artless talk and besides, for one accustomed to looking after herself, it was so very pleasant merely to sit quietly and have someone fuss over her.

'I was hoping that my lady would give me a reference,' Ruthie continued, beginning to gather up the heavy locks again. 'So I could become a proper lady's maid, but then of course there were that terrible accident.'

'Accident?' Lucy met her maid's eyes in the mirror. 'You mean Lady Adversane?'

'Yes, miss. She fell to her death, from Druids Rock.'

'Oh, heavens.'

Lucy had been wondering how Lady Adversane had died. She had decided she would ask Mrs Dean at some point, for she did not think she would be able to pluck up the courage to ask Lord Adversane.

She said slowly, 'How tragic. When did it happen?'

'Two years ago, on Midsummer's Eve.' Ruthie nodded, her eyes wide. 'Oh, 'twas perfectly dreadful, miss! They found her the next morning, dashed to pieces at the foot of the crag. I thought they'd all blame me, at first, for letting her go out alone, You see, I'd fallen asleep in my chair waiting for her to come up to bed.'

'I am sure it was in no way your fault,' Lucy told her.

'No, that's what Miss Crimplesham said. In fact, she was more inclined to blame herself. In a dreadful state she was, crying and saying she should've waited up for her mistress, but how could she undress her with her broken arm? No, we had a house full of guests, you see, and that night the players had come up from Ingleston to perform, and then after supper there was dancing far into the night, so it was very late before everyone went to bed. Only my lady didn't come upstairs but went off to see the sunrise, as she often did. Only this time she didn't wait to change her shoes and her thin little slippers wouldn't grip on the rock and she slipped and fell to her death.' The youthful face reflected in the mirror looked sad for a moment, then brightened. 'And now you're here, perhaps you'll keep me on as your maid, miss.' Ruthie placed the final pin into the topknot and stood back to cast a last, critical look at her handiwork. 'I'm sure I can pick it up very quickly.'

Lucy smiled. 'Have you not learned enough yet, then?'

'Oh, no, not by a long chalk. Miss Crimplesham said it would be *months* before I had learned enough to even *think* of offering myself as lady's maid. She'd started as my lady's nurse—called her "my baby", she did—and had spent years learning how to look after her, so even if Lady Adversane hadn't been dashed to pieces that night it wouldn't have done no good, for there wouldn't be time for Miss Crimplesham to teach me everything before they went away.' Lucy might have thought nothing of this artless speech, if Ruthie hadn't dropped her hairbrush and stared aghast into the mirror. 'Ooh, miss, I shouldn't't've said that. No one was meant to know. My lady said it was a secret.'

Lucy held her eyes in the mirror.

'Are you saying,' she spoke slowly, carefully, 'that Lady Adversane was planning to…to *run away*?'

'Yes—no!' Ruthie's face crumpled. 'Miss Crimplesham said I wasn't to tell no one. She was that angry when she found out my lady had let it slip. Said I should be turned off if I breathed a word of it, and I haven't, miss. I haven't said nothing until today, but I got so carried away, pinning up your hair and enjoying myself so much that it just came out.' As Lucy swivelled around on the stool to face her, the girl fell to her knees, sobbing. 'Pray, don't tell the master, miss! He'll be so angry that he'll turn me off for sure.

I'll be sent off without a character and I'll *never* get another position, not even as scullery maid!'

'I promise I shall not tell anyone,' Lucy assured her. She handed the maid one of her own handkerchiefs and bade her dry her eyes. It behoved her now to send the girl away, but instead she said quietly, 'It was an arranged marriage, perhaps.'

'Yes.' The muffled affirmative was followed by Ruthie blowing her nose very loudly. 'Only M-Miss Crimplesham said her mistress was very unhappy. And once my lady had determined to run away then she had no choice but to go with her, to look after her.' Lucy's thoughts raced, and as if reading them Ruthie continued. 'My lady never loved the master—well, who could? He is so stern and cold, and when he's angry...' She shuddered. 'He frightens *me*, and I'm not a beautiful, delicate little flower like my lady was.'

'And what happened to Miss Crimplesham after the accident?'

'She went back to my lady's family. They have another daughter, you see, so she's gone to be her maid now.' Ruthie sighed. 'And I became second housemaid again. And I suppose I shall have to go back to that now.' She fixed Lucy with an imploring gaze. 'Only *pray* don't tell Mrs Green why you are displeased with me—'

'I have no intention of turning you away,' Lucy told her, patting her hands. 'From what I have seen of you so far you have the makings of an excellent lady's maid, only you will have to learn to curb that runaway tongue of yours.'

'I swear to you, miss, I haven't said a word to a soul before today—'

'Very well then, we will forget everything that has been said, if you please. Now, you had best remain here until you look a little less distressed. Then go downstairs and have your own dinner. And remember, a good lady's maid must learn to be discreet!'

'Yes, miss, thank you.' Ruthie bobbed another curtsey, then impulsively clutched at Lucy's hand and kissed it. 'I'll never open my mouth again, I promise you.'

Lucy went off, leaving the girl happily tidying her room. She doubted that such a chatterbox could ever be totally relied upon not to gossip, but that did not worry Lucy overmuch. The girl's services would suit her very well for the duration of her stay.

Lucy made her way downstairs and found the drawing room deserted. She supposed Ariadne and Lord Adversane must still be in their rooms, changing for dinner, and rather than sit and wait, she decided to explore a little. She soon found the dining room, situated on the far side of the entrance passage. The servants were there, setting the table for dinner, and when they saw her

they all stopped to bow or curtsey, which made
her retreat hurriedly. Another door opened on
to a pretty chamber that she guessed might be
the morning room, since its windows faced east.
The next door she tried opened onto a room lined
with bookcases. At first she thought it was the
library, but then she realised it must be Lord Adversane's study, and the man himself was present. He was standing before the window but
turned as he heard the door open.

'Oh.' Lucy stopped in the doorway. 'I did not
mean to disturb you.' She tried a little smile. 'I
was exploring…'

'Come in, Miss Halbrook. You find me ex-
amining a new acquisition.' He stepped aside to
reveal a narrow table standing before the window, and on it a strange device consisting of a
brass tube fixed to a mahogany base. 'My new
microscope.'

'Is that what it is?' She came farther into the
room. 'I have read about them, and heard of
Hooke's masterful book full of the drawings he
made using a microscope to enlarge the tiniest
creatures, but I have never seen one.'

'Then come now and look.' He beckoned to
her to approach. 'Fix your eye over the eyepiece,
the mirror at the base will direct the light onto
the slide. Now, tell me what you see.'

'Something quite…monstrous.' She took her
eye away from the microscope and peered at the

tiny object in the slide. 'Is that what I am seeing—is it a beetle's head?'

'Yes. Magnified about a hundred times.'

'But that is quite astounding.' She studied it
again for a few moments.

'And there are others,' said Lord Adversane.
'Look here, this is a flea…'

Lucy was entranced as he positioned one slide
after another for her to study.

'But that is quite marvellous, my lord,' she exclaimed. 'I had no idea one could see so much.
Why, one might look at anything, a hair from
my head, for example!'

She straightened, laughing at the thought, and
found Lord Adversane standing very close. Too
close. Her mouth dried, she dared not raise her
eyes higher than his shirt front. Once again she
had the impression of standing before a solid
wall, only the slight rise and fall of the snowy
linen above his immaculate waistcoat told her
this was a living, breathing man. A sudden hot
blush spread through her body and all coherent
thought disappeared.

Ralph swallowed. Hard. He was shaken to
find how much he wanted to reach out and drag
the young woman before him into his arms.
She had shown such enthusiasm for the microscope, had asked intelligent questions and he
had been enjoying sharing his knowledge with

her, so that the sudden rush of lustful thoughts that now crowded into his head was quite inexplicable. And the hectic flush on her cheeks only heightened his desire to kiss her.

The air around them was charged with danger. She remained motionless before him in a way that suggested she, too, could feel it. He was powerless to move away and stood looking down at her, wondering what she found so fascinating about his neck cloth. The distant chiming of the long-case clock in the hall broke the spell. She glanced up, a look of fearful bewilderment in her green eyes.

Hell and confound it. This should not have happened!

Ralph knew it was his duty to put her at her ease, if he could. Turning aside, he drew out his watch.

'It is getting late. Ariadne will be in the drawing room by now and I must change for dinner.'

'Yes.' Her voice was quiet. She sounded dazed. 'I beg your pardon for delaying you—'

'There is no need. I enjoyed showing you the microscope. I will look out more specimens for you, if you are interested.'

'Thank you, yes, I would very much like—that is…perhaps.' With a faint smile and a muttered 'Excuse me' she hurried away.

Ralph closed his eyes. Good Lord, what was he about, offering to show her more slides?

Surely he should avoid putting them in this situation again. But it would not be the same, he argued. She had taken him by surprise. Next time he would be prepared. After all, he was not the sort to lose his head over any woman.

Chapter Three

Lucy did not go directly to the drawing room. Instead, she went back to her bedchamber and splashed her cheeks with water from the jug on the washstand. Lord Adversane had said earlier that she would have to get used to being alone with him, since they were supposed to be engaged, but just then, in the study, she had felt a profound sense of danger in his presence. She wiped her cheeks and considered the matter. He had said nothing, done nothing that could be construed as improper, yet just having him stand so close had raised her temperature and sct her heart thumping in the most alarming manner.

'He is so, so *male*,' she said aloud, and almost laughed at her foolishness.

Lord Adversane had no interest in her at all, save as an employee. She must never forget that. She tidied her hair, shook out her skirts and went

downstairs again to find Ariadne waiting for her
in the drawing room.

'Ah, there you are, my dear. Ralph has just
this minute gone up to change, so we have plenty
of time to get to know one another, and I know
you are anxious to be well versed in your role. I
agree that it is most important if you are to convince everyone it is for real. Now, what would
you like me to tell you first?'

Lucy recalled Ruthie's earlier disclosures.

'I am naturally curious to know a little more
about Lady Adversane,' she explained, 'but I am
loath to mention such a delicate subject to my
host.'

'Oh, I quite understand, my dear. One does
not want to open old wounds, and Ralph was
quite devoted to her, you know.' She signalled
to Lucy to sit beside her on the sofa.

'How long were they married?' asked Lucy.

'Less than twelve months.' Mrs Dean sighed.
'They met at Harrogate in the spring and were
married before the year was out. I believe that
as soon as he saw her, Ralph was determined to
make Helene his wife.'

'So it was not an arranged marriage.' Lucy
felt a little lightening of her anxiety. Perhaps
Ruthie had embellished her story out of all pro-
portion. She knew that old retainers could be
very jealous of their charges, and it was very
likely that Miss Crimplesham had not wished

to acknowledge her mistress's affection for her new husband.

'But of course it was arranged,' said Mrs Dean. 'After a fashion. There is no doubt that the Prestons went to Harrogate in search of a husband. I wondered at the time why they did not take Helene to London. She was such a diamond that in all likelihood she could have caught a far bigger prize than a mere baron—although it is unlikely it would have been a *richer* one. But London is such a distance and Helene was never very strong. I think perhaps her parents decided she would not cope with the rigours of a season in Town. Or mayhap they were planning to take her there later, when she was a little more used to society. Only once Helene had met Ralph, she persuaded her papa to let her have her way, and it was always obvious to me that Sir James could deny her nothing.'

'So they fell in love?'

'Oh, yes, they were devoted to one another.' Mrs Dean nodded. 'And there is no doubting they were well suited, Helene so beautiful and Ralph wealthy enough to make the required settlements. I *did* think that perhaps Helene's sweet, compliant nature might—' She broke off, gazing into space for a moment before saying with a smile, 'Ralph was so gentle with her, so patient. I have no doubt that he loved her very much indeed. One only has to think that in the two years since she died he has not so much as *glanced* at another woman.' The butler entered at that moment, and she added swiftly, 'Until now, of course, my dear.'

Conversation stopped as Byrne served the ladies with a glass of wine, and when Adversane came in they talked in a desultory manner until the butler had withdrawn again. As her host took a chair on the opposite side of the fireplace, Lucy thought how well Ruthie's description of Lord Adversane suited him. Stern and cold. There was no softness in the craggy features, no yielding in his upright posture, the muscled shoulders filling the black evening coat so well that not a crease marred its sculpted form. He might have been hewn from the grey rocks she had seen on her journey to Adversane. At that moment he looked across the room and smiled at her. Immediately his face was transformed, the hard lines softened and the grey eyes warmed with amusement. She could not prevent herself from smiling back.

'So, ladies, what have you been discussing?'

'You,' said Lucy. 'Or rather, your wife.'

The warm look that had made her speak so recklessly was immediately replaced by a black frown, yet she had no choice but to continue.

'I—I thought, for the role you have engaged me for, that I needed to know a little more about Lady Adversane.'

'Do you think anyone would dare mention her to you?'

The haughty reply should have warned her to desist, but instead she considered the question.

'They might.' She met his challenging look steadily. 'And it would certainly appear most odd if I did not evince some interest in my predecessor.'

The icy look vanished, replaced by a more disquieting gleam in his eyes.

'You are quite right, Miss Halbrook. Unless we put it about that you are marrying me for my money. In which case you need show no interest at all in me or my family.'

'Oh, dear me, no. I would not wish to feature as a fortune-hunter.' He laughed at that, and, emboldened, she continued, 'I looked in the Long Gallery on my way here tonight. I thought I might see a portrait of Lady Adversane.'

Mrs Dean fidgeted beside her, and Adversane's gaze shifted from Lucy to his cousin.

'You shall see her likeness,' he said coolly. 'But not tonight, for here is Byrne again to tell us dinner is served.'

By the time they had dined, the days of travel were beginning to catch up with Lucy, and when Mrs Dean suggested that instead of retiring to the drawing room after the meal she might like to go to bed, Lucy agreed. Ruthie was waiting in her bedchamber, taking such pains to say nothing while she helped her undress that Lucy was amused, but too exhausted to tease the girl. Once she had ascertained that Ruthie would be sleeping in the dressing room, she fell into bed and was asleep almost before her head touched the pillow.

Lucy woke very early the following morning. She had asked Ruthie to leave the window shutters open and not to pull the hangings around the bed and the sun was streaming into the room. Lucy stretched and plumped up the pillows, then she lay down again, thinking of the change in her circumstances. A maid was sleeping in the dressing room, there for the sole purpose of looking after her, and once dressed Lucy would be obliged to do very little except amuse herself. All day.

And she was being well paid for it.

With a contented smile she put her hands behind her head. She had imagined herself struggling to control a schoolroom of spoiled children, or running back and forth at the bidding of a querulous invalid, instead of which she was living the life of a rich and cossetted lady.

She slipped out of bed and walked over to the window, throwing open the casement and leaning on the sill to breathe in the fresh summer air. Her room overlooked the front of the house, where the gravelled drive snaked away between neatly scythed lawns and out through the gates. Beyond the palings lay the park, bordered by an expanse of woodlands, and beyond that she could see the craggy moors stretching away to meet the sky. How could anyone be unhappy in such surroundings?

Lucy had a sudden desire to be outside, while the dew was still on the grass. Rather than disturb her sleeping maid she dressed herself in a morning gown of primrose muslin, caught her hair back with a ribbon and, picking up her shawl, she left her room. There would be a quicker way of getting to the gardens than down the main staircase and through the Great Hall, but Lucy did not yet know it and was afraid of losing herself in the maze of unfamiliar corridors. It was still early, and although she heard the servants at work she saw no one as she made her way to the long through-passage and out of the doors that opened onto the formal gardens.

A broad terrace ended in a shallow flight of steps leading down to flower beds separated by wide gravel paths. A series of statues decorated each bed and at the far end of the gardens was a small pond and fountain. It was very beautiful and the air was already heavy with the scent of flowers, but the formal layout did not fulfil her wish to be at one with nature, so she made her way around to the front of the house, where she could stroll across the smooth grass, leaving a trail of footprints in the heavy dew.

Although it was early, a skylark trilled ecstatically somewhere above her and she thought how wonderful it would be to live here through the seasons. Immediately upon the thought came another, less welcome idea, that the late Lady Adversane had not thought so. From what Ruthie had said Helene had been very unhappy here, although Lucy suspected that it was not because of the property but its owner. As if conjured by her thoughts two horses emerged from the distant trees, galloping across the open park, their riders bent low over their necks.

Even at a distance there was no mistaking Ralph, Lord Adversane. He was riding a magnificent black hunter and was a good horse's length ahead of his companion. Man and beast were as one, flying across the turf with strong, fluid movements that made their progress look effortless. He slowed as he approached the drive, waiting for his companion to come up to him before they trotted between the stone pillars of the main entrance.

Lucy knew they must see her, a solitary figure standing in the middle of the lawns, but she determined not to scuttle away like some timid little mouse. She thought they would ride around the side of the house to the stables, and she was not a little surprised when they turned their horses onto the grass and came directly towards her.

Lord Adversane touched his hat.

'You are about early, Miss Halbrook.'

'Not as early as you, my lord.'

His brows rose a little, and she wondered if he had expected her to explain her presence. As if—and she bridled a little at the idea—as if she had no right to be there. However, he did not appear to be offended by her response and replied quite cheerfully.

'I often ride out in the morning. It is a good time to see just what is happening on my land.' He indicated the man beside him. 'This is Harold Colne, who acts as my steward here at Adversane.'

Lucy nodded. 'Mr Colne.' She shot him a quick, questioning glance. 'Acts? Is that not your main role?'

'Harry is also a lifelong friend and a business partner for some of my ventures.' Ralph grinned. 'In fact, the partnership is flourishing so much that I fear I shall soon have to find myself a new steward. However, for the present Harry manages everything here at Adversane. If you are in need of anything, you may ask him.'

'I will be delighted to help you in any way I can, Miss Halbrook.'

Mr Colne touched his hat and gave her a friendly smile. Lucy warmed to him immediately. He looked to be a similar age to Lord Adversane, but instead of short black hair he had brown curls and a kindly face that looked as if it was made for laughter.

'I have a great curiosity about this place, Mr Colne,' she told him. 'And I shall undoubtedly seek you out, if you can spare a little time.'

'As much as you require, ma'am, although I assure you Lord Adversane knows everything there is to know about the estate.' He held out one hand to his companion. 'If you will give me your reins, my lord, I will see to the horses and leave you free to walk with Miss Halbrook.'

'What? Oh. Of course.'

Lucy kept her countenance until the steward had ridden away, then she said, her voice rich with laughter, 'I suppose you told Mr Colne I was your fiancée, Lord Adversane?'

'Not as such. It was implied, and I did not deny it.'

'Then you cannot blame him if he assumes you wish to spend time with me.'

'Of course not.'

She chuckled.

'Your expression tells me you would like to add "and very inconvenient it is, too!" Although, of course I am sure you would use much stronger language.'

Again that swift grin transformed his countenance.

'You are right, much stronger!'

'Well, I am very happy with my own company, sir, so if you have business requiring your attention, please do not feel you have to humour me.'

'No, there is nothing that cannot wait.'

Lucy dropped a curtsey.

'I vow, my lord, I do not know when I have received such a handsome compliment.'

She wondered if her impetuous remark might bring his wrath upon her, but although his eyes narrowed there was a gleam of appreciation in them.

'Vixen,' he retorted without heat.

He held out his arm to her, and she laid her fingers on the rough woollen sleeve. She remarked as they began to stroll towards the house, 'If Mr Colne is such a good friend I wonder that you did not confide your plan to him.'

'It has been my experience that secrets are best shared as little as possible. It was necessary to take Mrs Dean into my confidence, but no one else need know of it.'

'Your reasoning is impeccable, but to deceive your friends must cause some uneasiness.'

'And are you not deceiving your family?'

She bit her lip. 'I am, in a way.' She added, firing up, 'But at least there is some truth in what I told them. I *am* employed.'

'And do I figure as your elderly invalid?'

She gave a little choke of laughter at the absurdity of the idea.

'I suppose you must be, although you are far too—' She broke off, blushing.

'Far too what? Come, Miss Halbrook. You intrigue me.'

'Healthy,' she said lamely. It had not been the adjective she had intended to use. Young. Strong. Virile. They were the words that had come to her mind, but impossible to tell him so, and she was grateful that he did not press her on the matter.

'So what *are* you doing out here so early?' he asked her.

'Communing with nature.' Her soulful response earned her a sudden, frowning look, and she abandoned her teasing. 'It is such a lovely day that I wanted to be outside. From what Mrs Dean told me yesterday I believe breakfast will not be for another hour or so yet.'

'Breakfast can be whenever you wish,' he replied. 'Did your maid dress you?'

She stopped, glancing down at her gown. 'No—why, is there something wrong?'

'Not at all. I prefer your hair like that, with a bandeau and hanging loose down your back.' He reached up and caught a lock between his fingers. 'It curls naturally?'

'Why, y-yes.' She was thrown off balance by the gesture, which seemed far too intimate. 'I usually wear it in a knot because it is more...'

'More suitable for a governess, perhaps,' he finished for her. They began to walk on. 'While you are here you will oblige me by *not* looking like a governess.'

'Very well, if that is your wish, my lord.'

'Now I have offended you.'

'Not at all.'

'You should know from the outset, Miss Halbrook, that I have no turn for soft words and compliments.'

'That is quite evident.'

Her sharp retort earned nothing but a swift, sardonic glance. Lucy knew she was fortunate; she guessed he was more than capable of delivering a brutal snub if she pushed him too far.

Lucy curbed her hasty temper. After all, it was not for her to criticise her employer. She decided to enjoy the morning stroll. Lord Adversane led her around the perimeter of the lawn and seemed disinclined to talk, but Lucy had no intention of allowing him all his own way. A gravelled spur off the main drive caught her attention and her eyes followed it to a small wicket gate set into the palings.

'Where does that lead?'

'To the moors.' Did she imagine the heartbeat's hesitation before he added, 'And Druids Rock.'

'Oh, is it far?'

'Too far to walk there now.'

She was beginning to recognise that implacable note in his voice. It told her he had no wish to continue with the conversation, but that was understandable, since Druids Rock was where his wife had met her death. Their perambulations had brought them round in a circle and she could see that they were now wending their way back towards the house. She decided to make the most of the remaining time alone with her host.

'This might be a good opportunity for me to learn something about you,' she began. 'Perhaps you should tell me...' she paused, waving one airy hand '...the sort of things a fiancée would want to know.'

'The state of my fortune, perhaps?'

'That is the sort of thing my parents would want to know,' she corrected him. 'No, tell me about *you*.'

'I am thirty years of age. I inherited Adversane some nine years ago and it has been my principal home ever since. I have other estates, of course, and a house in London that I use when the House is sitting or to attend lectures and experiments at the Royal Society—what have I said to amuse you, Miss Halbrook?'

'Nothing, only I am at a loss to see what would have brought us together.'

'I appreciate art—you will admit that we have that in common, madam.'

'But that is such a wide-ranging subject that I

am not at all sure we would enjoy the same artists,' she countered, unwilling to concede anything just yet.

He shrugged. 'I enjoy riding—'

'Ah, then we do have a common interest.'

'You ride, then?'

'It was amongst the accomplishments I listed for Mrs Killinghurst.'

'But do you ride *well*?'

'That you will have to judge for yourself.' She sighed. 'It is not something I was able to do very often in London.'

'There are plenty of horses in the stables that my sisters use when they are at Adversane. We shall ride out this afternoon. That is—you have a riding habit?'

'Yes, an old one. I wore it to travel here.'

'Very well, then.' They had reached the garden door, and he opened it and stood back for her to precede him. 'I have business with Colne to attend to, but it should be finished by four. I will send for you to come to the stables as soon as I am free.'

Her brows went up. 'Send for me? Perhaps I will not be able to respond to your...your *summons*, my lord. I may have found another occupation by then.'

Ralph heard the frosty note in her voice. What cause had she to complain? If he wanted to *summon* her he would do so, by heaven. She was, after all, only an employee. He gave a shrug and responded, equally coldly.

'I have already said you will get no fine speeches from me, Miss Halbrook.'

'Then you will understand if I respond in kind, Lord Adversane!'

Her spirited retort surprised him, but he did not resent it. In fact, he rather liked it and raised her fingers to his lips.

'I shall be delighted if you do so, ma'am.'

He strode off then, but not before he had seen the look of shock on her face. He felt a smile growing inside him. He was beginning to enjoy his encounters with Miss Lucy Halbrook!

Lucy's boots were sodden from walking on the grass, and she went upstairs to change them before making her way to the breakfast room. She did not know what to make of her host. He was blunt to the point of rudeness, showed no inclination for polite conversation, yet that kiss upon her fingers was as gallant as any she had ever received. It had shaken her, along with the disturbing glint she had more than once seen in his eyes. She could believe he was autocratic and impatient, but she did not think him cruel. However, she was not really engaged to him, merely an actor, hired for a few weeks. Perhaps she might feel differently about Lord Adversane if she was his wife, and in his power.

* * *

Over breakfast it was agreed that Mrs Dean would take Lucy for a gentle drive into Ingleston.

'It is but three miles away and a very useful place to buy little things like stockings and gloves and ribbons,' Mrs Dean explained. 'We can also call upon Mrs Sutton, the dressmaker—'

'No need,' said Adversane, coming in at that moment. 'I have arranged for Mrs Sutton to call here tomorrow.'

Mrs Dean stared at him. 'Oh, have you, Ralph? Well, then…I suppose we need not see her today…'

Lucy chuckled. She was now on very good terms with Mrs Dean and did not scruple to tease her.

'Ariadne is deeply shocked,' she murmured. 'She does not know whether to attribute your actions to consideration for my comfort or to an arrogant high-handedness.'

The widow protested and cast an anxious glance at Adversane, but he merely looked amused.

'And which of those would you choose, Miss Halbrook?'

She met his gaze, quite fearless with Mrs Dean present and the width of the breakfast table between them.

'Oh, I think the latter, my lord.'

'Baggage,' he said, grinning at her.

Lucy was inordinately pleased with his reaction, but thought it best not to say any more. Instead, she gave her attention to the bread and butter on her plate, which was all she required to break her fast. As she finished drinking her coffee she asked Ariadne how long she thought they would be out.

'Oh, not long, my dear. We shall drive around the town, that you may see it, and then if you wish we shall stroll along the High Street and look at the shops. There are not that many, and we may well be back by two o'clock or soon after.'

'Oh, that is excellent,' said Lucy. She rose. 'I shall fetch my coat and bonnet and meet you in the hall, Ariadne.'

As she passed Adversane's chair he reached back and caught her wrist.

'Four o'clock, Miss Halbrook, do not forget.'

The touch of his cool fingers brought the heat rising in Lucy's cheeks. His grip was loose, casual, the sort of informal gesture that might occur between good friends, but her heart missed a beat and now it was hammering far too heavily, preventing her from thinking clearly. Thankfully, Adversane did not notice her confusion, for he was explaining to his cousin that he had invited Lucy to ride out with him.

'Oh, perhaps then, my dear, we should put off our drive to another day,' suggested Ariadne.

'There is not the least need for that,' cried Lucy, struggling to recover her composure. 'I am not one of those lacklustre females who is prostrate after the slightest exertion!'

She had spoken in jest, but an uneasy silence fell over the breakfast room. Ariadne looked taken aback and the air was taut as a bowstring. Adversane released her, his chair scraped back and without a word he strode out of the breakfast room.

'What is it, Ariadne? What did I say?'

Mrs Dean dabbed at her lips with her napkin.

'Lady Adversane was not very strong,' she said quietly. 'At least, she could walk well enough when it suited her, but she would often take to her room for the rest of the day after the most gentle exercise, pleading exhaustion. You were not to know, of course.' She rose and came round the table to Lucy, taking her arm. 'Come along, my dear, we'll go upstairs to fetch our things and be away.'

Ariadne was right, of course. Lucy had spoken in all innocence, but she could not forget the effect of her words. She did not mention it again to Mrs Dean, but later, when she changed into her riding habit and went out to the stables,

she knew she would have to say something to
Lord Adversane.

He was waiting for her at the stable yard,
holding the reins of his black hunter while the
groom walked a pretty bay mare up and down.
When Lucy appeared, the groom brought the
bay to her immediately and directed her to the
mounting block. As soon as she was in the saddle Adversane handed his reins to the groom
and came close to check the girth and stirrup.

She said quietly, as the groom moved away,
'My Lord, what I said at breakfast—I must apologise, I did not know…about your wife.'

'I am aware of that, Miss Halbrook.'

'I did not intend any offence.'

'None was taken.' He gave the girth a final
pat and stood back. 'Shall we go?'

Discussion ended, she thought sadly. He had
withdrawn from her again.

It was a long time since Lucy had last ridden, and for the first ten minutes she gave her
attention to staying in the saddle and control-
ling the bay's playful antics as they trotted out
of the gates. Adversane waited only to assure
himself that she was comfortable before he set
off at a canter across the park. Lucy followed,
and when he gave the black hunter his head she
experienced a surge of delight as she set the
mare galloping in pursuit. She forgot their ear-

lier constraint and when at last her companion slowed the pace she came alongside and said with heartfelt gratitude, *'Thank* you, my lord! I do not know when I have enjoyed myself more!'

'Really? But you ride very well, you must have learned that somewhere.'

'Yes, on friends' ponies and for a short time when Papa had funds enough for me to have a horse of my own, but we only ever rode on the lanes or rough pasture. To be able to gallop— really *gallop* across the park like that—it was… it was exhilarating!'

'I am pleased, then, Miss Halbrook, and happy for you to ride Brandy whenever you wish. You do not need to refer to me. Send a message to the stables when you want to ride out and Greg, my groom, will arrange for someone to accompany you.'

'Was Brandy your wife's horse?'

For a moment she thought he had not heard her.

'No,' he said at last. 'Helene had a grey. Beautiful to look at, but no spirit at all. Now, which way would you like to go?'

She accepted that he did not wish to talk more about his wife and looked about her before answering his question. 'I am not sure…which is your land?'

'All of it.' He glanced up at the sun. 'There is

time to ride as far as the Home Wood and around
the southern perimeter, if you wish.'

'Oh, yes, please—I feel as if I could ride for
ever!'

Lord Adversane grinned, putting his severe
expression to flight, and Lucy wondered if it was
just such a look that had made his first wife fall
in love with him.

The idea surprised and embarrassed her.
Her hands clenched on the reins and the mare
snatched at the bit, unsettled. She gave her attention to quietening the horse and by the time she
brought the bay alongside the black hunter again
she had regained her equilibrium. They left the
park and soon found themselves on a high ridge,
with the moors climbing even higher on one side,
while a vista of wooded hills and steeply sided
valleys opened out before them.

Lucy was enchanted and eager to know more
about the country—she asked him the name of
the thick wood in the distance, and what river
it was that tumbled through the valley, and did
he really own everything as far as the eye could
see? She was relieved that he did not appear to
be offended by the questions that tumbled from
her lips. He responded with patience and good
humour, even expanding his answers and offering more information when he realised that she
was genuinely interested.

* * *

Ralph found himself looking closely at this slight figure riding beside him. Her faded habit only enhanced the peach bloom in her cheeks and the sparkle in her green eyes. He usually went out alone, or with Harry, but riding with Lucy Halbrook, seeing his world afresh through her eager eyes, was surprisingly enjoyable.

As they continued their ride he told her about the family members she would meet at the forthcoming house party. She listened to him intently, her head a little on one side as if trying to commit it all to memory. It was with something very like regret that Ralph noticed the sun's shadow had moved on and he told her they should turn for home.

'Will we have time to visit the moors today?'

'I'm afraid not.' He saw the disappointment in her face and added, 'The moors are so extensive they deserve at least a day to themselves. However, we can ride back across the fields, and there will be a few dry stone walls to jump, if you are able.'

Immediately, the absurd chit was smiling at him as if he had offered her a casket of jewels.

'Oh, yes, please, only…perhaps you can find a couple of *tiny* walls for me to jump first, since I am so horribly out of practice!'

Laughing, Ralph set off across country, choosing a route that would not overtax the mare or

her rider. He soon realised that he needn't have
worried. Lucy was a natural horsewoman. She
rode beside him, jumping everything fearlessly
and with such delight that he wished the return
journey was twice as long. All too soon they
were back in the park with the house just visible
on the far skyline and in between a vast expanse
of green, springy turf. He reined in his horse.

'You appear to be at home upon Brandy now,
Miss Halbrook. Would you like to lead the way
to the stables?' He saw the speculation in her
eyes, the quick glance she threw towards his own
mount. 'Don't worry about Jupiter. He will be
happy enough to follow in your wake.'

'I was thinking rather that we might race for
the gates.'

His brows went up.

'Oho, are you so confident of your ability,
madam?'

'Yes, if you will give me a head start.'

He regarded her with a slight frown. Sheer
foolishness, of course. Childish, too. It would
be reckless in the extreme to hurtle at break-
neck speed across the park. One stumble could
mean disaster. He opened his mouth to say so,
but found himself subject to such a hopeful gaze
that he could not utter the words. Instead, he
pointed to a single tree standing alone some distance away.

'I'll give you to the oak.'

She needed no second bidding. He watched her careering away from him and found himself enjoying the view. She had almost outgrown the faded habit, for it clung to her figure, accentuating the tiny waist and the delectable roundness of her buttocks, seated so firmly in the saddle. She rode well, and he imagined her in his bed, thought how satisfying it would be to rouse that same passion and spirit in her by covering her soft, pliant body with kisses.

The image enthralled him and it was Jupiter's fretful protest that made him realise Lucy had reached the oak. With a word he gave the hunter his freedom and Jupiter leapt forward. He was soon in his stride and catching up with the smaller bay. Ralph leaned low, urging his horse on while keeping his eyes upon Lucy's shapely figure, trying to prevent his imagination from picturing what he would like to do when he caught up with her.

Jupiter stumbled and Ralph held him up, steadying him with a word. They were on the bay's heels now, the hunter's longer stride giving him the advantage. Sensing a victory, the black lengthened his neck and strained to come up with the bay. Ralph was so close now he could almost reach out and touch Lucy's back. The open gates were looming. She would check soon, and he would shoot past. But Lucy did not slow—she pushed Brandy on and they raced through the narrow entrance side by side, with only inches to spare.

Lucy was laughing as they brought both horses to a stand on the lawn. Glancing back, Ralph could see where they had ridden by the deep gouges the hooves had made in the turf. Old Amos would ring a peal over him for this. He had been head gardener for decades, and Ralph could almost hear him, demanding in outraged accents to know just what my lord was about, behaving like a schoolboy.

And looking into Lucy's smiling eyes, Ralph realised that was just how he felt, like a schoolboy ripe for a spree, rather than a man bent upon a plan of action that was no laughing matter.

Sobered by the thought of the dangerous game he had in mind, Ralph began to walk Jupiter towards the stables. Lucy brought the bay alongside.

'I am afraid your groundsman will be most unhappy with us, sir.'

He knew she was looking up at him, but he thought it best not to meet her eyes. She had an uncanny power to disconcert him. When they reached the stable yard, the grooms ran out to take the horses. Ralph jumped down and walked around to Lucy, holding out his arms to lift her down. It was a duty, he told himself. It was what any man would do for the woman he intended to marry and therefore it was necessary for him to do so, to convince his staff that all this was real.

She was light as a feather and her waist was so tiny his hands almost spanned it. Ralph needed all his iron will to stop himself from holding her a moment longer than was necessary. In fact, so eager was he to ensure Lucy could not misunderstand his intentions he released her a little too soon and she stumbled, off balance. Immediately, his arms were around her, even as her own hands clutched at his riding jacket. The flush on her cheeks deepened, and he was shaken to the core by a strong desire to kiss the cherry-red lips that had parted so invitingly. The grooms had walked the horses into the stables, there was no one to see them. Why should he not lower his head and take advantage of the situation?

The way his body hardened immediately at the thought caught him off guard. He had to conjure every ounce of resolve to prevent himself from giving in to it. He tried to summon up a reasonable response, but could only find anger—at himself for his weakness and at Lucy for tempting him. With rigid control, he brought his hands back and put them over hers, pulling her fingers from his lapels.

He said coldly, 'Please do not throw yourself at me, Miss Halbrook. That might be how one conducts oneself in your world, but at Adversane we expect a little more decorum.'

Her face flamed, those green eyes lost their shy smile and darkened with hurt and bewilderment. Damnation, why had he not cut his tongue out before allowing himself to utter such words? She had put out her hands to steady herself, he knew that, but he had been thrown off balance by the hunger that had slammed through him when she was in his arms. He had not known such strength of feeling since the heady days of his youth and, unnerved, he had attacked her cruelly, coldly, in a manner designed to depress any pretensions she might have.

These were the thoughts of an instant. He felt as if time had stopped, but it could only have been a moment. He said quickly, 'I should not have spoken so. It was unforgivable—'

But she was already backing away from him, her cheeks now white as chalk, and her hands raised before her, as if to ward him off.

'No, no, you are quite right. I beg your pardon.'

Her voice was little more than a thread. She turned and hurried away, head high. He should go after her, tell her it was not her fault, that the blame was all his, but he did not move. What could he say? That he had lost control? That he had suddenly been overwhelmed with the desire to ravish her? She was an employee, here for a purpose. If she thought him in any way attracted to her it would compromise her position.

She would be unable to play her part for fear of the consequences. All his planning would come to naught.

Ralph watched her walk through the arched entrance and out of sight. Only then did he move, striding into the stables, stripping off his coat as he went. He made his way to Jupiter's stall and tossed his coat over the partition. He would rub down the horse himself, brush the black coat until it shone and then he would put his head under the pump in the yard. After that he thought he might just be able to face meeting Lucy Halbrook at the dinner table.

Chapter Four

'I will not cry.'

Lucy kept repeating the words to herself as she made her way back to her room. She kept her head up, teeth firmly biting into her lip to off-set the bitter shame and revulsion that brought hot, angry tears to clog her throat and prickle behind her eyes.

They had been getting on so well, it had been the most perfect outing until Adversane had lifted her down and she had lost her balance. She had been exhilarated, in love with the whole world, and when she had put her hands against his chest to steady herself she had had no thought other than to laugh and apologise for being a little giddy.

Then she had looked up into his slate-grey eyes and her world had fallen apart. Her fool-ishly heightened sense had thought that he had taken her in his arms instead of trying to hold her upright, and she had imagined *such* a look that it had turned her bones to water. Instead of being able to stand up straight, she had been in even greater danger of falling over and had clutched at his coat like a drowning man might cling to a wooden spar. In her silly, dizzy brain she had thought herself a princess about to be kissed by her fairy-tale prince. That, of course, was pure foolishness. No one, absolutely no one, would ever think of the saturnine Lord Adversane as a prince.

'At least he is not a rake,' she muttered as she ran up the grand staircase. 'You were standing there, looking up at him, positively *inviting* him to seduce you. Thankfully he is too much of a gentleman for that.'

She flinched as she remembered his reprimand, but it was justified. In fact, she would be very fortunate if he did not pack her off back to London immediately.

She went down to the drawing room before dinner in a state of nervous apprehension. When Ariadne asked her if she had enjoyed her ride, she answered yes, but hurriedly changed the subject, and when Lord Adversane came in she retired to a chair by the window and hoped that if she kept very still he would not notice her.

It seemed to work. Apart from an infinitesimal bow Lord Adversane ignored her until dinner was announced, when he gave his arm to his cousin. Lucy was left to follow on as best she might. Thankfully, Mrs Dean was never short of small talk at the dinner table. She chattered on, rarely requiring a response, while Byrne kept the wineglasses filled and oversaw the elaborate ritual of bringing in and removing a bewildering array of delectable foods. Lucy was too unhappy to be hungry and ate almost nothing from the dishes immediately before her. She was pushing a little pile of rice about her plate when Byrne appeared at her elbow with a silver tray.

He said quietly, 'His lordship recommends the salmon in wine, miss, and begs that you will try it.'

Lucy glanced along the table. Lord Adversane was watching her, unsmiling, but when he caught her eye he gave a little nod of encouragement. She allowed the butler to spoon a little of the salmon and the sauce onto her plate. It was indeed delicious and she directed another look towards her host, hoping to convey her gratitude. Her tentative smile was received with another small but definite nod. Whether it was that, or the effects of the food, she suddenly felt a little better.

When dinner was over the ladies moved to the drawing room. Having boasted earlier of her stamina, Lucy did not feel she could retire before Lord Adversane joined them. Mrs Dean settled herself on one of the satin-covered sofas but Lucy could not sit still. To disguise her restlessness she pretended to study the room. There was plenty to occupy her: the walls were covered with old masters and the ornate carving of the overmantel was worthy of close attention. Adversane did not linger over his brandy and soon came in. He made no attempt to engage Lucy in conversation and took a seat near his cousin, politely inviting her to tell him about her day. Ariadne needed no second bidding and launched into a long and convoluted description of her activities.

It was a balmy evening, and the long windows were thrown wide, allowing the desultory birdsong to drift in on the warm air. Lucy slipped out onto the terrace. The sun was dipping but was still some way from the horizon and she could feel its heat reflecting from the stone walls of the house. The earlier breeze had dropped away and a peaceful stillness had settled over the gardens spread out before her, the statuary and flowerbeds leading the eye on to the trees in the distance and, beyond them, the faint misty edge of the high moors. Lucy drank in the scene, trying to store every detail in her memory. She suspected such summer evenings were rare in the north and she wanted to remember this one.

It was very quiet in the drawing room and she wondered perhaps if Lord Adversane had

had enough of his cousin's inconsequential chatter and retired. She stepped back into the room, and gave a little start when she realised that it was Mrs Dean who was missing. Her host was standing by the empty fireplace.

'You are very quiet this evening, Miss Halbrook.'

She sat down and folded her hands in her lap. She must take this opportunity to say what was on her mind.

'I was wondering, my lord, if you wished me to leave. If I go now there is still time for you to find someone else.'

'Do you wish to go?'

She shook her head. 'My circumstances have not changed. I am still in need of employment.'

'And I am still in need of a fiancée. It seems logical, therefore, that we should continue.' He paused. 'You are smiling, Miss Halbrook. Have I said something to amuse you?'

'You make it all sound so simple. A mere business arrangement.'

'Which is what it is.'

She looked down at her hands.

'But this afternoon, in the stable yard—'

'A little misunderstanding,' he interposed. 'Brought on by the excitement of the ride. It will not be allowed to happen again.'

'No, my lord?'

'You sound sceptical.'

'I am, a little.' She continued, with some difficulty, 'I know—I have been told—that when a man and a woman are thrown into a situation, when they are alone together…'

She blushed, not knowing how to go on.

'I understand you,' he said quietly, 'but you have nothing of that nature to fear. Let us speak plainly, madam. I have no designs upon your virtue and no intention of seducing you.'

His blunt words should have been reassuring, but she was contrary enough to feel slighted by them. She kept her eyes lowered and heard him exhale, almost like a sigh.

'Believe me, Miss Halbrook, you will be quite safe here. I can assure you that even strong passions can be assuaged with hard work and exercise. And if not… Well, for a man at least there are establishments that cater for his needs.' Lucy bent her head even more to hide her burning cheeks. He continued after an infinitesimal pause, 'But perhaps that is a little too much plain speaking, and a subject not suited to a young lady's ears.'

'Not at all. I value your honesty, sir.'

She had not raised her head and now she heard his soft footsteps approaching. She looked up to find him standing over her.

'And I value yours. You are a sensible young woman, which is what I require in my hostess.

A simple business transaction, Miss Halbrook. Can you manage that?'

She did not answer immediately. It should be easy, he made it sound so reasonable. Yet some instinct urged caution. She stifled it. If Lord Adversane could approach this in a logical fashion, then she could, too. After taking a few deep breaths she straightened her shoulders.

'Yes, my lord, I can.'

A simple business transaction.

The words echoed around Lucy's head when she lay in her bed through the dark reaches of the night. She could do this. The remuneration was worth a little sacrifice, surely. And if she was honest, the only sacrifice was that she should not allow herself to flirt with Lord Adversane. He roused in her a girlish spirit that had no place in her life now. When he was near she wanted to tease him, to make him laugh and drive away the sombre look that too often haunted his eyes. But his sorrow was none of her concern and she must be careful not to compromise herself.

'I must not be alone with him, that is all,' she told herself.

Surely that was no very arduous task when he had even brought in Ariadne to act as chaperone. All she had to do was to live like a lady in this beautiful house for another few weeks and she would walk away with more money than she could earn in a year. She turned over and cradled her cheek in her hand, finally falling asleep while engaged in the delightful task of thinking just what she might do with such a sum.

Lucy awoke to another brilliantly sunny day. Her spirits were equally bright. For a while, yesterday, she had thought she would be leaving all this luxury behind. Instead, she had a delectable prospect ahead of her. A visit from the dressmaker.

'Byrne, where is Lord Adversane?'

Miss Halbrook's enquiry echoed around the stone walls of the Great Hall. If the butler noted her flushed cheeks or the martial light in her eye he showed no sign of it and calmly informed her that she would find his lordship with Mr Colne.

It took Lucy a little time to find the steward's office for she had not before entered the service wing of the house, but the delay did nothing to cool her temper. She knocked briefly and walked in without waiting for a response.

Lord Adversane and Mr Colne were standing by a large table, studying a plan of the estate.

'I would like to speak to you, my lord,' she said without preamble.

He raised his brows.

'Can it not wait?' One look at her face gave him his answer. He turned to Mr Colne. 'Harry, will you go on to the stables and have the horses saddled? I will join you in five minutes.' As the door closed behind the steward he leaned back against the table. 'Very well, Miss Halbrook, what is it you want to say to me?'

'It concerns the dressmaker.'

He glanced at the clock. 'Has she not arrived?'

'Oh, yes, she is here, my lord. She informs me that you have given her instructions—precise instructions—on the gowns she is to provide, down to the very colours and fabrics to be used.'

'What of it?'

'What—?' She stared at him. 'It is usual, my lord, for ladies to make their own decisions on what they wear.'

'Do you not like the colours?'

'That is not the point—'

'And are the gowns too unfashionable for you?'

'Not at all, but—'

'Then I really do not see the problem.'

Lucy drew in a long and angry breath.

'The *problem*,' she said, with great emphasis, 'is that I have no choice. I am to be measured and pinned and fitted like a—like a doll!'

'Surely not.' He picked up his hat and gloves from a side table. 'I have no doubt Mrs Sutton will ask your opinion on trimmings and beads and so forth.'

'Minor details!'

'But it must suffice.'

He began to move towards the door and she stepped in front of him.

'What you do not understand—'

'What *you* do not understand,' he interrupted her curtly, 'is that this discussion is ended.'

She glared at him. 'When I accused you of high-handedness yesterday, my lord, I did not think it would go so far!'

He fixed her with a steely gaze and addressed her in an equally chilling voice.

'Miss Halbrook, remember that I am paying you very well for your time here. If I wish you to wear certain colours and styles of gown while you are under my roof then you will do so. Do I make myself clear?'

He was towering over her, as unyielding as granite. The cleft in his chin was more deeply defined than ever and there was no softness about him, not even in the grey wool of his riding jacket. He would not give in; she knew that from the implacable look in his eyes, but she would not look away, and as their gazes remained locked together she found other sensations replacing her anger.

Such as curiosity. What it would be like to kiss that firm mouth, to have his arms around her, to force him to bend to the will of her own passion...

Shocked and a little frightened by her

thoughts, Lucy stepped back and dragged her eyes away from that disturbing gaze. There must be no repeat of yesterday. He must not think she was trying in any way to entice him. Better to summon up the resentment that had brought her here in the first place.

'You have made yourself very clear, my lord.'

She ground out the words, staring at the floor, but he put his fingers under her chin and obliged her to look at him again.

He said softly, 'I am not an ogre, Miss Halbrook. I have my reasons for this, believe me.' He held her eyes for a moment longer before releasing her. He went to the door and opened it. 'Now go back upstairs and continue being—ah—fitted and pinned. You are going to have more new clothes than you can count. When this is over you may take them all away with you. Most women would be delighted with the prospect.'

She found she was trembling. Despising her own weakness, Lucy dragged together her pride and managed to say with creditable calm, 'I am not most women, my lord.'

'No.' His mouth twisted into a wry smile as she stalked out of the room. 'No, you are not, Miss Halbrook.'

Lucy went back to the morning room where Mrs Dean and the dressmaker were engaged in

discussing fabric samples and looking through
the portfolio of drawings that Mrs Sutton had
brought with her. She was shaken by her encounter with Lord Adversane, and a little chastened,
too. He was, after all, her employer, and quite
within his rights to dictate what she should wear.
A little spirit flared to argue that it would have
been better if he had explained all this at the outset, but it was a very tiny spark and soon died.

She gave herself up to the task of looking
at the various designs and samples of fabrics.
She soon discovered—as she had known all
along, if only she had thought about it—that
she did indeed have a degree of freedom in the
choice of ribbons and trimmings to be added to
each gown. By the end of the session her head
was spinning with all the talk of closed robes,
morning and day dresses, walking dresses and
evening gowns, as well as the pelisses, cloaks
and shawls required to go with them. Also—a
last-minute addition that Lord Adversane had
ordered in a note, delivered hotfoot to the dressmaker yesterday evening—a riding habit.

Although she knew she had no real choice,
Lucy nodded and approved all the samples and
sketches put before her. They were without exception elegant creations, not overly burdened
with frills and ribbons, which suited her very
well. As the dressmaker and her assistant began

packing away the drifts of muslin, samples of fine wool, worsted and sarcenet, Lucy spotted a large square of red silk. She picked it up.

'What is this?'

Mrs Sutton looked around and gave a little tut of exasperation.

'Heavens, miss, as if I should forget that!' She pulled out the sheaf of loose papers again and selected a coloured drawing, which she handed to Lucy. 'Lord Adversane was most insistent that you should have this gown.'

Lucy gazed at the impossibly slender figure in the painting. She was swathed in red silk, the high waistline and low neck leaving little to the imagination.

'It is shown exactly as his lordship directed,' said Mrs Sutton, waiting anxiously for Lucy's reaction. 'Even to the diamond set of earrings, necklace and bracelet.'

'Scarlet and diamonds.' Lucy pictured herself in such a gown, the jewels sparkling in the candlelight, her skirts floating about her as she danced around the ballroom. 'Very striking but…it is not suitable for an unmarried lady. What say you, Ariadne?' She handed the picture to Mrs Dean, who stared at it in silence. 'Ariadne?'

The widow gave a little start.

'Oh, I do not…' She tailed off again, her troubled glance fixed upon the drawing.

'It is far too grand for me to wear,' Lucy continued. 'If we were in London, perhaps, but here in the country, what use can I have for such a creation?'

'Unless Adversane means to invite the neighbourhood,' murmured Ariadne.

Lucy frowned. 'Why should he do that?'

Ariadne made a visible effort to pull herself together, saying robustly, 'I suppose he thought you must have it. Who knows what invitations you might receive? And everyone wears such colours these days. You will not always want to be wearing those pale muslins, now will you? And I recognise the diamonds. They are a family heirloom. As Ralph's fiancée I have no doubt he will wish you to wear them.'

'Yes, of course.' Lucy dismissed her doubts, relieved by Mrs Dean's approval of the scarlet gown. To appear in public so beautifully apparelled was every girl's dream. And what did it matter that it was all a sham, a charade? It would be a wonderful memory for her to take away with her.

When the dressmaker had departed Ariadne carried Lucy off to the shrubbery, declaring that one needed to clear one's head after being bombarded with so much detail.

'I must confess,' she added, as they strolled arm in arm along the gravelled paths, 'when you went off so angrily I thought I should be sending Mrs Sutton away and ordering the carriage to take you back to London forthwith.'

Lucy's free hand fluttered.

'It was foolish of me to allow such a little thing to make me angry. I assure you, I never had any intention of leaving over such a matter.'

'Oh, no, my dear, I was not thinking of *your* intentions. I thought Ralph might order you to go. I thought he would call a halt to this whole business—not that that would be a bad thing.' She muttered these last words almost to herself and when she found Lucy's considering gaze upon her she coloured and said, as if in apology, 'My cousin is not used to having his will crossed.'

'I am well aware of that. Autocratic to the point of tyranny!'

'But he is not a bad man, Lucy. It is just that… You should understand, my dear, that he was the only surviving male child, and much loved. Although he was brought up on strict principles he was allowed to go his own way from an early age. I suppose you might say he was too much indulged—'

'I should,' put in Lucy emphatically.

'But he was not rebellious, you see, so his sainted parents never needed to curb him. They had him late in life, too, which I think made them a little more inclined to spoil him, and then, of course, they were carried off within weeks of each other by a vicious bout of influenza, and he inherited the title soon after he was one-and-twenty. From being a carefree young man he suddenly found himself with half a dozen estates and hundreds of people dependent upon him. And things were not so comfortable as they are now. The old lord had spent so much on improvements to Adversane that the finances were severely stretched when Ralph took over. He has had to struggle to rebuild the family fortunes. He needed a steady nerve and a firm hand on the reins to bring it back to prosperity. He demanded that everything should be done his way and it has worked. The fortune is restored.'

'But he rules his household with a will of iron,' objected Lucy.

'All the Cottinghams are strong-willed, my dear, and as the heir and only son, Ralph's will has never been opposed. Is it any wonder that he has grown used to his own way? That was why his marriage to Helene was so fortuitous. She was all compliance and perfectly suited to his temperament.'

'Perfectly suited to make him even more despotic,' declared Lucy. 'The poor lady must have been wholly downtrodden.'

Ariadne quickly disclaimed.

'He never bullied her, I am quite certain of

it. But then, Helene was so very sweet-natured, I doubt she ever gave him cause to be angry.'

'Well,' said Lucy, thinking of the small sum she had sewn into the hem of her travelling cloak, 'Lord Adversane may be as autocratic and demanding as he wishes, but I shall not allow him to bully *me*, and so I shall tell him!'

However, Lucy had no opportunity to tell Lord Adversane anything that evening, for when she joined Mrs Dean in the drawing room before dinner she learned that their host had gone off to visit friends and would not be back for two days. The news left her feeling a little disconsolate and she gave a little huff of exasperation.

'And how am I supposed to learn everything I need to know if he is not here?'

'My dear, no one will expect you to know everything about Ralph,' replied Mrs Dean, looking amused. 'In fact, I doubt anyone could do that.'

'I beg your pardon, Ariadne, it is just that… Well, I had worked myself up to challenge him about his high-handed ways and now I feel a little…cheated.'

'You *enjoy* confronting him?'

Her shocked expression made Lucy smile.

'I like matters out in the open wherever possible.'

She thought of her uncle's unwanted attentions

and felt a little guilty that she had not brought that out into the open, but it would have caused too much distress to her mother and her aunt. Lucy had every reason to be discreet in that case. Lord Adversane, however, was another matter entirely. She added a little pugnaciously, 'If that means confronting your cousin, I will not shirk from it.'

'Then perhaps it is as well Ralph is away, or we should see the sparks fly,' retorted Mrs Dean, chuckling. 'Never mind, my dear, there is plenty for us to do. You can help me with the arrangements for the forthcoming house party. The guests have already been invited, of course— Ralph has seen to that—but there are the rooms to be allocated, furniture to be arranged, menus to be planned.'

'And just who is invited, Ariadne?'

'Well, there are Ralph's two sisters and their husbands,' said Mrs Dean, counting them off on her fingers. 'Adam Cottingham—Ralph's cousin and heir—and his wife, or course. And Sir James and Lady Preston.'

'Do you mean the late Lady Adversane's parents? But surely they will not wish to come to Adversane—'

'Oh, yes, they will! They are even bringing their daughter Charlotte with them.'

'But—do they know, about me?'

'Oh, lord, yes. Ralph told them himself when he invited them to come and stay.'

'And they still accepted his invitation?'

'Yes. I doubt they hesitated for a moment.' She patted Lucy's arm. 'I do not think I am speaking out of turn if I tell you that the Prestons virtually *threw* Helene at Adversane. They wanted her to marry well. Lady Preston would have preferred a higher title, perhaps, but the Cottinghams are an old family. Their line goes back to the Conqueror. And besides that, Ralph's wealth made him a very acceptable *parti*.'

Lucy frowned. 'But surely they will not be comfortable staying here, knowing what happened two years ago.'

'As to that, they must feel it, of course, as we all do, but life must go on. Ralph's sisters are already pressing him to marry again, which is why he has installed you here. And I hear even Lord Preston has been hinting that young Charlotte could fill her sister's shoes.'

'But that is monstrous.'

'It is hard-headed sense,' replied Ariadne drily. 'Preston will naturally want to maintain his connection with Adversane, if he can.'

Byrne came in to tell them that dinner awaited them and no more was said that evening about the house guests, but Lucy thought she understood a little better now just why Adversane had hired her.

* * *

The following days were spent in preparations for the forthcoming house party. Ariadne took Lucy on a tour of the east wing, preparatory to allocating the guest rooms. There was also a trip to Ingleston to buy additional gloves and slippers to go with all her new clothes. It was like being caught up in a very pleasant whirlwind, thought Lucy. She loved being busy and happily threw herself into all the arrangements. She discussed menus with the housekeeper and accepted the gardener's invitation to show her around the gardens and select the flowers she would require for the house. Lucy discovered that the staff was eager and willing to help, and once she had accustomed herself to the thought that she was regarded as the next Lady Adversane she found she could work very well with them all. It was impossible for Lucy not to enjoy herself, but at the back of her mind was the realisation that this would not last. At some point she would have to leave Adversane.

She pondered the idea as she sat at her open bedroom window, where the night air was scented with summer flowers.

'And when that day comes I shall go with many happy memories,' she told herself, smiling up at the sliver of moon suspended in the clear sky. 'Until then, I shall continue to enjoy every minute of my stay here!'

* * *

Lord Adversane returned the following afternoon. His arrival coincided with the first delivery from the dressmaker. He walked into the morning room to find Lucy and his cousin surrounded by a chaotic jumble of gowns and boxes and tissue paper.

'Ralph, my dear, you are back!' Ariadne smiled at him and waved a hand at the disorder. 'Mrs Sutton and her assistants must have been sewing night and day to have so many things finished already.'

'Evidently,' he murmured. 'I trust the gowns are to Miss Halbrook's satisfaction?'

Lucy had been feeling a little shy and not sure how to greet him after their last confrontation, but the challenging look in his eye roused her spirit.

'They are indeed,' she replied. 'I have yet to try them on, but the styles and colours cannot be faulted. You have impeccable taste, my lord.'

'Handsomely said, madam.' He grinned at her, then cast a faintly bewildered glance about the room. 'I am definitely *de trop* here, so I will go away and change out of all my dirt.'

'Oh, dear, how remiss of me,' cried Ariadne, 'Have you been travelling all day, Cousin? Shall I ring for refreshments?'

'No need,' he said, going back to the door. 'I

shall ask Byrne to send something up to me. I shall see you at dinner.'

'My lord!' Lucy called him back. As he turned she held up two of the new creations, saying innocently, 'I have these new evening gowns now, sir. The white drawn-thread muslin with a twisted pink sash, or the cream sprigged muslin. Which would you like me to wear tonight?'

'I have not the least—' He broke off, his eyes narrowing. 'I see. You have not forgiven me for my high-handedness in dictating what should be made, is that it?'

'He who pays the piper may call the tune, my lord.'

He met her limpid gaze with a hard stare.

'But one would hope, Miss Halbrook, that the piper knows how to play. I have provided your wardrobe, madam, I leave it to you to present yourself to best advantage.'

He closed the door behind him with a decided snap.

Ariadne gave a little tut of reproof. 'Lucy, my dear, I really do not think you are wise to tease Ralph in that manner.'

'No?' A smile tugged at the corners of Lucy's mouth. 'I think it is high time someone teased your cousin. In my opinion he has had his own way for far too long!'

Lucy might well want to tease her host, but she was also eager to wear one of her new gowns,

and the look of relief upon Mrs Dean's countenance when she presented herself in the drawing room before dinner caused Lucy to chuckle.

'You see I have behaved myself and chosen
the cream muslin. The embroidery on the shawl
Mrs Sutton sent with it exactly matches the pink
sash.' She gave a twirl. 'Does it not look very
well? And Ruthie found a matching ribbon for
my hair, too. I hope his lordship will be pleased.'

'He is.'

The deep voice made her turn quickly to the
door. Adversane had come in and was walking
towards her. His dark evening coat contrasted
with the white waistcoat and knee breeches, and
his black hair gleamed like polished jet in the
soft light of the summer evening. Lucy found
herself thinking how attractive he was. That
made her laugh inwardly, for no one could call
Lord Adversane's craggy face handsome. Strong,
yes. Striking, even. Yet the impression persisted
and she quickly sat down on the sofa next to Ariadne, conscious that she was blushing.

Ralph raised his quizzing glass to look at her.
He did not need it, and the gesture was more to
cover his own confusion. He had entered the
room in time to see her spin around, the skirts of
her gown lifting away from a pair of extremely
neat ankles and her honey-brown curls bounc-
ing joyously about her head. Once again he had
been surprised by the way she roused his desire.

She was no beauty, certainly not a diamond as his wife had been, but he had never seriously expected to find anyone to equal Helene. Yet there was a vivacity about Lucy Halbrook, and he found himself wondering if that liveliness would translate itself to passion if he was to take her in his arms.

Impossible. She was a lady, not a courtesan, and he had never dallied with gently bred ladies— not even Helene, although he had known from the start that he would marry her. Ruthlessly, he suppressed all improper thoughts and when he spoke his tone was at its most neutral.

'My compliments, Miss Halbrook. You look very well tonight.'

'Any tributes are due to Mrs Sutton and to my maid, sir, the one for providing the gown and the other for arranging my hair.'

She answered calmly enough and the becoming flush on her cheeks was dying away. He was relieved. It formed no part of his plan to become entangled with his employee. He helped himself to wine from the decanter on the side table and addressed his cousin.

'I have had a letter from Caroline. She and Wetherell are coming on the nineteenth.'

'Was there ever any doubt?' Ariadne turned to Lucy to explain. 'Lady Wetherell is Ralph's sister and eight years older than he. She is very eager to meet you, Lucy, but I should warn you that Caroline can be a little forthright—'

'She is damned interfering,' he said brutally.

'A family trait, perhaps,' murmured Lucy.

His eyes narrowed. The minx was teasing him again, but he acknowledged the justice of her remark with the flicker of a smile while Ariadne continued, unheeding.

'You may recall, Lucy, I told you that Ralph's sister Margaret is also coming. She is only four years older than Ralph but equally...'

'Interfering?'

Ralph laughed. 'There you have it, Miss Halbrook. Perhaps now you see why I need a fiancée to protect me?'

'Your sisters are concerned for the succession,' put in Ariadne.

'They need not be. I have an heir.'

'Adam Cottingham? He is merely a cousin.'

'He bears the family name. That is sufficient.'

'But they would prefer to continue the direct line, Ralph—'

His cousin's persistence hit a nerve. He had heard all these arguments before.

'Enough,' he said impatiently. 'I have married once for the sake of an heir. I do not intend to do so again. I shall never take another wife.' He rose quickly before anyone could respond. 'Shall we go in to dinner?'

Lucy accompanied Lord Adversane into the dining room, her fingers resting lightly on his sleeve. She could feel the tense muscles, strong as steel beneath the expensive Bath coating. He was angry, and she had some sympathy with him. His wife had been dead for but two years and he was being nagged to marry again. He must have loved her very much.

In an effort to divert his mind she asked him about his trip. He told her that he had been in Leeds, discussing the prospect of a steam railway. She dragged from her memory whatever she had learned of steam power in order to ask questions that would not result in his dismissing her as a fool. She succeeded very well, and the conversation continued during dinner. Lucy included Ariadne where she could, but although Mrs Dean professed herself interested, she was content to allow the discussion to continue around her while she concentrated upon her meal.

'Steam power has a lot to offer,' concluded Lord Adversane, when the covers had been removed and they were sitting back in their chairs, choosing from the dishes of sweetmeats left on the table. 'It has even more potential than the canals, I think, and we will be able to move huge quantities of goods to and from the new manufactories.'

'And will it mean the demise of the horse?' asked Lucy.

'Good God, no. Or, at least, not for a long time.' He pushed a dish of sugared almonds towards her. 'Which reminds me. Did I see your new riding habit amongst all those new clothes delivered today?'

'Why, yes, sir.'

The high-waisted style was very different from her old habit, and the soft dove-blue linen not nearly so hard-wearing as the olive-green velvet, but, she thought wryly, the future Lady Adversane did not need to worry about such practicalities.

'Good,' remarked her host. 'Then perhaps you would like to ride out with me tomorrow. Greg tells me you have not been near the stables since that first ride.'

Lucy hoped her face did not show her embarrassment at the memory.

'No, I did not like to presume.'

'It is no presumption, madam. Brandy needs exercising and you may as well do that as the stable hands. You may order the mare to be saddled whenever you wish, and Greg will find someone to accompany you.'

'Th-thank you, my lord.'

'So? Are you free tomorrow? It will have to be after breakfast. Colne and I have business before that, but I should be free soon after ten.'

Mrs Dean gave a little cluck of admiration.

'You are so industrious, Ralph, to be conducting your business so early.'

'If I do not then the day is lost.' He looked again at Lucy, who met his enquiring glance with a smile.

'I shall be ready, my lord.'

Lucy was already in the stable yard and mounted upon the bay mare when Lord Adversane appeared the following morning.

'I wanted to accustom myself to this new habit,' she told him as she waited for him to mount up. 'The skirts are much wider than my old dress. I hope Brandy will not take exception to them if they billow out.'

'She is used to it, having carried my sisters often enough.'

They trotted out of the yard and as soon as they reached the park Lord Adversane suggested they should gallop the fidgets out of their mounts. The exercise did much to dispel any lingering constraint Lucy felt, and her companion also seemed more relaxed. When they left the park he took her through the little village of Adversane, where she noted with approval the general neatness. All the buildings were in good repair and it did not surprise her to learn that most of the property belonged to the estate. They met the parson on his way to the church, whose square tower was visible beyond a double row of cottages. They drew rein, introductions were performed and the reverend gentleman smiled up at Lucy.

'So this is your second week here, Miss Halbrook.'

'It is.'

Her eyes flickered towards Adversane, who said easily, 'I was away last Sunday, Mr Hopkins, and Miss Halbrook was reluctant to attend church alone.'

Lucy cast him a grateful glance. It was almost true. Mrs Dean had cavilled at taking her into the church and, as she put it, continuing the pretence of the betrothal in such a holy place.

'We will wait until Adversane is here to escort you,' Ariadne had said. 'The Lord's wrath will come down upon his head then. Not that he will care much for that!'

Mr Hopkins was directing a sympathetic look towards Lucy and saying gently, 'Ah, yes, quite understandable, in the circumstances. You were afraid everyone would be gawping at you, Miss Halbrook. And they would be, too, I'm afraid. Perhaps you would like to come and see the church now? It has some quite wonderful examples of Gothic architecture. And I doubt if there will be anyone there at present—'

'Thank you, Mr Hopkins, but next Sunday will have to do for that. We must get on.'

'Ah, of course, of course.' The parson nodded

and stepped back. 'And there is plenty of time for all the arrangements, my lord. You need only to send word when you wish me to come to discuss everything with you.'

Lucy knew not what to say and left it to Adversane to mutter a few words before they rode off.

'He meant the arrangements for the wedding, I suppose,' she said, when they were safely out of earshot.

'Of course.' His hard gaze flickered over her. 'Feeling guilty?'

'Yes, a little,' she admitted.

'Don't be. Our betrothal has given the locals something to talk about, and when it ends they will have even more to gossip over. A little harmless diversion, nothing more.'

'I suppose you are right, my lord.'

'I think it is time that we abandoned the formality, at least in public.'

'I beg your pardon?'

'You cannot keep calling me "my lord". I have a name, you know.'

Lucy felt the tell-tale colour rising up again.

'I do know,' she managed, 'but—'

'No buts, Lucy. There, I have used your name, now you must call me Ralph. Come, try it.'

She felt uncomfortably hot.

'I—that is, surely we only need to do so when other people are near—'

'And how unnatural do you think that would sound? We need to practise.'

'Of course. R-Ralph.'

He grinned. 'Very demure, my dear, but you look woefully conscious.'

'That is because I am,' she snapped.

'Which proves my point,' he replied in a voice of reason that made her grind her teeth.

Observing her frustration, he merely laughed and adjured her to keep up as he trotted out of the village.

It was impossible to remain at odds. There was too much to see, too many questions to ask. The hours flew by and Lucy was almost disappointed when Adversane said they must turn for home.

'We are on the far side of Ingleston,' he told her. 'It will take us an hour to ride back through the town, longer if we skirt around it. Which would you prefer?'

'The longer route, if you please.' Lucy recalled her meeting with the parson and had no wish to be stared at and pointed out as the future Lady Adversane.

They kept to the lanes and picked up the road again at the toll just west of Ingleston. Lucy recognised it as the road she had travelled when Mrs Dean had taken her to the town. She recalled there was a narrow, steep-sided valley ahead, where the highway ran alongside the river. It had felt very confined in the closed carriage, with nothing but the green hillside rising steep and stark on each side, and Lucy was looking forward to seeing it from horseback. She turned to her companion to tell him so and found that his attention was fixed upon something ahead, high up on the hills. Following his gaze, she saw the moors rising above the trees, culminating in a ragged edifice of stone on the skyline.

'Is that Druids Rock, my lord?'

'Yes.'

She stared up at the rocky outcrop. The sun had moved behind it, and the stone looked black and forbidding against the blue sky.

'Your cousin told me that the old track to Adversane ran past there, before this carriageway was built.'

'That is so.'

'And can one still ride that way?'

'Yes, but we will keep to the road.'

She said no more. His wife had died at Druids Rock and it must be very painful to have such a constant and visible reminder of the tragedy. She longed to offer him some comfort, at least to tell him she understood, but he had urged Jupiter into a fast trot, and quite clearly did not wish to discuss the matter any further.

By the time they arrived back at Adversane Hall Lucy felt that she had achieved a comfortable understanding with her host. Glancing up

at the clock above the stable entrance, she wondered aloud if there would be time for her to
bathe before dinner.

'I have not ridden so far in a very long time,'
she explained.

'You had probably forgotten, then, how dusty
one can get.'

'And sore,' she added, laughing. 'I have a lowering suspicion that this unaccustomed exercise
will leave my joints aching most horribly!'

'I shall tell Byrne to put dinner back an hour
and have Mrs Green send up hot water for you.'
He helped her dismount and led her towards a
small door at the back of the stable yard. 'This
is a quicker way,' he explained. 'A path leads
directly from here to a side door of the house,
which opens onto what we call the side hall, and
from there we can ascend via a secondary staircase to the main bedchambers. It is much more
convenient than appearing in all one's dirt at
the front door.'

'I guessed there must be a way,' she told him
as she stepped into the house. 'Only I had not
yet found it. Does it lead to the guest wing, too?'

'No. They have their own staircase, over
there.' He pointed across the side hall to a
panelled corridor, where Lucy could see another
flight of stairs rising at the far end. 'My guests
have perfect freedom to come and go as they
wish.'

There was something in his tone that made her look up quickly, but his face was a stony mask. She began to make her way up the oak staircase, conscious of his heavy tread behind her.

'How useful to have one's own staircase,' she remarked, to break the uneasy silence. 'Was it perhaps the original way to the upper floor? Mrs Dean did say that the grand staircase was added when the house was remodelled in the last century.'

She knew her nerves were making her chatter, but when her companion did not reply she continued, glancing at the dark and rather obscure landscapes on the wall. 'And of course it gives you somewhere to hang paintings that are not required elsewhere...'

Her words trailed away as they reached the top of the stairs, and her wandering gaze fixed upon the large portrait hanging directly in front of her. But it was not its gilded frame, gleaming in the sunlight, nor the fresh, vibrant colours that made her stop and stare. It was the subject. She was looking at a painting of herself in the scarlet gown.

Chapter Five

'My wife.'

It did not need Adversane's curt words to tell her that. Only for an instant had Lucy thought she was looking at herself. A second, longer glance showed that the woman in the picture had golden curls piled up on her head, and eyes that were a deep, vivid blue.

'I had forgotten it was here.'

She dragged her eyes away from the painting to look at him.

'Forgotten?' she repeated, shocked. 'How could you forget?'

His shoulders lifted, the faintest shrug.

'My cousin had it moved from the Long Gallery the day you arrived. She thought it would upset you. Personally I would not have done so. You were bound to see it at some time.'

She found her gaze drawn back to the painting.

'She is wearing the gown I saw in Mrs Sutton's sketch.'

'Yes.'

'And the diamonds.' She swallowed. 'My hair is a little darker but…there is a striking resemblance between us.'

'Is there?'

Anger replaced her initial astonishment.

'Come now, my lord. Please do not insult my intelligence by saying you have not noticed it.' She had a sudden flash of memory: the open door in Mrs Killinghurst's office, the gilded picture frame on the wall of the inner sanctum. 'Did you deliberately set out to find someone who looked like your wife?'

'Pray, madam, do not be making more of this than there is.'

He indicated that they should move on, but Lucy remained in front of the portrait. He had not denied the allegation, so she could only surmise that his reasons for hiring her were not quite as straightforward as he had said.

'And your choice of gowns for me—are they all the same as those worn by your wife? Every one?'

'If they are it need not concern you.'

'My lord, it *does* concern me.'

'Well, it should not.' He frowned. 'I have already explained what is required of you. I can assure you there is nothing improper in it.'

'I am very glad to hear it!'

'So, does it matter what you wear?'

'No-o…'

'Then pray do not concern yourself further. Instead, enjoy living in luxury for a few weeks!' With that, he turned and strode off, leaving her to make her own way to her bedchamber.

Damn the woman, must she question everything?

Ralph stormed into his room, tearing off his neck cloth as he went. He had enjoyed their morning ride, much more than he had expected. Lucy Halbrook was spirited and intelligent and for a few hours he had put aside his cares and given himself up to pleasure. So successful had it been that he'd completely forgotten Ariadne had moved the painting and he'd been unprepared to see Helene staring down at him, large as life, from the top of the stairs. He had looked up and seen the portrait when he put his foot on the first tread, but by that time it was too late. Lucy was already before him, and all he could do was to try and think what on earth he would say to her when she saw the painting.

He was not surprised at her look of astonishment. Even Ariadne had questioned why he had hired someone who looked so much like Helene to play his fiancée. Lucy had seen the resemblance immediately and had turned to him, a

question in her eyes. Green eyes, he recalled, and
they changed with her moods. They looked like a
stormy sea when she was angry and today, when
she was exhilarated from the ride, they shone
clear and bright as moss. Nothing like Helene's
blue eyes, which he had once thought so alluring.

He gave his head a little shake to dispel the
unwelcome thoughts that came crowding in.
Kibble's voice intruded and Ralph looked up to
see his valet coming out of the dressing room.

'I have prepared a bath for your lordship.'

'Thank you. Go down and tell Mrs Green to
send up water to Miss Halbrook's room, if you
please.' When Kibble hesitated he said curtly,
'Damn it, man, I can undress myself, you know!'

Not visibly moved, Kibble gave a stately little
bow and retired. Going into the dressing room,
where scented steam was gently rising from a
hip bath, Ralph threw off his clothes and lowered himself into the water.

Kibble knew him well enough not to be offended by his rough tone, but what of Lucy? He
had spoken harshly to her on several occasions
now. A slight smile tugged at his mouth. She
appeared quite capable of standing up to him,
but that last look she had given him nagged at
his conscience. If he told her everything, would
she understand?

He could not risk it. He had known the woman
barely two weeks, it would not make sense to

trust her with such a dangerous secret. Safer to keep his own counsel. Much more logical.

He heard a movement in the bedchamber, and Kibble appeared in the dressing room doorway.

'A bath is even now being carried up to Miss Halbrook's room, my lord.'

Ralph was immediately distracted by the image of Lucy undressing and stepping into the warm water. There was a golden sheen to the skin of her neck and shoulders. Did that extend, he wondered, to the rest of her body...?

Kibble spoke again, in a voice with just a hint of rebuke. 'Mrs Green hopes there will be enough hot water, since she did not anticipate anyone other than your lordship requiring a bath today.'

Ralph sat up with an oath, not so much angry with his valet as with himself for not being able to dispel the thought of Lucy Halbrook.

Finding his master's wrathful eye turned towards him, Kibble unbent sufficiently to add, 'With so few guests in the house, Monsieur deemed it wasteful to light the new range in the kitchen and has been cooking on the old open range—it has a much smaller water cistern, my lord.'

'I know precisely what the difference is,' barked Ralph. 'You may tell Monsieur that since I pay him an extortionate wage to run my kitchens, I can afford to use that new range whatever

the number of guests in residence, do you understand?'

'Yes, my lord.'

'Very well.' Ralph nodded towards the pail
of hot water standing on the hearthstone. 'Miss
Halbrook can have that to top up her supply.'

'Won't you be needing it, my lord?'

'No, I won't.' The vision of Lucy bathing was
still tantalising Ralph. Great heavens, what was
wrong with him? 'In fact, you had best pour in
the rest of the cold water before you go.'

Lucy rubbed herself dry, her skin and spirits
glowing. To be able to call up a bath at a moment's notice was luxury indeed and she could
forgive her employer a great deal for that.

She could not forgive him everything, however, and the idea that she had been brought here
to imitate his dead wife made her decidedly uneasy.

She left the chaos of the bath, buckets and
towels in the dressing room and went into her
bedchamber, where Ruthie had laid out a selec-
tion of gowns upon the bed. They were all new,
and had all arrived that day. Lucy was tempted
to wear the French cambric that she had brought
with her, but she knew enough of her employer
by now to be sure that if she did so, he would
order her back upstairs to change.

In the end she chose a simple round gown of

green silk over a white chemise. Ruthie dressed her hair in loose curls, caught up in a bandeau of matching ribbon, along with a pair of satin slippers dyed the same colour as her gown.

Looking at herself in the mirror, Lucy wondered if Helene had worn a gown like this, but of course she already knew the answer to that. Lucy derived some small, very small, satisfaction from the fact that however well the gown might have looked with guinea-gold curls, it could not have enhanced cornflower-blue eyes as it did green ones. Dismissing the thought as unworthy, Lucy placed a fine Norwich shawl about her shoulders and set off for the drawing room.

As she descended the main stairs she heard voices in the hall. One, which she recognised as Lord Adversane's, came floating up to her.

'Adam. What the devil brings you here?'

Adam. Lucy searched her mind and remembered that Adam Cottingham was Adversane's cousin and heir. A cheerful male voice now made itself heard.

'Don't sound so surprised, Cos. I came to take pot luck with you, as I have done often and often.'

'Aye, but not since the accident.' She heard Ralph hesitate over the last word. 'I thought you had vowed not to come here again.'

'No, well…the past is over and done. Time to

let it rest, eh? We should not allow it to cause a rift in the family.'

'I was not aware that it had done so.'

'Well, there you are, then. And here I am. I take it you can spare a dinner for me, Cousin?'

Lucy continued to descend, smiling a little at Adversane's rather guarded response.

'Of course, it will be a pleasure to have you stay.'

'Thank you. So, Ralph, you old devil. What is this I have heard about a betrothal? Judith tells me you wrote to say you have installed your fiancée— *Good God*!'

This last exclamation was occasioned by Lucy's appearance in the Great Hall. She found herself being stared at by a fair-haired stranger. He picked up his eyeglass the better to study her and said sharply, 'Ralph, what the devil—?'

Lucy was tempted to run away from such astonished scrutiny, but Lord Adversane was already approaching and holding out his hand to her.

'My dear, this boorish fellow is my cousin. He has come to join us for dinner.' He pulled her fingers onto his sleeve, giving them a little squeeze as he performed the introduction.

Mr Cottingham dropped his eyeglass and made her an elegant bow.

'Delighted, Miss Halbrook.'

Lucy's throat dried as she responded. Suddenly, she felt very ill prepared. Now that she had met one of Adversane's relatives in the flesh she was very nervous at the thought of being caught out. When Ralph smiled and patted her fingers she realised that she was clutching his arm rather tightly.

'Let us go to the drawing room,' he suggested. 'I expect Mrs Dean is waiting there for us.'

The short walk across the hall gave Lucy time to collect herself, and once Ariadne had greeted their guest, expressed her surprise at his arrival and assured him that there was plenty of time for him to change before dinner, she was able to sit down and join in the conversation with reasonable calm.

'Such a long time since I have seen you, Adam,' said Mrs Dean, fluttering back to her seat. 'I suppose there is no surprise about that. After all, we used to meet here at Adversane regularly, but of course all that changed when…' She trailed off, looking self-conscious.

'When Helene died,' said Ralph bluntly. 'I am aware that I have not entertained since then.'

'Indeed, Cousin, you have become something of a recluse,' declared Mrs Dean, recovering. 'But thankfully all that is ended now.' She turned back to Mr Cottingham. 'And will you stay overnight, Adam? I can have a room prepared in a trice.'

'No, no, I will not put you to that trouble. The

long evening will give me time to get home before dark.'

'Do you live nearby, sir?' asked Lucy.

'At Delphenden, about fifteen miles hence. I am on my way home after visiting friends in Skipton and thought, since I was passing—'

'That is hardly passing,' Ralph broke in. 'You have come a good deal out of your way to get here.'

Adam laughed. 'True, but your letter intrigued me and I wanted to know more—and to meet your future bride, of course.'

He turned to Lucy as he said this, but although his words were uttered with a smile Lucy thought the look in his eyes was more speculative than welcoming.

'There is very little more to know,' Ralph responded calmly. 'Miss Halbrook and I met in London and she has done me the signal honour of agreeing to become my wife.'

'No, no, Ralph, you will not fob me off like that,' cried Adam, laughing. 'What a fellow you are for keeping things close! I am determined to know all about this engagement.'

'And so you shall.' Ralph smiled. 'There is nothing secret about it.'

'No, no, I never— That is…' Adam coloured. 'I was not suggesting there was anything… The news came as something of a surprise, that is all.'

'Miss Halbrook's father died twelve months

ago and she has only recently come out of mourning. That is why we have made no announcement yet.'

Ralph's tone indicated that this explained everything. Lucy was well aware that it did not and was relieved when Mrs Dean asked Mr Cottingham about his wife.

'How is dear Judith, Adam?'

'She is well, thank you.'

'Oh, that is good. I vow I have not seen her since the last house party here at Adversane—and how are the children?' She turned to Lucy. 'Adam has two fine boys, my dear. I suppose they are both at school now, are they not?'

'Yes, Charlie joined his brother last term…'

The conversation turned to family matters and Lucy felt she could relax, at least for a while, although she was aware of Adam Cottingham's thoughtful gaze frequently coming to rest upon her. She was not surprised, therefore, when he turned his attention towards her once more but by that time she was more prepared to answer his questions, adhering to Ralph's advice that they should tell the truth wherever possible.

When Mr Cottingham went off to change for dinner, Lucy sank back in her chair and closed her eyes.

'Good heavens, I feel completely exhausted!'

'You did very well, my dear,' Ariadne told her.

'Although I thought it a little impolite of Adam to ask you quite so many questions.'

'He is my heir,' Ralph reminded her. 'He has more of an interest in the matter than anyone else.'

Lucy sat up again. 'Do you think he suspects the engagement is a sham?'

Ralph's brows went up. 'Why should he?'

'It was the way he kept looking at me.' Lucy hesitated. 'I think he noticed my resemblance to the late Lady Adversane.'

'She has seen the portrait, Cousin,' said Ralph in response to Mrs Dean's gasp of mortification.

'And it is hardly surprising if he did notice, since all the clothes I have to wear are identical to Lady Adversane's.' Lucy lifted her chin and met his eyes defiantly. 'What is it you are not telling me, my lord?'

'There is nothing that need concern you,' said Ralph dismissively. 'However, I do think the portrait should be reinstated in the Long Gallery.'

Mrs Dean looked at Lucy. 'As long as that will not upset you, my dear?'

Lucy shook her head. 'I think it would cause a great deal more comment if you do not put it back.'

'I agree.' Ralph rose. 'Now if you will excuse me, since we will have to wait for my cousin before we can eat, I shall use the time to attend to a little more business.'

He went out, leaving the two ladies to sit in silence.

'Did you know?' said Lucy at last. 'Did he tell you he hired me because I look like his wife?'

Ariadne shook her head, her kindly eyes shadowed with anxiety.

'At first I thought it was merely a coincidence. Then, when Mrs Sutton brought the sketches for your gowns—I asked Ralph what he meant by it, but he merely brushed it aside.'

'I wonder what game he is playing?'

'Oh, surely nothing more than he has already told you,' Ariadne was quick to reply.

'I am sure it is,' said Lucy, adding bitterly, 'No doubt he thinks I am not to be trusted with his secrets!'

'I think it is merely that he misses Helene a great deal more than he is prepared to admit.'

Lucy had already considered that idea and found it did not please her.

Mrs Dean sighed. 'Adversane prides himself upon his logical mind, you see. He says every problem can be solved by the application of logic, so to find him grieving so much for his late wife is quite touching, is it not?'

'It is also a little embarrassing,' replied Lucy tartly. 'Everyone will think he is marrying me because I look like Helene. They will pity me, which I shall dislike intensely.'

'Yes, but he is not going to marry you,' Ariadne reminded her, brightening. 'So it does not really matter, does it?'

Lucy could not disagree with this reasoning, but she knew, deep down, that it did matter to her, although she had no idea why it should.

Lucy enjoyed Adam Cottingham's company at dinner. He was an entertaining guest, witty and knowledgeable, and although she thought his manner a little insincere she was grateful to him for making sure she was not left out when the conversation turned to family matters.

'You will meet Adversane's sisters, of course, when they come here for the house party,' he said as they helped themselves to sweetmeats once the covers had been removed. 'Fearsome ladies, both of 'em.'

'No, Adam, you know that is not so,' protested Mrs Dean, laughing. 'You are not to be frightening Lucy out of her wits.'

'Of course not, but it is as well to be forewarned.' Adam grinned at Lucy. 'They can be very outspoken, but you will do very well as long as you stand up to them.'

'Now you have terrified me,' she replied, chuckling.

'You need not fear,' said Adam. 'I shall be here to protect you.'

The look that accompanied these words was surprisingly intense. Lucy suspected he was trying to flirt with her and was at a loss to know how to respond. However, Adam's attention switched to Lord Adversane when he announced that he had invited the Ingleston Players to entertain his guests on Midsummer's Eve.

'The devil you have!' exclaimed Adam.

The room was filled with a sudden tension that Lucy did not understand. Adversane's dark brows rose a fraction as he regarded his heir.

'Do you have any objections to them coming?'

'No, of course not. It is a tradition that goes back generations...'

'Precisely. They were very sorry not to be performing here last year.'

'Who are these players?' asked Lucy. 'Are we to have theatricals?'

'Yes, indeed,' Ariadne responded. 'Ingleston has its very own troupe of thespians who perform plays at certain times of the year, such as Easter and Christmas time.'

'They have been performing here every Midsummer's Eve for as long as I can remember,' put in Lord Adversane. 'Last year was the exception.'

Midsummer's Eve. Lucy felt a little chill run down her spine. So Lady Adversane had died on the night of the performance. No wonder he had not wanted them to play there last year. Surely their appearance would bring back unwelcome memories? She glanced across at her host. There was no telling what he was thinking from that stern, inscrutable countenance.

An uncomfortable silence began to fill the room, and Lucy was thankful when Ariadne stepped into the breach.

'And when shall you and Judith be coming to stay, Adam?'

'Three weeks' time, Cousin. On the nineteenth.'

'Oh?' Ariadne sounded surprised. 'But that is when the other guests are expected.'

'Adversane suggested it.'

'Yes,' said Ralph shortly. 'There will be no need for you to arrive weeks in advance this year.'

Adam turned to Lucy to explain.

'In the past we spent a deal of time at Adversane, it was almost a second home. My wife was a great help to Lady Adversane, especially with all the arrangements for the summer house party. We would spend weeks here so that Judith could assist her, but of course Cousin Ariadne is taking care of everything this year, and she has you to support her, Miss Halbrook.'

'Precisely.'

An awkward silence followed Adversane's curt response. Mrs Dean rose and quietly invited Lucy to come with her to the drawing room. She said nothing as they crossed the hall, but immediately they were alone in the drawing room she burst out with unwonted spirit, 'If Judith Cottingham did anything to help anyone I should be surprised. Whenever I've seen her here at Adversane she has either spent her time lying down in her room, or wandering about the garden, looking forlorn.'

Lucy blinked at her.

'Why, Ariadne, I have never heard you speak in such a forthright manner before.'

'No, well, usually I am prepared to give anyone the benefit of the doubt, but to hear Adam talking in that fashion—!' Her pursed lips and frowning expression told Lucy just what she thought. She continued scathingly, 'Judith Cottingham is a poor little dab of a woman with a perpetual air of gloom about her. And I did not think Helene was ever that fond of her. In fact, I think she resented her interference, because she told me once that she could not prevent Adam and his wife from coming here so often because they were Ralph's nearest relatives. Heavens, to listen to Adam you would think Judith was essential to the running of Adversane!'

'Mayhap Mr Cottingham is very much in love with his wife. I believe such affection can blind one to a partner's faults.'

Her companion gave a most unladylike snort. 'The only person Adam Cottingham is in love with is himself! His father was a wastrel, you know. Quite profligate, but thankfully he went to his grave before he lost everything. However, although Adam managed to keep the house at Delphenden, there was never enough money—at least not to keep Adam in the manner he wished. Even his marriage did not bring him the fortune he expected, so Ralph set up an annuity for him. Not that Adam was ever grateful. It is my belief that he envies Ralph his fortune and his lands, although I doubt he appreciates just how hard Ralph has worked to make Adversane so prosperous.

'Adam positively *haunted* the place while Helene was alive, for the house was always full of visitors and that gave him the opportunity to shine, which there is no doubt he does in company. But since the accident I believe he has not been near the house, when you would have thought he would be here to support his cousin in his grief. As Ralph's heir I think he should have done more to help him over the past two years, rather than to stay away. To my mind it shows a sad lack of family loyalty—but there, it is not my place to say so, and Ralph has not encouraged visitors for the past two years. He was in great danger of becoming a recluse, you know, which would have been a very bad thing for the family, so we must be grateful that he is holding the summer house party again this year and I shall say no more about Adam's behaviour.'

Lucy was inclined to think Mrs Dean a little harsh in her judgement of Mr Cottingham. Despite his propensity for flirting, as the evening progressed Lucy decided that he was a very friendly, cheerful gentleman and a complete contrast to his cousin, whose unsmiling countenance and taciturn manner were even more marked than usual.

Lucy found only Mrs Dean in the breakfast room the following morning, Lord Adversane having already gone off to Ingleston on business with Harold Colne. Her thoughts turned to the forthcoming house party.

'Is there anything you would like me to do, ma'am?' she asked.

'I rather thought we might go over the arrangements together later today,' said Ariadne. 'I have several urgent letters that I must write this morning so Byrne can have them taken to catch the mail. I am sorry, my dear—'

'No, no, that suits me very well,' replied Lucy. 'It is such a lovely morning that I thought I might walk to Druids Rock.'

'Alone?'

'Of course, alone. It is Adversane land, I believe, so surely it is safe enough.'

'Well, yes, my dear, of course it is *safe*, as long as one does not ascend the rock itself—but I have always thought it such a forbidding place, especially since Helene's accident…such tragic memories.'

'It holds no such memories for me, although I admit I was reluctant to ask Adv—Ralph to take me for that very reason.'

'If you will only wait until later I will come with you—'

Lucy chuckled. It had not taken her long to discover that while Ariadne liked to busy herself around the house, her idea of exercise was a gentle stroll in the shrubbery.

'No, no, ma'am, I would not dream of troubling you,' she said now. 'Besides, it promises to be very hot later, and we would be better employed indoors than walking in the midday sun. No, I shall go this instant and thoroughly enjoy myself.'

Shortly after, attired in her sensible boots and carrying a shawl in case the breeze should be fresher on the moor, she made her way out of doors, pausing only to ask directions from one of the footmen, explaining with a twinkle that she did not wish to lose her way and put the staff to the trouble of finding her.

'Nay, ma'am, that's not likely, for Hobart's Moor ain't large and the path is well marked.'

'I believe the lane leading from the wicket gate will take me there,' she prompted him.

'Aye, ma'am, that it will. Follow the lane through the trees and that'll bring you to

Hobart's Bridge. Cross that and you'll be on t'moor. There's a good track then that brings you round to Druids Rock.'

Armed with this information, and the footman's assurance that she could not miss her way, Lucy set off. The gate was in fact wide enough for a horse and she guessed the path through the trees had originally been intended as a ride. However, the undergrowth now encroached upon it and the trees grew unchecked, their branches almost meeting overhead. She was glad of her shawl for the morning shade was cool. The trees ended where the ride joined an ancient track that curved away around the belt of woodland in one direction and in the other it stretched out before her, winding down across a picturesque stone bridge and cutting through the distant moors.

She walked on and crossed what she guessed to be Hobart's Bridge, pausing to look over the side at the fast-flowing little stream that tumbled over its rocky bed. Lucy followed the track, striding out briskly beneath the cloudless blue vault of sky. The path ran around a natural ridge in the moor, the land falling away to gorse bushes and the stream on one side while rugged slopes covered with rough grass and heather rose up on the other.

As the path wound onwards the views of Adversane were left behind and the dramatic landscape of hills and steep-sided valleys unfolded before her. She stopped several times, taking in the view and thinking how much her father would have loved to paint such scenery. She had captured some of it in her own sketchbook, but everywhere she looked there was another vista. So many views, she knew she would not be able to sketch them all before the house party was over and her employment at Adversane was ended.

She rounded a bend to find the ground ahead rising steeply and suddenly there was Druids Rock soaring above her. There could be no mistaking it, for it towered over the path at this point, dark and brooding, even in the sunshine. The old track ran to the south of the rock and continued down into the wooded valley below, which she guessed was the way to Ingleston, but Lucy chose a narrow path winding up through the heather. As she drew closer to Druids Rock she could see it was not one solid piece but a jumble of huge stones, pushed together as if by some giant hand. The southern face reared up like a cliff, but the northern side swept upwards in a gentle slope, easily ascended. Lucy did not hesitate. She walked up to the top of the ramp and stood there, revelling in the feel of the fresh breeze on her skin. It was like standing on top of the world.

Behind her, the natural rise of the moors blocked her view of the track and only the chimneys of Adversane were visible. Looking south, with the sheer drop at her feet, the valley opened up and beyond the belt of trees directly below her she could see the town of Ingleston nestling between the hills. Leading from it was the white ribbon of road that she had ridden with Ralph yesterday.

Lucy sat down on the edge of the rock, enjoying the peace and solitude. Below her, a few wagons and horses were moving silently along the road while the surrounding land below the moors looked green and well-tended, a network of tidy walls and neat farmsteads. Most of it, she knew, belonged to Adversane. Ralph. It was a good spot from which to see the extent of his domain, but she understood why he did not come here, if his wife had fallen from this very rock. Glancing down, she remembered Ruthie's incautious words. Helene had come here in her evening dress. Had she really been so unhappy that she—?

No. She would not speculate. That would be a despicable thing to do. She scrambled to her feet and left her high perch. She would go back to the house and ask Mrs Dean what exactly had happened. She regained the track and set off back the way she had come. She had not gone far when she heard the thunder of hooves. Looking around, she saw the dark figure of Adversane cantering towards her. Lucy stopped and waited while he brought his horse to a plunging halt beside her.

'Was it you, on top of the rock?'

He barked out the words, a thunderous scowl blackening his countenance.

'Yes.' She fought down the urge to shrink away or apologise. 'It was such a lovely morning I wanted to explore.'

'Explore! Don't you know how dangerous those rocks can be?'

She replied calmly, 'I am sure in the wet they are extremely treacherous, but the ground is dry, and my shoes are not at all slippery.' She twitched aside her skirts to show him the sturdy half-boots she was wearing.

He glared down at her, and Lucy waited for the furious tirade that she felt sure he wanted to utter. After a moment's taut silence she said quietly, 'I am very sorry if I alarmed you.'

She thought she might have imagined his growl as her apology robbed him of the excuse to harangue her. He jumped down and by tacit consent they began to walk, with Jupiter following behind them.

'I saw someone on the rocks and thought it was you. I came up to make sure you were safe.'

'That was very considerate, sir, when I know you do not normally use this track. Is that because of what happened to your wife here?'

He threw a swift, hard glance at her.

'Who told you? What have you heard about that?'

'My maid said Lady Adversane fell to her death from the rock.' She added quickly, 'Please do not blame Ruthie. If she had not told me I should have asked Mrs Dean.'

'I am surprised you were not told I'd killed her.'

Lucy stopped in her tracks. He gave a harsh laugh.

'Oh, not literally. I was at the house when she fell, but it was known she was not happy.'

'You mean they think she killed herself.' Lucy's parents had often deplored her blunt speaking and she glanced a little uncertainly at Lord Adversane, but he did not appear shocked so she continued. 'Would she have done such a thing?'

'*I* do not think so, but—'

Lucy put out her hand to him. 'If she did take her own life, you must not blame yourself, sir.'

He was looking down at her fingers where they rested on his sleeve. Gently, she withdrew them. It had been an impulsive gesture, but he was, after all, almost a stranger. They began to walk on again and despite a little awkwardness Lucy did not want to let the moment pass.

'Will you tell me?' she asked him. 'Will you explain what happened the night she died?' When he did not reply immediately she added, 'I beg your pardon. I have no right to ask—'

'But you want to know, don't you? If I will not speak of it then you will find out from someone else.'

She could not lie.

'Yes.'

'Then it is best you hear it from me. Helene walked here a great deal. Her father, Sir James, is—calls himself—a druid. Have you heard of The Ancient Order of the Druids, Miss Halbrook? Not so ancient, in fact. They were founded about five-and-twenty years ago by a man named Hurle and they are an offshoot of an older order, which Hurle considered too profane. They have their own beliefs and rituals, many based on nature and astrology. And of course they believe there is a link with the ancient standing stones.' His lip curled. 'There are no such stones at Adversane, but we do have Druids Rock. The name of the place goes back generations. No one seems to know why it was called thus, but certainly there have been no druidic rituals here in my lifetime, or my father's. When Preston learned that Druids Rock was on my land he was even more eager for me to become his son-in-law. Even before the marriage had taken place he began to come to Adversane regularly to visit the rock. As did Helene during that last spring and summer when we were living at Adversane. She even went there in the dark, ostensibly to watch the sunrise.'

'Ostensibly? You did not believe it?' Lucy closed her lips. That was not the sort of thing one asked a man about his wife.

'I did not question her beliefs,' he said shortly. 'But I did insist that she never went there unaccompanied. She agreed always to take her maid with her, and I was content with that.' A faint, derisive smile curled his lip. 'The locals fear the place is haunted by fairies and hobgoblins, but I never heard that they injured anyone. If she wanted to get up before dawn to go there I would not forbid it.'

'That is what she is thought to have been doing on Midsummer's Eve. It is thought to be the reason she was still wearing her evening gown.'

'Why did you not come with her?'

'I have no time for superstition, Miss Halbrook.'

'But what about romance?' Those dark brows rose and she blushed. 'Some would think it romantic to watch the dawn together.'

'That would be as nonsensical as my wife's druidical beliefs.' His hard look challenged Lucy to contradict him, and when she said nothing he continued. 'She was not missed until just before breakfast time, when her maid realised she had not gone to bed. I organised search parties, but it did not take long to find her. Druids Rock was the first place we looked.'

'How dreadful for you.'

'Not only for me, but for everyone who was staying at Adversane.'

'And yet, you have invited the same people to join you here again?'

'Yes.'

'And you have invited the players to come in, just as they did the night she—the night Helene died.'

'The Midsummer's Eve play is a tradition, Miss Halbrook. It goes back generations, far beyond the tragedy of my wife's death. It is not logical that it should cease because of one tragic event.'

'But surely—'

He stopped her, saying impatiently, 'Enough of this. We will talk of something else, if you please, or continue in silence.'

She chose silence, and Ralph found himself regretting it. She might infuriate him with her incessant questions but she was only voicing what others would think. It was as well that he had the answers ready. He acknowledged to himself that he had been misled by her appearance. In Mrs Killinghurst's office, she had looked positively drab in the enveloping grey gown and quite demure. If he had known she would show such spirit he would never have employed her. A faint smile began inside him. He should be honest with himself. He *did* know, from that very first encounter in the alley.

He had deliberately positioned himself at the door of Mrs Killinghurst's office so that he could observe the candidate for this post and he had seen Miss Lucy Halbrook walking towards him. He had noted the slight hesitation as she found her way blocked, then the way her head had come up as she approached him, determined not to be intimidated.

Yes, he knew from that first moment that she was not one to accept his demands without question. He should have told Mrs Killinghurst to send her away, to find someone more biddable. Even as the thought formed he realised that after Lucy Halbrook, anyone else would seem very dull indeed.

Lucy hardly noticed the continuing silence. Her mind was too full of what she had heard to make idle conversation. Lord Adversane was lost in his own thoughts and did not appear to object so she occupied herself with studying her surroundings, the rough grass and darker patches of heather, the view of the distant hills. Everything was new and interesting. Suddenly a swathe of white caught her eye, a shifting, snowy carpet nestling in a wide, flat depression a short distance from their path.

'Oh, how pretty. What is it?'

'Cotton grass.' He strode across to the dip and picked a handful of the fluffy, nodding heads. 'It grows on boggy ground. It can be used to stuff pillows, though it is not as good as goosedown.'

'It looks very fine,' she observed.

'It is. Feel it.'

The breath caught in her throat as he brushed the white heads against her cheek. The touch was gentle, as light as thistledown, but it sent a thrill running through her body. She became shockingly aware of the man standing beside her. She wanted to reach out and touch him, to connect herself to his rugged strength. It was an immense struggle to compose herself and respond calmly.

'It, um, it is as soft as silk.'

He held her eyes for a moment, a look she could not interpret in his own, then he turned away.

'Unfortunately the strands are too short to be spun into thread.'

A faint disappointment flickered through her as he cast aside the grasses and began to walk on.

Did you expect him to present them to you like some lovesick swain?

With a mental shrug, she fell into step beside him again, walking on in silence until they had crossed Hobart's Bridge and were approaching the belt of trees that separated the moors from Adversane Hall.

'Does that way lead to the Hall, too?' she asked, pointing to the old track where it disappeared around the trees.

'Yes. It leads to the main gates, but it will be quicker if we go through the old ride.'

'Is that what it is called? I came out that way,' said Lucy. 'I suppose Lady Adversane rode through it when she went to Druids Rock.'

'No, my wife was a nervous rider and preferred to walk. I never come this way.'

She looked up at the overhanging branches.

'And you have not had many guests since the accident, so consequently it is much overgrown.'

'You are right. The only people to use it now are the servants, if they are walking to Ingleston.'

'But it is such a delightful route, my lord. It seems such a shame that one cannot ride this way any more.'

'It is a loss I can bear.'

They had reached the gate leading into the grounds of the house. Ralph was about to open it, but Lucy was before him, lifting the latch and walking through, as if declaring her independence. He found himself smiling as he watched her. She was a strange mix, quiet and a little shy, yet not afraid to challenge him, and not at all cowed by his sharp retorts. He had not spoken to anyone of Helene's death for so long that it had been a relief to talk of it, so much so that he had had to stop himself from confiding his suspicions. But he could not do that, he was playing far too dangerous a game to involve anyone else. If he was wrong then innocent names would be mired by suspicion. It was his plan and he would share it with no one. He alone would take the credit for it. Or the blame.

Ralph guided Jupiter through the gate and closed it firmly behind him. Lucy was waiting for him. The wind had sprung up and she was busy trying to untangle her shawl.

'Here, let me.' He dropped Jupiter's reins so that he could use both hands to take the shawl and drape it around her shoulders.

'Thank you. There are rainclouds on the horizon. I am glad we are back in time to avoid a soaking.'

She was laughing, completely unaware of how pretty she looked, her windswept curls rioting around her bare head and her skin glowing from the fresh air.

Kiss her.

She was knotting the ends of her shawl, oblivious of his hands hovering over her shoulders. He snatched his hands away as she turned her head to address him.

'What say you, my lord, will it last? Shall we be confined indoors by the inclement weather?'

She was peeping up at him through her lashes and he felt his blood stirring. It was unconsciously done, he would swear to it, but by God that look was damned inviting! With a silent oath he tore his eyes away from her. She was here for a purpose and he would not allow himself to be distracted.

'There is rain on the way, certainly.' He picked up Jupiter's reins. 'You can see the house from here, so there is no reason for me to come farther with you.'

Without another word, he threw himself into the saddle and dug his heels into the horse's flanks. Soon they were flying across the park, and he had to concentrate to keep the big hunter steady. As Jupiter settled into his stride Ralph found the unwelcome feelings were receding. It was the novelty of having a young woman in the house, that was all.

Since Helene's death he had thrown himself into his work on the estate and shunned female society. He saw now that it had been a mistake. If he had not been so reclusive he would not now find himself so desirous of Lucy Halbrook's company, and he would not be so quickly aroused when they were together. After all, she was no beauty. It was her resemblance to Helene that had persuaded him to employ her, but the longer she was here the less he could see any similarity. Damnation, had he been mistaken? No, Adam had seen the likeness, he was certain of that.

'She will have to do,' he muttered as he bent low over Jupiter's glossy black neck. 'Only another couple of weeks and it will be finished. She will leave Adversane and I need never see her again. All I require of Lucy Halbrook until then is that she plays her part.'

Chapter Six

'Well, was there ever anyone so rude?'

Lucy watched Ralph gallop off across the park. She had thought they were getting on well. They had talked quite freely during their walk, which had gone a long way to allowing her to put aside some of her own reserve, but now he had rebuffed her. Lucy tried to be angry, but honesty compelled her to admit that she was more wounded by his abrupt departure.

'But why should he walk you back?' she asked herself as she turned her steps towards the house. 'If he was truly your fiancé it would be a different matter. You would have every excuse to feel aggrieved. As it is, he is paying you very well and that should be sufficient. Surely you do not want to spend more time with such a difficult man.'

She thought back to what he had told her about his late wife. Ariadne thought them a devoted couple, but Lucy was sceptical. Ralph himself had admitted Helene was not happy and she had detected no sign of affection in his manner when he talked about his wife. She stopped and uttered her thoughts to the open air.

'But if that is the case, why does he want me to look like Helene?'

She fixed her eyes on the darkening sky, as if the black clouds might give her an answer. The only response was a fat raindrop that splashed on her nose. She hurried on, reaching the house just as the heavens opened.

The heavy rain continued for the rest of the day, making the sky so dark that when Lucy went down to the drawing room before dinner she found that Ariadne had ordered the candles to be lit.

'These summer storms are so depressing,' said Mrs Dean, staring despondently at the rain cascading down the windows.

'Best to be thankful there is no thunder and lightning,' remarked Ralph, walking in at that moment. 'That sends even the most sensible females into a panic.'

Lucy, still smarting from the way he had left her that morning, bridled immediately.

'Not all females, my lord.'

He raised his brows, looking at her as if her comment was not worthy of a response. She watched him sit down beside his cousin and engage her in conversation.

Good. She was glad and did not wish to talk to him when he was determined to be so disagreeable. She had to admit that he was being perfectly civil to Ariadne, but whenever he was obliged to acknowledge Lucy he did so with such brevity that it bordered on curt. Byrne came in to announce dinner and Lucy hung back. With only the briefest hesitation Ralph offered his arm to his cousin.

It was what Lucy had intended, what she wanted, yet following them across the hall she felt decidedly alone. The rain did not help, for it made the Great Hall cold and gloomy, and when they reached the dining room she was glad to find that an abundance of candles burned brightly, giving the room a cosy glow that offset the sound of the rain pattering against the window. Mrs Dean remarked that they would need to ensure they had a good supply of candles for the forthcoming house party.

'Colne sent off an order for another twelve dozen only yesterday,' replied Ralph. 'Which reminds me, have you made up the guest rooms yet?'

'Lucy and I allocated the rooms today. There is a little furniture to be moved, but apart from that nothing need be done now. We shall make up the beds the day before your guests arrive.'

He nodded. 'And when does Mrs Sutton anticipate the rest of your gowns will be ready, Lucy?'

'She has promised them next week, my lord.'

He did not respond immediately, but when Byrne followed the servants out of the room he said, 'I thought we were agreed that you would call me by my name?'

'I beg your pardon, my—Ralph. It slipped my mind.'

'Then pray do not let it happen again.'

Ariadne shook her head at him.

'Fie upon you, Cousin, how can you expect Lucy to address you informally when you are acting so cold and...and *lordly* this evening?'

'I am paying her to do so.'

And very handsomely, Lucy acknowledged silently. However, it did not mean that she would be browbeaten. She remarked, as the servants returned with more dishes, 'Ralph cannot help being *cold and lordly*, ma'am. It is all he knows.'

With Byrne filling the wineglasses and the footmen in attendance, only the narrowing of Adversane's eyes told Lucy that her comment had hit home.

The dinner was excellent, as always, but Lucy felt a tension in the air. Perhaps it was the weather. It was very close in the dining room, but the driving rain made it impossible to open the windows.

Ariadne did not seem to notice, but whenever Lucy looked at Ralph, he appeared to be frowning and distracted. He contributed little to the

conversation and by the time the covers were removed Lucy was so incensed by his conduct that
she barely waited for the door to close behind
the servants before asking him bluntly what he
meant by his boorish behaviour.

Those black brows flew up.

'I beg your pardon, ma'am?'

Ariadne fluttered a warning hand at Lucy,
but she ignored it.

'You have barely said two words together during dinner,' she retorted. 'If there is something
pressing upon your mind then do please share it
with us. Otherwise it would be courteous to give
us at least a little of your attention.'

'If there are matters *pressing upon my mind*,
madam, they are my business, and not for general discussion.'

'Dinner is a social occasion,' she retorted.
'My father always said if you cannot talk about
a problem then it should be left outside the dining room. He considered family dinners to be
most important.'

'When he was sober enough to attend them!'

He saw her flinch as if he had struck her, and
it did not need Ariadne's outraged gasp to tell
him he was at fault.

'Lucy—Miss Halbrook, I beg your pardon,
I—'

She held up a hand to silence him. Slowly, she
rose to her feet.

'If you will excuse me, Ariadne, I think I shall retire.'

'My dear!' Mrs Dean put out her hand, then let it fall and looked instead to her cousin. 'Ralph, how could you say such a thing? You must apologise.'

'I have done so, Cousin.'

'It is unnecessary, I assure you,' said Lucy in freezing accents.

Keeping her head high, she left the room. She closed the door behind her with exaggerated care, determined to keep her anger in check. To her annoyance she could feel the hot tears coursing down her cheeks. She dashed them away but more followed. The through-passage was empty but she could see shadows moving in the Great Hall and hesitated, unwilling to allow the servants to witness her distress.

She heard the dining room door open and a hasty tread upon the boards behind her. Heedless of decorum, she turned and raced through the passage, heading for the gardens.

'Lucy!'

She wrenched open the garden door and flew across the terrace, heedless of the drenching rain. The only light came from the house windows, illuminating the terrace with a pale gleam but leaving the rest of the gardens in darkness. Without thinking Lucy plunged down the shallow steps into the blackness. She had reached the bottom step when Ralph caught up with her, catching her arm and forcing her to stop. She kept her back to him, rigidly upright, anger burning through every limb.

'Forgive me.'

She shook her head, unable to trust her voice, but thankful that the rain had washed away all evidence of her tears. She would not allow him to think she was so weak.

'Lucy, you are right, I have had something on my mind. I have been distracted, ever since our meeting at Druids Rock this morning, but it is not something I could share with you in company.'

'That does not give you the right to throw my father's weakness in my face.'

'I know, but I was taken aback by your reproof.' An unsteady laugh escaped him. 'No one has dared to admonish me at my own dinner table before.'

'More's the pity. Now leave me alone!'

She shook off his hand, only to find herself caught by the shoulders and whirled about so violently that if he had not maintained his hold she would have fallen.

'Damn you, woman, you shall not leave me like this!'

'Like what, my lord?'

'Will you not at least be open with me?'

The injustice of his words made her swell with indignation.

'It seems to me, my lord, that it is *you* who will not be open with *me*! You bring me here, make me masquerade as your wife yet you will not tell me *why*. I abhor these secrets, sir!'

She glared up at him, trying to see his face, but the darkness was too deep. She could see only his outline and the gleam of his rain-soaked hair. Then she could not even see that, for he swooped down, enveloping her in darkness as his lips met hers. The shock of it was like a lightning bolt. Her limbs trembled and she leaned against him, clutching at his wet coat as she reeled under the shocking pleasure of his kiss.

But only for a moment. Then she was fighting, some unreasonable panic telling her that she must get away from him or risk destruction. He raised his head, but he was still holding her arms and she began to struggle.

'Let me go!'

'Lucy, I beg your pardon. I should never—'

Anger swelled within her as she tried to shake off his hold. He was her employer; he owed her his protection, yet he was betraying her trust— just as her uncle had done—by attempting to ravish her as soon as she was under his roof. And had her father not betrayed her, also, by keeping his gambling a secret instead of sharing it with her, allowing her to help him?

Her sense of injustice grew. She tried again to break free but he held her firm, and she said furiously, 'Do you think to impose your will upon me by this ruthless seduction?'

His hands fell from her shoulders and she took the opportunity to turn and flee to the safety of her room, where she relieved her anger and distress in a hearty bout of tears.

The rain had gone by the morning and the sun was shining in a clear sky, but the prospect did little to raise Lucy's spirits. She had not slept well; the night had brought counsel and she knew what she must do. Quietly, she rose from her bed, heavy-eyed and depressed. It was still early and she could hear Ruthie snoring noisily in the dressing room, so she went to the linen press and brought out the grey wool robe she had worn for her interviews with Mrs Killinghurst. She needed no maid to help her into it, and she could dress her own hair, too, catching her curls back from her face with a black ribbon. A glance in her glass confirmed her sober, even severe appearance. Squaring her shoulders, she quietly left her room.

She found Lord Adversane in the Great Hall.

'Good morning, my lord. I wonder if you could spare me a few moments, alone?'

When he turned to face her she thought he

looked a little haggard, and there were dark shadows under his eyes, as if he, too, had not slept well. His searching gaze swept over her but with a silent nod he led the way to his study.

He closed the door and invited her to sit down.

'Thank you, my lord, I would rather stand.'

He walked over to the large mahogany desk and turned to face her, leaning on its edge and folding his arms across his chest.

'That, and your funereal garb, tells me this is important.'

'Yes. I am resigning my position here.'

'Indeed?' One word, uttered quietly. No emotion, no surprise. Lucy found it difficult to keep still while he subjected her to a long, long look. 'Is that because of my behaviour yesterday?'

'In part, yes.'

'For which I have apologised, and I will beg your pardon again, here and now. My behaviour was unforgivable and I give you my word it shall not happen again. Will you believe that?'

Her eyes slid to the floor.

'It makes no difference.'

'You still wish to leave Adversane.'

'Yes. Today.'

He pushed himself upright.

'Strange. I had not thought you the sort to give up at the first hurdle.'

'I am not giving up,' she replied indignantly. 'I do not believe I am the right person for this post.'

'Adam Cottingham found no fault with you.'

'He saw me for only a few hours. In a longer period he would realise that it was a sham.'

'And why should he do that?'

'Because our characters are not suited.'

'I fail to see that it matters.'

She looked at him rather helplessly.

'How are we going to convince everyone that we are betrothed?'

He was looking at her, something she could not read in his eyes.

'It is like marriage, madam. We shall have to work at it.'

'My lord, I *cannot* pretend to be your fiancée.'

'May I ask why not?'

She blushed. 'I do not feel for you any of the… the warmer feelings that are necessary to make everyone believe that I—that we—'

'Really? That was not the impression I had last night. I thought your feelings for me were very warm indeed.'

'They are, sir,' she retorted, goaded. 'I dislike you, intensely!'

'That is not important. As long as we are polite to one another people will assume it is a marriage of convenience. You are here to meet my neighbours and relatives, your chaperone has been taken ill at the last moment and Ariadne has kindly stepped in. Come, Miss Halbrook, is it so very onerous a task? I thought we were agreed the settlement I am prepared to make will more than make up for any gossip that may arise when you jilt me.'

'The gossip does not worry me but being caught out in this charade does. I should find it very difficult to hide my true feelings.' Lucy raised her head, determined to be brutally honest. 'I find you rude and overbearing, my lord. In fact I find you totally abhorrent!'

Her declaration did not appear to disconcert him in the least.

'Then you will just have to act a little, Miss Halbrook.' He laughed at her stunned silence and stepped towards her, reaching for her hand. 'You have spirit, Lucy Halbrook. I like that, although sometimes I find it hard to accept your home truths about my character. My temper is cross, as you know to your cost, but I have apologised, and I will try to curb it for the next few weeks. You have my word on that, if you will but reconsider.'

His thumb caressed the inside of her wrist, causing an extraordinary reaction. Her pulse was jumping erratically, his touch awakening an inexplicable longing from somewhere deep inside her. She was aware of a pleasant languor spreading through her body and it was difficult to think clearly. However, she had to try.

'It is not just your temper, sir. You took advantage of me.' The memory of it sent the hot blood pounding through her body again, enhanced this time by the continued assault upon her wits caused by the light-as-a-feather touch of his circling thumb.

'A kiss,' he said shortly. 'A brief sensory exploration, brought on because our senses were heightened by the ongoing disagreement. It could happen to any two people caught in those circumstances. We have my cousin here as your chaperone and as long as we are civil to one another it will not occur again.'

It all sounded so reasonable, thought Lucy, yet they were being civil now, and her senses were still heightened. He was standing very close, surrounding her with his strong masculine presence. His broad-shouldered torso blocked out the light, the grey riding coat reminding her of the shadowed cliff-like face of Druids Rock. He smelled of soap and clean linen. She could almost taste the faint hint of citrus and spices that clung to his skin, feel the strength emanating from his powerful form. Her eyes were on a level with the diamond pin nestled deep in the folds of his neck cloth, and she fixed her gaze upon it, trying to cling to some semblance of reality and stop herself stepping closer, inviting him to enfold her in his arms and repeat the embrace they had shared in the rain. She heard the soft rasp of his breath as he exhaled.

'We can do better than this, Lucy.' His voice

was low and soft, melting the last of her resistance. 'Say you will stay. It is only for two more weeks, and we need only give the appearance of being happy together when we are in company. If I am boorish, then I give you leave to upbraid me as much as you wish.'

She looked up at that, grasping at a mischievous thought to put an end to her languor.

'Do you mean you will accept my strictures meekly, my lord?'

He was smiling down at her and the warm look in his grey eyes set her pulse jumping again.

'I never promise the impossible. We shall battle most royally, I fear.'

To her surprise, Lucy did not find the thought daunting. She was aware of a tiny frisson of disappointment when he changed his grip on her hand and stopped caressing her wrist.

'So, cry *pax* with me, Lucy?'

No. Impossible. There can be no peace between us. Even just standing here I can feel it.

'Very well.'

'And you will stay and be friends?'

Friends. Lucy found the idea very tempting. Despite all she had said to the contrary she would dearly like to be friends with this man, to have him trust her.

No! The danger is too great. Go. Now.

'Yes. But I shall not allow you to bully me.'

Amusement gleamed in his eyes.

'Then it should prove a very eventful two weeks.'

He lifted her hand to his lips before releasing her. Lucy trembled inwardly as the gesture sent more shockwaves racing through her body. She did not think Ralph had noticed, for he had turned to his desk and was sorting through the papers.

He said, over his shoulder, 'Very well. If that is all, I have work to do before breakfast. You can go upstairs and change out of that abominable gown!'

No relief, no word of thanks—Lucy felt a gurgle of laughter bubbling up inside her as he resumed his usual autocratic tone. It would indeed be an eventful two weeks!

Having cleared the air, Lucy threw herself into life at Adversane. Ariadne was glad of her help with the arrangements for the house party, and Lucy cultivated the acquaintance of Amos, the aged gardener who promised her enough fresh flowers to fill the house. She also made a friend of Greg, Ralph's groom, who accompanied her on her daily rides.

Of Ralph himself she saw very little. He accompanied her and Ariadne to church on Sunday, but after that he spent most of his time with Harold Colne or on the estate, going out before breakfast and joining the ladies only in time for dinner each evening. When Ariadne jokingly remarked that he was neglecting them he said they would see more than enough of him when the guests arrived.

Lucy discovered that she missed his company. She began to take more care over her appearance when she prepared for dinner each evening. Ruthie proved herself a proficient *coiffeuse*, and Lucy was happy to sit still while the maid arranged her hair, chattering merrily all the while.

However, after her first incautious speech, Ruthie never mentioned her late mistress, and Lucy was increasingly curious to find out more about the woman whose place she was supposed to be filling. A casual remark to Mrs Green brought forth the information that Lady Adversane had been eager to learn how to run the household to his lordship's satisfaction.

'Not that the master wanted her to pander to him,' remarked the housekeeper, smiling at the memory. 'Quite nonplussed he was, whenever he found she put his comfort before her own. Told her she was mistress now, and must order things the way she wanted. He even gave her leave to have her bedchamber redecorated in any style she wished, but she wouldn't change a thing. To my mind I think she would have preferred to live in the London house, but she would not say so. Never one to make a fuss. But that was my lady's way.' She sighed and shook her head.

'A saint, she was, always looking to everyone else's happiness.'

Lucy found herself stopping in the Long Gallery to look at the portrait of Helene, now back in its original position. She tried to read her expression, to discern if she was happy or miserable, but the painted face merely stared down at her, a faint, wistful smile lifting her mouth. She wished she had the courage to ask Ralph about his wife, but even though she thought they had achieved an excellent understanding they only met at dinner or in the drawing room with Mrs Dean present, and Lucy did not feel she could mention it in company.

Mrs Sutton arrived towards the end of the following week, bringing with her all the remaining outfits, save the scarlet gown. She explained that she had had to send to London for the silk. However, she had brought so many other gowns and pelisses that Lucy was in no way disappointed. After trying them all on, she left the dressmaker and her assistant in the morning room, making the final adjustments while she went off to the stables. She had sent word earlier that she wanted to ride out and she found Brandy saddled and waiting for her. A young stable hand called Robin helped her to mount and explained that Mr Greg had gone off to Ingleston with Lord Adversane.

'So I'm to come with you today, miss,' he ended with a grin.

Brandy was fresh, and as soon as they entered the park Lucy gave him his head and enjoyed a gallop. It was only when she reached the trees and slowed up that she realised the young groom was quite some distance away. She stopped and waited for him to catch up with her. He was looking a little red in the face, and she laughed.

'I did not mean to leave you so far behind.'

'Nay, miss, that were my fault. Fair took me by surprise, you did, setting off so fast. I weren't expecting you to be such a good rider.'

He looked at her with new respect in his cheerful, open countenance, and as they turned and walked on Lucy could not resist asking if he had accompanied Lady Adversane on her rides.

'Aye, miss, for she wouldn't ride out alone. Wouldn't travel anywhere on her own, and that's a fact. Very nervy she was, which didn't suit my lord. Neck or nothing, he is. Bruising rider.'

'Yes, he is.' Lucy knew she should not ask, but Robin was a friendly lad, and there was no harm in her questions, surely. 'How did they get on, riding out together?'

'They didn't, miss. My lady was frightened of all his lordship's cattle, especially Jupiter. Horses knows, see, they can smell that sort of thing. The master said at first that my lady would have to get used to 'em, but it was no good, and after a few weeks he asked Sir James to send over the grey my lady had always ridden.' He wrinkled his nose. 'Overfed old mare, no pace at all. Mr Greg said he'd never expected to see such a slug in the master's stables, and 'twas no wonder my lord never rode out with his lady.' He stopped, flushing. 'I beg yer pardon, miss. I should not be saying this to you.'

Guiltily aware that she had encouraged his confidences, Lucy hastened to reassure Robin that she would not repeat it to anyone. She knew she should put all thoughts of Lady Adversane out of her mind, but Lucy was beginning to feel a little sorry for her, if she did not share her husband's love of horses. She could well imagine Ralph's impatience, but surely he could have curbed it and indulged his wife in a gentle ride around the park occasionally? She shook her head. It was not her concern. She would only be here for another two weeks. After that nothing at Adversane would be her concern at all.

Lying in her bed, Lucy stared into the enveloping darkness.

'You would think,' she said aloud, 'that after spending the day helping Ariadne arrange all the guestrooms I would be exhausted. So why am I now wide awake?'

She clasped her hands behind her head. Perhaps working in the house had brought it home to her that Ralph's family would be arriving soon. She had grown very comfortable at Adversane with only her host and his cousin for company, but she would have to be on her guard once their guests arrived. She sighed, realising how happy she had been for the past week, but it could not continue. She had been employed for a reason, and she must play her part. Lucy blinked. The inky blackness around her was almost total, only relieved by the bluish square of the window. Silently, she slipped out of bed and padded across the room. After wrestling for a moment with the catches, she threw both casements wide.

Balmy night air flooded in, bringing with it the heavy fragrance of the newly scythed lawns and the faint, tantalising hint of roses from the flower garden. Lucy curled up on the window seat and rested her arms on the sill, leaning out to catch the cool air on her face. With a sigh, she dropped her chin on her arms and gazed across the drive to the park beyond. She felt the heavy weight of the single plait of her hair slide over her shoulder to dangle into nothingness. The darkness was not so thick out of doors, for although there was no moon the clear sky was sprinkled with stars.

"Well, Rapunzel, what are you doing out of bed at this hour?"

Lucy jumped and looked down to see a figure standing beneath her window. His face was little more than a pale blur in the darkness, but the deep voice was instantly recognisable.

'One might ask the same of you, Lord Adversane,' she retorted. 'And *what* did you call me?'

'It is from a German folk tale. Rapunzel is a maiden who is locked in a high tower and the only way her lover can reach her is to climb up her hair.'

Lucy laughed. 'That sounds very painful. Besides, my hair is far too short for that.' However, she still flicked the braid back over her shoulder, out of sight. 'I might ask you what you are doing beneath my window.'

'Jupiter lost a shoe on the way back from Halifax this afternoon. I have been to the stables to check up on him.'

'No serious damage, I hope?'

'No, Greg will take him to the smith in the morning. I am more concerned at why I should find you at your window in the middle of the night.'

'I could not sleep.'

'Are you anxious about anything? Can I help?'

His response was unexpected and surprised her into replying more freely than she had intended.

'No, thank you, sir. I have no idea why I am awake, I have been busy all day and in truth I should be very sleepy, but I am not. So I am star-gazing.'

'A good night for it. The moon will make an appearance tomorrow.' He paused. 'If you are truly awake…'

'I am.' A sudden sense of anticipation made the breath catch in her throat.

'We could take my telescope onto the roof and you could look at the stars properly.'

'Oh, I should dearly like to—' She stopped, aware of just what he was suggesting. Why, it must be nearly midnight. Regretfully she shook her head. 'That is, no, my lord. Thank you, but I cannot keep you from your rest.'

He ignored her objection.

'Put on a wrap and be ready. I will come for you. And do not light a candle, you need to keep your eyes accustomed to the dark!'

This is madness, thought Lucy as she stood by the door, listening. As soon as she heard a soft tread in the passage outside her room she opened the door a fraction and peeped out. The darkness there was leavened by a small lanthorn that gave out sufficient dim light for her to see Lord Adversane, still wearing his evening dress. Nervously, one hand went to her neck as if to assure herself that the enveloping wrap covered her from chin to toe.

'Good, you are here,' he murmured. 'Come

along then. The staircase is at the far end of the east wing.'

I should not be doing this, she thought even as she stepped out of her room. Her wrap looked ghostly pale in the dim light, and she began to feel a little nervous until her fingers were taken in a firm, warm grasp.

'It will be easier if I hold on to you,' he whispered. 'Follow me.'

He led her through the gallery and into the east wing, where a long corridor brought them to a door.

'My workshop,' Adversane told her. 'There are stairs to the roof in the far corner.'

She followed him into the room. He placed the lanthorn down on a table, and Lucy looked around her. A large cupboard filled one wall. She had seen something similar once before—a cabinet of curiosities, it was called, and it could be filled with all sorts of odd things, from antiquities to rare books and stuffed animals, whatever caught the owner's interest. How she would love to come and explore here in daylight! Reluctantly, she turned away and spotted a large circular stone on the table by the lanthorn. She picked it up, turning it so that the feeble rays of the lamp showed her that it was formed like a coiled snake.

'That is a fossil,' he said, coming up. 'An ammonite, sometimes called a serpent stone. It is the petrified remains of a creature that lived in the very distant past.'

'Oh, I have heard of these,' cried Lucy. 'Is this not evidence of the flood, as it is told in the Bible?'

'Some might believe that.'

'But you do not?'

'I think this might be evidence of much older life forms.'

'Really? But I thought someone—a clergyman—had calculated the exact age of the earth.'

'I am a product of the Enlightenment, Miss Halbrook. I believe in logic and need to be convinced by reasoned argument and experiment. There are a great many theories on the origins and age of the earth, and much work yet to be done to prove them.'

'But surely not everything can be explained by reason and logic, my lord.'

'Not yet, perhaps, but one day. The Royal Society's own motto is "Nullius in verba" which means "take no man's word for it". A good maxim, I think.' He picked up the lanthorn and held it out to her. 'Time is going on. We must take the telescope up to the roof. Can you light the way?'

He ushered her across the room to a door that opened onto a flight of stairs. Indicating that she should precede him with the lamp, he shouldered the large brass instrument and followed her. The stairs were steep and narrow, and it was as much as Lucy could do to hold up her skirts and keep the light steady. At last she reached the top and opened the door to find herself upon the roof. Outside the starlight was faint, but bright enough to make the lamp unnecessary. It was possible to make out a flat walkway around the perimeter of the building, and Lucy was relieved to note that it was edged by a sturdy stone balustrade.

Ralph stepped in front of her and strode off, leaving Lucy to follow as best she might. They soon reached a small platform, where Lord Adversane set the telescope upon its tripod and began to angle it towards the sky. She put down the lamp and watched him.

'Mercury and Venus are only visible at twilight,' he said, turning back to her. 'But there is a good view of Saturn tonight, and I shall be able to show you the major constellations.'

'I know some,' she said, looking upwards. 'There, that is Ursa Major, is it not, leading to the North Star? Papa taught me that. He said if I knew which way was north I would always be able to find my way home.' She laughed. 'Not that I have ever needed to do so. As I told you, my lord, this is the farthest from London I have ever travelled.'

'And would you like to travel more, Miss Halbrook?'

'Oh, yes. When the war is over I would love

to go to the Continent, especially Naples and Rome.'

'To do the grand tour, perhaps?'

'Oh, no, I shall not have that much money, but what you are paying me for being here will be a good start to my savings—' She broke off, suddenly conscious of her situation, alone in the dark with her employer. Alone in the dark with Ralph Cottingham, fifth Baron Adversane. She thought back to his explanation of their encounter in the rain-soaked garden. It had sounded very reasonable at the time, but no amount of reasoning could dispel her unease. She said briskly, 'But that is all for the future and I should not be wasting your time with it. Now, let me see, what other patterns can I recognise? That is Ursa Minor, is it not?'

'That's right. And there, the brighter stars that make an elongated letter "W", is Cassiopeia....'

He continued to describe the night sky, standing behind her and directing her eyes up to the heavens. He pointed out Draco, Hercules and Cygnis, as well as the bright star Arcturus in the constellation of Bootes, the herdsman. Lucy tried to concentrate, but when he laid one hand casually on her shoulder it took all her resolution to stand still. It was a relief when he finished his brief tour of the skies and invited her to look through the telescope.

'But the stars are not much clearer,' she exclaimed, a laugh in her voice. 'I fear you have misled me, Lord Adversane.'

'That is because they are so distant. Now, look at Saturn.' He turned her around and stood behind her, pointing over her shoulder. 'Look, there it is. Follow my finger, do you see it? A bright spot in the south.'

'Yes, yes, I do.'

'Now.' He realigned the telescope and beckoned her over. 'Now, what do you see?'

She peered through the lens and caught her breath in a gasp.

'But it is beautiful,' she breathed. 'I can see it so clearly, and it has hoops around it—' She straightened and moved away from the telescope to stare once more at the night sky. 'It is quite marvellous, my lord.'

He laughed and, clearly encouraged by her eagerness to learn, pointed out even more constellations to her.

'But this is not the best time of year for stargazing,' he told her. 'Once the darker nights are here you have more opportunity to see the planets and track them across the heavens.'

They stood in silence, gazing up. Lucy felt a strange contentment and was emboldened to ask, 'Did Lady Adversane share your enthusiasm, sir?'

She felt him drawing away from her, even before he moved.

'No,' he said shortly. 'I brought her here once or twice, but she found it tedious and very cold. We have done enough for tonight. Come along.'

Putting a hand under her arm, he took her back to the stairs, scooping up the lanthorn as they went.

'What about your telescope?'

'I shall come back for it later. For now I must get you indoors.'

The easy camaraderie they had shared was quite gone, and Lucy knew she had caused the change by asking him about his late wife. Silently, they descended to his workshop, where Lucy thanked him politely for showing her the stars.

'I only hope you have not caught a chill in that flimsy wrap.'

'Not at all. The night is very warm.'

He put down the lamp.

'Let me feel your hands.' He reached out and took them in his own warm grasp. 'You are cold.'

'No, no, I assure you it is only my fingers.'

Lucy stared at his hands. Her throat dried, a voice inside was screaming that she should pull away, and she knew she was standing far too close for safety. The darkness swirled around them, edging her closer still, like a solid hand on her back. How easy it would be to lean into him, to rest her cheek on the smooth silk of his waistcoat and feel the hard chest beneath. Perhaps she might even hear the thud of his heart. The very thought sent her own skittering around like a frightened bird and when Ralph released her hands and reached for her, she quickly moved away.

'I—I must get back.'

'Of course.'

She tried to avoid any further contact, but as soon as they stepped into the dark corridor he put out his hand and hers slid into it, as if of its own accord. The silence of the house pressed in around them, the only sound the faint rustle of their moving. When they reached Lucy's room Adversane stopped, standing between her and the door.

'It will soon be dawn. I hope you will sleep now, Miss Halbrook.'

'I am sure I shall.'

I don't want to sleep. I want to stay awake and live again everything that I have seen and experienced with you!

She was shaken by the sudden thought and could only hope she had not spoken aloud. She forced herself to release his hand. He nodded.

'Very well, I shall leave you now.' His fingers grazed her cheek. 'Goodnight, Rapunzel.'

Lucy slipped into her room and closed the door. She leaned against it, listening for the sound of his footsteps moving away, the soft thud of his door closing. Her heart was singing with happiness. Quite foolish, of course, but she could not help it.

She smiled and whispered, 'Goodnight, my lord.'

Chapter Seven

Ralph's sisters and their husbands arrived the following afternoon, a day early, while Lucy and Ariadne were on a shopping trip to Ingleston.

'Perhaps it is not such a bad thing,' remarked Mrs Dean, when Byrne informed them that their guests were in the drawing room with Lord Adversane. 'You have not had time to get into a panic.'

Lucy tried to smile. She could not forget Adam Cottingham's remark that Ralph's sisters were fearsome ladies. However, there was no going back, for Mrs Dean had taken her arm and was marching her towards the drawing room.

The next ten minutes passed in a flurry of introductions and exclamations. Lucy was presented to Lord and Lady Wetherell and Sir Timothy and Lady Finch. The ladies had the same rather hawk-like features as their brother, but their smiles were warm, and however fearsome they might be, she took comfort from the fact both Sir Timothy and Lord Wetherell had the genial, well-fed look of contented spouses.

'Enough of this formality,' declared Lady Wetherell, coming forward and kissing Lucy on the cheek. 'You must call me Caroline, my dear, and my sister is Meg—or Margaret, which is what I call her when she has annoyed me! Now, Miss Lucy Halbrook, let me look at you. What persuaded you to agree to marry my brother? Did he bully you into it?'

Lucy blinked at such a direct question and could only be thankful when Ralph answered for her.

'My dear Caroline, how do you expect her to respond to such a question?' He came forward and took Lucy's hand. 'I admit I had to work hard to persuade her to accept my offer, but I don't think I bullied you, did I, my dear?'

He was smiling down at her, the mischievous glint in his eyes inviting her to enjoy their shared secret. She found herself relaxing.

I can do this.

'No more than usual, my lord.'

'Bravo,' cried Lady Finch, putting her sister aside so that she, too, could greet Lucy with a kiss. 'You must never be afraid to stand up to Ralph, my dear. His last wife was too complaisant for her own good.'

Lucy froze. The room fell silent, and Sir Timothy murmured a quiet remonstrance to his wife, who looked around her, brows raised in surprise.

'What have I said that isn't common knowledge?' She turned back to Lucy. 'You will learn that we like plain speaking in this family.'

'But not if it embarrasses Miss Halbrook,' retorted Ralph.

'Quite right,' agreed Caroline. 'Sit down, Meg, and give Miss Halbrook time to grow accustomed to us.'

'And how are the children?' asked Ariadne, as if to deflect attention from Lucy.

'Oh, they are all healthy and ripe for a spree,' replied Sir Timothy cheerfully. 'We sent the boys off to stay with Caroline's three young scamps.'

'That's good,' said Ralph. 'They can ruin Wetherell's coverts and leave my birds in peace.'

Mrs Dean shook her head at him. 'Fie, Ralph, you know you love them all dearly.'

'How many children do you have?' asked Lucy.

'Two fine young boys,' replied Sir Timothy, pushing out his chest a little.

'And Caro has two girls and a boy,' declared Margaret. 'Delightfully noisy and boisterous, thank heaven.'

'Yes, they are, which is why we thought it would be quite unfair to subject Ralph's future wife to such lively children until she was better acquainted with the rest of us.' Caroline laughed. 'They might well have scared her off!'

An hour later, when Mrs Dean suggested that they should all retire to change for dinner, Lucy's head was reeling. She liked Caroline and Margaret very much and she enjoyed their lively banter, but it had not taken her long to realise that they were as strong-willed as their brother. She was about to follow them out of the room, but Ralph caught her hand and held her back.

'Pray do not pay too much heed to my sisters,' he said. 'Do not let their chatter worry you.'

'It doesn't. I find them very entertaining.' She chuckled. 'Although I now understand completely why you want me here.'

'You do?' His swift, frowning look unsettled her, but it was gone in a moment. 'Of course. You did not believe me, then, when I said I need protection?'

'Having met your sisters, I think we may both need protection if they discover they have been deceived.'

He pulled her hand onto his arm. 'Then let me escort you upstairs to add credence to our story.'

She walked with him across the hall and up the grand staircase, but when they reached the Long Gallery she deemed it time to protest.

'Apart from a few servants in the hall, no one has seen us, my lord.'

'Ralph,' he reminded her. 'And someone may come upon us at any time. We need practice, to make sure we always look at ease together.'

She gave a little tut.

'I mean, *Ralph*, that everyone is in their room. We have no audience, sir.'

She freed her arm, but he caught her hand and held on to it as they entered the inner corridor leading to her bedchamber. With no windows on this passage the light was dim, and Lucy felt her pulse quickening. She stopped.

'I do not think we need to continue this any further, my lord.'

'No?'

His softly spoken response made her heart flutter alarmingly, and she stepped away, only to find her back against the wall. She was dismayed to hear how unsteady her voice was when she replied to him.

'There is no one here to impress with our charade.'

'But as I said, we need to practise. It is really quite logical.'

His free hand cupped her cheek, quite gently, but the shock of it held her motionless. She was unable to drag her gaze away from his face. Even in the dim light she noted how his eyes had darkened. He was lowering his head, he was going to kiss her and instead of making any effort to escape she ran her tongue over her lips, as if in preparation.

Then his mouth was on hers. A gentle touch, nothing like the tumultuous kiss they had shared in the rain. She closed her eyes and a tremor ran through her, like a sigh for something long desired. Her lips parted under his gentle insistence, she felt his tongue invading, exploring, and a slow burn of excitement began deep inside, heating her blood. When he raised his head she almost groaned with disappointment. Her eyes flickered open and stared up at him, too dazed to move.

His face was immobile, dark as stone in the deep shadow. He looked at her for a long, long moment. She cleared her throat, forcing herself to speak.

'Ralph—'

His hand was still cupping her face, and now he caressed her bottom lip with his thumb. Without thinking, she caught it between her teeth. Something flared in his eyes, something primeval, triumphant. She released him immediately, and he laughed softly as he drew away from her.

'I was wrong. You need no practice.'

As he turned away she forced out a few more words.

'I—I don't understand.'

He stopped and looked back.

'No, you wouldn't.' He spoke almost sadly,

before adding in his usual brusque tone, 'Tell Ariadne she is not to let you out of her sight!'

'Damn, damn, damn!'

Ralph kicked the door closed behind him as he entered his room. He had made great efforts to keep away from Lucy Halbrook and allow her to forget that kiss in the garden. Not that he could forget it, for that encounter had shaken him badly. She unsettled him, which was why he had ripped up at her and then, knowing that his remark about her father had hurt her, he had wanted to make amends, only to find himself making a bad situation worse by taking her in his arms. Since then he had done his best to act with perfect decorum—apart from that midnight madness when he had taken her up onto the roof. His mind was diverted by the thought. She had been so delightful with the starlight shining in her eyes, and it had been a struggle not to succumb to temptation and kiss her, but he had behaved perfectly rationally.

Ralph told himself he wanted her at Adversane because he needed her to play her part in the forthcoming house party, but the truth was he wanted her to stay for her own sake, because he found her company stimulating. The more he saw of Lucy the more he wanted her. He tried to fight it. During the day he busied himself with his work and he had made sure they only met when Ariadne was present in the evenings, but today he had again broken his own rule and allowed himself to be alone with her.

And look at the result. His body was still tense with desire, and when he closed his eyes all he could see was her face upturned to his, those lustrous green eyes dark and inviting, the tip of her tongue flickering over those full, red lips.

By heaven, how he wanted her!

He absolved Lucy of all intent to seduce him. She was too innocent, completely unaware of her power over him. But for all that he found her presence intoxicating. A ragged laugh escaped him. If his sisters could see him behaving in this idiotic way they would have no difficulty believing the engagement was real.

Ralph frowned. He was growing fond of Lucy and did not want to hurt her by raising hopes he had no intention of fulfilling. He had already decided he could not marry again. He would never risk making another woman as unhappy as Helene had been.

'You are being foolishly conceited if you think she would even consider you as a husband,' he muttered to his reflection as he struggled with the knot of his neck cloth. 'She has already told you she does not even like you!'

And the way she responded to your kiss? The demon in his head would not be silenced. *How do you explain that?*

'Pure animal instinct. She had no idea of what she was doing. Hell and confound it, where *is* Kibble?' He tugged savagely at the bell-pull to summon his valet.

The restless mood would not leave him, and he strode to the window, leaning an arm on the frame and dropping his head against it. One thing was certain: when Lucy Halbrook did eventually find a suitor who pleased her, he would be a very, very lucky man.

Lucy kept one hand on the wall as she made her way back to her bedchamber. Her knees felt far too weak to support her, and her body still pulsed with an energy she did not understand. Ruthie bustled in from the dressing room, too excited with her own news to notice her mistress's pallor.

'Ooh, miss, I'm to sit with the ladies' maids at dinner tonight. Imagine! Mrs Green says when the other guests arrive tomorrow, us ladies' maids will have to have a table to ourselves. Was there ever anything like it?'

'No, never.' Lucy tried to be glad for her maid. 'Help me out of this gown, Ruthie, then I think I shall lie down for a little while before I change for dinner.'

'Yes, miss. Oh, and Mr Kibble passed on a message from his lordship. He says you are to wear the blue silk tonight, miss, with the silver stars.'

'Yes, yes.' Lucy stepped out of her robe and waved her maid away. 'Hang that up, Ruthie, then come back in half an hour.'

Lucy crawled onto her bed and curled up, hugging herself. *Such* feelings she had experienced when he had kissed her. Such emotions had welled up. When she had first raised the idea of finding employment, her mother had warned her of the dangers that lurked in a gentleman's household. She had told her how persuasive men could be, had explained something of the dangerous charms of a seducer, but Lucy had pictured then a leering, lecherous man like her Uncle Edgeworth. Mama had not told her that she must also beware of the treacherous longings of her own body.

The mere memory of Ralph's kiss made her writhe and hug herself even tighter. How would she be able to face him, to be in the same room with him, without wanting to touch him? She knew she would stare longingly at his mouth, desperate for him to kiss her again.

All too soon Ruthie returned with a jug of hot water. Lucy managed to wash with tolerable calm, and she allowed her maid to help her into the high-waisted evening gown of midnight-blue embroidered with silver thread. As the skirts

shimmered into place Lucy was reminded of
standing on the roof with Ralph, gazing up at
the blue-black vault of the night sky. She had
felt such happiness then, with his hand resting
upon her shoulder and his deep voice murmuring in her ear as he talked to her about the stars.

'Miss, miss? Will you sit down, miss, so that
I can dress your hair?'

Lucy gave herself a mental shake and sank
down on the stool before her mirror. She watched
patiently as Ruthie caught her hair up in a blue
ribbon and nestled little silver stars amongst her
curls. She frowned.

'I remember being fitted for the gown, but I
cannot recall Mrs Sutton supplying the hair ornaments.'

'No, miss, they belonged to Lady Adversane.
It seems the master has kept them all this time.
Fancy that!'

Lucy stared in the mirror and a cold chill of
reality began to trickle through her veins.

'And this gown, Ruthie. Do you remember
Lady Adversane wearing one similar?'

'Of course, miss. She said she chose the midnight-blue to match her eyes.' Ruthie gave a gay
little laugh. 'She was that beautiful, but of course
the stars didn't show up quite so well against
her gold curls as they will in your darker ones.'

If Ruthie meant this as a comfort it fell far
short. Lucy stared at her reflection and felt some-

thing inside turning to stone. Ralph wanted her to look like Helene. It was his late wife he had imagined he was kissing earlier. He did not want her at all, merely someone who looked enough like Helene to arouse him.

Lucy sank her teeth into her bottom lip to stop it from trembling. She wanted to sweep her arm across the dressing table, to send the pots and brushes and the rest of those exquisite little silver ornaments flying across the room. Instead, she folded her hands in her lap. This was what she was being paid for—to recreate the image of a dead woman.

The murmur of voices when she went downstairs to the drawing room told Lucy she was not the first, but that was what she had planned. She had deliberately left it as late as she dared to put in an appearance. As she entered the room a silence fell. Lord Wetherell raised his looking glass to stare at her. Sir Timothy goggled, and Margaret exclaimed, in her frank way, 'Good God, she is just like Helene!'

'Do you think so?' murmured Ralph, coming towards her. 'I do not see it.'

He was smiling, and Lucy forced herself to smile back. She had no wish now to gaze at him adoringly, to think of his kiss. When he would have taken her hand, she moved away slightly and made her own way into the room. Caroline patted the seat beside her and smiled invitingly.

'Everyone wears these styles and colours, Margaret. Leave the girl alone.'

But Lucy saw the speculative glance Caroline threw at her brother.

Lucy discovered that playing a role was much easier than being herself. She existed only as Ralph's fiancée; quiet, complaisant and totally without emotion. When Ralph escorted her in to dinner and asked her if she was all right, she smiled sweetly and told him she was very well. Conversation ebbed and flowed around her. After dinner the ladies retired to the drawing room, where Lucy recited without a blush the story she and Ralph had concocted about how and where they had met.

'So it was love at first sight,' said Margaret.

'Not exactly.'

'Well, I must say I was surprised to learn that Ralph had found himself another bride,' remarked Caroline. 'I thought Helene's death had put him off marriage for ever.'

'Did he...? Did he love her very much?' Lucy thought it quite reasonable that a fiancée might ask the question of Ralph's sisters.

'I never thought so,' replied Caroline frankly. 'She was exquisitely beautiful, of course, but when one got past that she had very little else to recommend her.'

'My dear, she was the sweetest girl,' protested Ariadne.

'Yes, the sweetest little nodcock.'

'Well, I think we have only ourselves to blame that he married her,' said Margaret, coming to sit on the other side of Lucy. 'We urged Ralph to marry, and to please us he went to Harrogate, looking for a wife. Preston hurled the gel at his head and with her beauty it is hardly surprising that Ralph should fall head over heels in love and offer for her.'

'And she bored him within a month of the ceremony,' declared Caroline. 'Whereas you, my dear…' She turned and caught Lucy's hands. 'You have intelligence and a sharp wit, if I am not mistaken, that will keep a man interested for a lifetime.'

Shocked out of her role, Lucy blushed.

'How can you say so when you hardly know me?'

'I knew it as soon as we met. You have a ready sense of the ridiculous and although you are no chatterbox, what you do say shows you have an active and enquiring mind.'

'But many men do not want an intelligent wife, Caro,' said Margaret. 'The very thought frightens them.'

'Not Lucy,' cried her sister, smiling, 'Who could be frightened of her?'

Lucy laughed and disclaimed. How she would have liked to make real friends of these women, but it could not be. When the time came for her to jilt Ralph they would despise her, she knew it.

'Let us have some music!' cried Margaret, jumping up and going to the piano. 'Do you play, Lucy?'

'A little, but not that well.'

'Then we are all evenly matched. Come along, there is some music here somewhere...'

When the gentlemen came in some time later they found all four ladies gathered about the piano, singing folk songs. Margaret immediately called across the room to them.

'Ralph, your fiancée has the sweetest voice. Do come and join her in a duet.'

Lucy forgot to be complaisant and said hurriedly, 'Oh, no, I couldn't—'

'Do you mean to say you and Ralph have not sung together yet?' Caroline caught Lucy's hand to stop her running away. 'Fie upon you, brother, isn't it Shakespeare who says music is the food of love? Come and sing with her. Margaret shall play for you.'

There was no avoiding it. The sisters shepherded Lucy into place beside Ralph, music was thrust into their hands, and Margaret began to play, while the others took their seats in eager expectation. A lively version of 'Cherry Ripe' was followed by 'Early One Morning'. They were familiar songs, and Lucy soon lost her nervousness and enjoyed herself, her voice blending with Ralph's powerful tenor to produce a wonderful sound that rang around the room. When they had finished their audience clapped enthusiastically.

'Do you know, that was really rather splendid,' declared Sir Timothy, beaming at them. 'I think we shall enjoy some wonderful musical evenings here at Adversane in the future.'

'There is a lovely duet from *The Magic Flute* here somewhere,' cried Caroline, pulling more music from a cupboard. 'It would suit you both beautifully—'

'Not tonight,' said Ralph firmly. He signalled to his brothers-in-law to come forward. 'We have performed, and now it is your turn to join your ladies.'

Lucy had enjoyed herself far too much. The way Ralph had smiled at her had made her pulse race again, disastrous for her peace of mind. She went over to sit next to Ariadne on the sofa. It was only large enough for two and Ariadne's ample frame took up most of the space, so she would be able to enjoy the singing without being distracted by Ralph's disturbing presence.

However, when the couples had agreed who would sing, and Caroline had replaced her sister at the piano, Ralph came across and perched himself upon the arm of the sofa beside her. Lucy kept her gaze fixed rigidly on the piano, but she was very much aware of his thigh so close to her shoulder. He leaned back and rested his arm on the back of the sofa, his fingers playing with the curls at the nape of her neck.

It was all very nonchalant, if a little daring, for a gentleman to lounge in such a manner so close to a lady, but at an informal house party, and when the lady in question was his fiancée, Lucy knew no one would object.

She sat upright, removing her curls from his reach, but her skin still tingled at the knowledge that his fingers were so close and, even more disturbingly, she was very aware that no more than a few inches and a thin covering of kersey separated her from that long, muscular thigh.

Her mind was in turmoil. She had no idea what was sung, or even how long it went on. Part of her wanted it to be over so that Ralph would get up and move away.Another part of her, a much more invidious part, wanted it to go on for ever so that she might lean back again and feel those strong, lean fingers playing with her curls, perhaps even caressing the back of her neck.

The singing ended. Ralph eased himself off the arm of the sofa and walked over to congratulate the performers. Lucy told herself she was delighted, relieved. Margaret returned to the piano to play a sonata and the others disposed themselves gracefully around the room. It was a warm evening, and Sir Timothy threw open the long windows and stepped outside. It was growing dark, and a servant entered with a taper to light the candles. Lord Wetherell invited his lady to accompany him onto the terrace and watch the bats. For the first time Lucy saw Caroline show signs of nerves.

'Bats—horrid creatures! They swoop upon one so silently.'

'But I shall be there to protect you,' murmured her husband, holding out an imperious hand. 'Come along, Caro.'

They wandered out. Ariadne went off to tidy away the music and Lucy was left alone on the sofa. Ralph sat down beside her.

'No, please do not go.' He put his hand on her arm as she went to get up. 'I enjoyed singing with you.'

'Did Helene sing?' The question was out before she could stop it.

'Of course. She was most accomplished.'

He removed his hand and her skin felt cold where his fingers had rested. Lucy suddenly felt very depressed. One could not compete with a dead love. Compete? The very idea was ludicrous. She was an employee, little more than a servant. Ralph would never think of her as anything else.

'I should retire.'

'But it is early yet.'

'I am very sleepy.'

She rose, and Ralph followed her to the door.

'I will escort you—'

'No, please—' She turned, knowing tears were not far away. 'I would prefer to be alone. Please remain with your family.'

He raised her hand to his lips, and the now-familiar heat shot through her veins. She said, to distract herself, 'We have more guests arriving tomorrow. I will need to have my wits about me for that.'

'You managed very well tonight.'

She glanced down. The skirts of her midnight-blue silk looked black in the dim light. Mourning colours for a dead wife. She raised her head, forcing a smile.

'I am doing what you employed me for, my lord.'

He did not correct her, and she went out, closing the door quietly behind her.

'Ralph, where is Lucy?' Margaret called across the room as she closed the lid of the piano.

He had no idea how long he had been standing at the door. Long enough to imagine Lucy crossing the hall and climbing the stairs, her silken skirts whispering about her and the little silver stars in her hair twinkling in the light of her bedroom candle.

'She has gone to bed.' He added lightly, 'No doubt you have tired her out with your endless questions.'

'Pho, we have been unusually restrained,' Meg retorted, coming across the room and taking his arm. 'There are so many questions we *could* have asked. Such as, why have you chosen a woman who looks so much like your late wife?'

'She would not have been able to answer that.'

'No, but you can.' She squeezed his arm. 'Well, Ralph?'

'She is nothing like Helene.' He saw Margaret's cynical smile and shrugged. 'Very well, there is a passing likeness.'

'Helene is gone, Ralph. You cannot bring her back.'

Margaret was the sister nearest to him in age and temperament. He was not used to seeing sympathy in her eyes, but it was there as she murmured the quiet words.

'I have no wish to bring her back,' he muttered. 'I just want—' He stopped. This was his burden, and he would not share it. Instead, he smiled at his sister. 'I want you and Caro to look after Lucy. This house party will be something of a trial for her.'

Chapter Eight

Lucy rose early the following morning. After a night's repose nothing seemed quite so bad and she decided to go out. She dressed quickly, but when she went downstairs she found that Margaret and Caroline were before her.

'Ah, so you are going out walking, too,' Caroline greeted her cheerfully when she met them in the hall. 'We are going to Druids Rock. Will you join us?'

The prospect of congenial company was too tempting. The three ladies went off together, the sisters setting a brisk pace, which suited Lucy very well.

'This is a favourite walk of ours,' said Caroline as they headed for the wicket gate on the far side of the lawn.

'Really? Even after the accident?'

'Well, that was very sad, of course,' said Margaret. 'We always spare a thought for Helene when we go this way, but we enjoy the walk, and the views from Druids Rock are spectacular.'

'Besides,' said Caroline, 'I am sure many dreadful things have happened there in the past. The Druids, you see.' She lowered her voice and said with relish, 'Dark deeds, sacrifices and satanic rituals!'

'Hush, Caro, you know that is all nonsense. Pay no heed to my sister, Lucy. She has a penchant for horrid mysteries and Gothic tales.'

'But you must admit it does add a touch of excitement,' said Caroline. 'Oh! What has happened here?'

They were approaching the gate into the old ride, and Lucy looked up with some surprise. The trees had been cut back, allowing the sunlight to pour onto the path.

'It has been opened up,' cried Caroline. 'And about time, too. Now we shall be able to ride this way again. This must be for you, Lucy. Ralph told us you are a bruising rider.'

Lucy blushed and shook her head, wishing he did indeed care enough to do such a thing for her.

'And the undergrowth has been cut back so we can walk three abreast,' declared Margaret, linking arms with her companions. 'It is quite shocking how overgrown it had become in the past couple of years. Since Helene did not ride much this path was rarely used, but after the ac-

cident Ralph closed the gate and never came this
way any more.'

'Accident!' Caroline gave a snort. 'Everyone
knows she killed herself.' When Margaret protested she waved her hand. 'It is best that Lucy
knows the truth, Meg, if she is going to live here.
It was recorded as an accident, of course, but Helene must have been very distressed to go out
without changing her gown.'

'You think she was distraught?' asked Lucy,
curiosity overcoming her reluctance to discuss
the matter.

Margaret looked at Caroline.

'We think she and Ralph had quarrelled that
day,' she said. 'Or rather, that he had upbraided
her, for she was such a soft little thing she never
argued with anyone. There was a brittle quality
to her at the play that evening, and Ralph was
looking decidedly grim. At the end of the night
we all thought Helene had gone to bed. Of course
with so many people in the house it was all noise
and confusion, and it wasn't until the following
morning we discovered she had gone out.'

'It was quite dreadful when her body was
brought back to the house,' added Caroline. She
gave a shudder. 'I have never seen Ralph so pale.
And later, after dinner, he had the most terrible
row with Adam.'

'Adam Cottingham,' queried Lucy. 'His heir?'

'Yes. We were all gathered in the drawing

room, and Adam had clearly been imbibing far too freely, for suddenly he burst out, "You are to blame. You pushed her to this, you cold devil. If she had not married you she would still be alive!" And Ralph never said a word. He just stood there, that closed look on his face—you know the one, Sis—until Adam stormed out of the room.'

'That is right,' nodded Margaret. 'And Ralph said, in the quiet way he has, "He is right." And then not another word upon it.'

'So he blames himself for her death,' muttered Lucy.

'Yes, but he should not,' declared Caroline. 'No one could have been more kind or forbearing, and you will know by now that that is *not* Ralph's nature. He went out of his way to look after his wife. Helene was very mild-mannered and kind to a fault, but she had no *spirit*. She crumbled at the first hint of disapprobation.'

'Caro—'

'It's the truth, Meg. Oh, everyone loved Helene and I believe she was determined to be a good wife, but she was unhappy. Ralph did his best, as soon as he realised what a nervous little thing she was he did everything in his power to set her at her ease. We never heard him raise his voice to her, did we, Meg?'

'No, he was most forbearing.'

'It's my belief she was unstable,' remarked

Caroline, considering the matter. 'She would burst into tears at the slightest provocation. I found her extremely tiresome, and I only saw her occasionally. How Ralph kept his temper with her I do not know!'

'Caroline!'

'Well, Meg, it is most unfair that Ralph should be blamed because she jumped off the rock.'

'No one blames him,' said her sister. 'But he blames himself and has been punishing himself quite dreadfully. He even declared that he would never marry again, and I am thankful that he has thought better of that decision! We are so glad that he has brought you to Adversane, Lucy, and that he is hosting another house party. It is a sign that he is getting over it at last!'

'Is he?' Lucy tried to smile, but all she could think of was the portrait of Helene in the scarlet gown, and all those dresses he had insisted she should wear.

They walked on in silence, over the pretty bridge and onto the moors. The sun was climbing and by the time they reached Druids Rock it had burned off any remaining mist from the valley. They scrambled up onto the rock and the two sisters pointed out various landmarks to Lucy: the paddock where Greg had taught them to ride, the old ruin on the hill where they had played hide and seek and the neat property on the edge of Ingleston where Ralph's steward lived.

'Harry Colne is Ralph's oldest friend,' said Margaret. 'They used to go everywhere together as boys, fishing, hunting, riding—and here, of course. This was always one of their favourite places.'

'And ours, too,' said Caroline. 'This was our castle, or a pirate ship, or whatever we wanted it to be.' She laughed. 'Do you remember, Meg, when the boys were climbing the south face and Ralph fell and broke his collarbone?'

'Lord, yes. Papa was so angry. Said it served him right for being careless. Oh, it was not that he didn't love us,' she added, catching sight of Lucy's startled face. 'As soon as Ralph was well enough he brought him here and taught him the correct way to scale the rock.'

'That was Papa's way,' explained Caroline. 'He was kind, but not a great one for displays of affection. Ralph is very like him—even more so, in fact, because once he inherited the title he had such responsibilities on his shoulders that he became quite serious and lost his sense of fun… which perhaps explains why Helene found him so difficult to live with.'

Silence followed her words, broken only by the sighing of the wind, until Margaret jumped to her feet.

'Breakfast!' she declared, making her way off

the rock. 'Then we must prepare for the arrival of the Prestons, and Adam and his wife.' When they were on the track again she took Lucy's arm, saying cheerfully, 'We are so very glad you are here, Lucy. We really could not like the thought of our cousin inheriting Adversane.'

'Oh?' said Lucy. 'I met him earlier this week. He seemed a very pleasant gentleman.'

'Oh, he is pleasant enough,' said Caroline. 'And very charming, if you like that sort of thing, yet he is not the man to fill Ralph's shoes. But now that Ralph is going to marry you,' she ended sunnily, 'we need no longer worry about that. Come, let us get back for breakfast. There is nothing like a good walk to sharpen the appetite!'

'I'd forgotten what a noisy family I have.'

Ralph entered the breakfast room to find everyone gathered there and he hardly expected to be heard above the clatter of dishes and cheerful voices.

'Good morning, Ralph.' Margaret waved her fork at him. 'Will you join us? There are still some eggs and ham left, I think, and the most delicious pie, if Timothy has not taken the last piece.'

'Thank you. I broke my fast at Ling Cottage,' Ralph said, smiling at the merry scene.

'And how is Harry, and Francesca, his lovely

wife? Will they be joining us for dinner?' Caroline turned to Lucy. 'Harry is more like family than Ralph's steward, but he is very busy with his own life and can rarely be persuaded to dine here.'

'Well, you will be pleased to know I have, er, *persuaded* them to come along tonight,' Ralph informed them.

His eyes rested on Lucy, noting the colour in her cheeks. He had seen her going off with his sisters that morning, and thought how much better she looked for the exercise. So much brighter than last night, when the sadness in her eyes had unsettled him. 'I came to ask Miss Halbrook if she would spare me a few moments when she has broken her fast.' All the female eyes turned on him, full of rampant curiosity. He felt obliged to add, 'There has been a delivery for her.'

'For me?'

She looked quite delightful, with the colour mounting to her cheek and her eyes wide with astonishment.

'A surprise,' declared Caroline. 'Do wait a moment, Lucy my dear, and we will all come with you.'

Ralph frowned.

'You will not!'

'Is it a secret, Ralph?' Lucy's eyes were upon him, green and luminous with shy anticipation.

'No, of course not.'

'Would it embarrass her if we came along?'

Margaret's blunt question made him scowl.

'It should not do so, but I pray Lucy will not hesitate to say if she has had enough of your company for one day!'

Lucy chuckled at that, a soft, melodious sound that he found immensely satisfying.

'Of course I should,' she said. 'But I have no objection to them coming with me to see this mysterious delivery.'

Ralph was relieved when the gentlemen declared themselves happy to remain and finish their breakfast, but all the ladies rose as one to follow him to the hall. He wished now he had said nothing until Lucy was alone, but he was impatient for her to see what he had bought for her.

A large packing case rested on the floor next to the table in the centre of the hall. Lucy reached in and lifted out a brown paper parcel. Shaking off the packing straw, she placed the parcel on the table. Ralph unfolded his pocket knife and handed it to her.

'You may need this.'

He stood back as the ladies gathered around the table, their excited chatter reminding him of family birthdays long ago, when the house had been alive with laughter. Lucy cut the string and turned to give him back the knife, glancing up at him a little uncertainly. If it had been Caro or

Margaret they would have had the paper ripped off by now. He gave her a little smile and nod of encouragement. Carefully, she pulled the paper aside to reveal a square rosewood box, inlaid with mother of pearl. As she lifted the lid he heard her gasp.

'A paint box!' cried Margaret. 'How delightful—look, Caro, it even has little bowls to mix the colours.' She laughed. 'And we had to manage with oyster shells! What a lovely gift, Ralph.'

'I know Lucy brought only her sketchbook to Adversane,' he explained.

'I have never had anything like this,' she murmured, gently pulling open a drawer and revealing ranks of coloured paint blocks. She turned to face him. 'It is very thoughtful of you, Ralph. Thank you.'

'You will be able to take it with you.' He held her eyes. 'Wherever you travel.'

Lucy felt her heart skip a beat at his words. This was nothing to do with Helene. It was a gift for her, something of her own to keep.

'I shall treasure it always.'

'Well, that is no way to thank your fiancé,' cried Margaret, laughing. 'You must kiss him, Lucy.'

A blush stole up her body. She felt it burning her neck and then her whole face was aflame. She saw that a dull flush had also crept into Ralph's cheeks. He said softly, 'Well, Lucy?'

Everyone was watching. Lucy met Ralph's eyes. There was a smile in them, but a challenge, too, and she could not resist it. She stepped closer and placed her hands on his lapels, standing on tiptoe as she reached up to kiss his cheek. His hands came up to cover hers, he moved his head and captured her lips with his mouth.

Sparks flew. Cannon roared. She closed her eyes, wanting the kiss to go on for ever, but she could hear his sisters laughing and clapping, and even more disturbing was Ariadne's gasp and muttered protests. Lucy dropped back on her heels, blushing furiously. Ralph cleared his throat.

'Shall I carry the box up to your room?'

'No, no, I can manage.'

'Very well.' He released her hands. 'I must go and see Colne.'

She saw his brows contract as he heard his sisters giggling, and he bent a frowning look upon them.

'I hope you are satisfied, ladies,' he barked, then turned on his heel and strode off, shouting to Byrne to come and clear away the mess.

Chapter Nine

The final guests, Adam Cottingham and his wife and the Prestons, arrived later that day. Lucy was pleased she had already met Ralph's cousin, for she could then give more attention to his wife when the couple were shown into the drawing room. Judith Cottingham was a colourless little woman with a habit of looking to her husband after her every utterance. Her brown hair had lost any glow it might once have had and there were no roses in her cheeks. Lucy thought she looked distinctly unhappy, and put aside her own nerves in an attempt to make her smile. She did not succeed, and was relieved when Caroline drew her away.

'Do not trouble yourself with Judith Cottingham,' Caro murmured when they had moved off. 'She is such a timid little thing, and has no conversation at all.'

'She seems very dependent upon Mr Cottingham.'

Caroline flicked a glance over her shoulder.

'He is her sole delight—if you can call it delight.'

Lucy wanted to ask her what she meant but was distracted by the arrival of the last of the house guests, Sir James and Lady Preston and their daughter, Charlotte. The parents were an ill-assorted pair. Sir James was a solid gentleman with sharp eyes while his wife was a much paler creature, tall and very slim. Lucy thought she must have been pretty as a girl, but her beauty had faded to the palest pastel colours. However, Lucy's eyes were drawn to the daughter. She would have recognised Charlotte as Helene's sister even if the butler had not announced her name. She looked very much like a younger version of the portrait of Lady Adversane—the same golden hair, the same willowy figure, but she had much more animation in her countenance and had not yet outgrown the schoolgirl habit of giggling when a gentleman addressed her. Lucy observed it now, when Ralph greeted the newcomers and smiled at Charlotte, but it did not stop her feeling a little stab of something that she recognised as jealousy. What need had he to hire her when Charlotte was bidding fair to be Helene's equal?

No time to think of that. Ralph was talking to the Prestons, holding out his hand and inviting her to join them. Lucy approached nervously.

She had dressed with care for this occasion, choosing a fine cream muslin gown that was so universally fashionable no one could say it was a copy of the late Lady Adversane's. She had also dressed her hair differently, drawing it all back save for a fringe of curls, and the rest cascading in ringlets from a topknot. Ralph had given her a long look when she had appeared, but he had made no comment. Now she hoped that any resemblance to Helene was so minor it would be overlooked. Certainly Sir James and Lady Preston greeted her in a kindly manner, although she found herself blushing when Sir James declared with what she thought forced joviality that he was delighted to meet Adversane's fiancée.

'It is not yet official,' replied Ralph calmly. 'There is no announcement. Nothing is drawn up.'

'No, of course, of course.' Lady Preston fluttered her fan and gave a smile that didn't quite reach her faded blue eyes. 'You wanted to inform the family first, is that not so, my lord? So thoughtful of you. Hasn't he always been a most thoughtful brother-in-law, Charlotte?'

Charlotte responded with a giggle, but Ralph was already leading Lucy away, calling to Byrne to bring more refreshments for his guests.

'There,' he said quietly, when he had drawn her aside. 'Your ordeal is at an end.'

She glanced up at him.

'How did you know I was nervous?'

'What fiancée would not be in such a situation?'

'Oh, dear, I hope it did not show too much.'

'Only to me.' He squeezed her hand. 'There is only one more couple expected today and that is Harry, whom you know, and his wife, Francesca. They are driving over from Ling Cottage to join us this evening.'

'Then he has no excuse to be late,' said Caroline, overhearing. 'If he takes the shortest way.'

Lucy frowned, trying to picture the route.

'That would be past Druids Rock, would it not?' Even as she spoke she was aware that the very name had brought conversation around them to an end. 'Oh, I beg your pardon, I did not intend...'

Sir James approached, smiling.

'Pray do not think you should not speak of that place in front of us,' he told her kindly. 'We are quite accustomed to having lost dear Helene there, and the rock has far greater significance to the world. It is not a place to be shunned.'

'Ah, the druids,' said Caroline and earned a scowl from her brother.

'No, no, my boy, do not frown her down,' said Sir James. 'Lady Wetherell is quite right, even though I do not think she takes it seriously.' The smile he directed at Caroline was full of smug superiority. 'Despite Adversane's dependence upon empiricism and new discoveries, there is a great deal the ancients can teach us.'

'There is no evidence that Druids Rock was ever used by any ancient order,' retorted Ralph.

'No written evidence, perhaps,' replied Sir James, unabashed. 'However, when one has studied the ancients as I have done, one can sense their presence. I shall be visiting Druids Rock to watch the sunrise at the summer solstice.'

'As a guest you are, of course, free to go where you please,' said Ralph.

'Well, I shall remain in my bed, soundly asleep!' Lady Preston gave a tinkling laugh and turned the conversation to safer channels.

More refreshments appeared; wine and ratafia, and tea for those who, according to Lord Wetherell, preferred to corrupt their insides with the pernicious brew. His wife threw him a saucy look as she drew Lucy away from Ralph and carried her off to where Ariadne was pouring tea.

'You can relax now, my dear,' she said when they had collected their cups and withdrawn to an empty sofa.

'You sound just like your brother.' Lucy laughed. 'I admit I was a little nervous to meet Sir James and Lady Preston. I was afraid they would resent my presence.'

'If they do it is because they wanted Ralph to offer for Charlotte.' Caroline noted Lucy's look of disbelief and nodded. 'She may only be seventeen, but Sir James would like to maintain his links with Adversane.'

'That is what Mrs Dean told me.' Lucy sighed. 'There is a financial incentive, I am sure.'

'Yes, but not just that. Sir James would like to invite his friends to Druids Rock.' She smiled. 'Oh, we may think it a fine joke, but Sir James was one of the founder members of The Ancient Order of the Druids and he would very much like to hold a druidical ceremony at the rock. Ralph will not countenance it, although I know Helene tried to persuade him on her father's behalf. Sir James wrote again to Ralph last summer and asked if he might bring a party to celebrate the summer solstice at Druids Rock.'

'Celebrate?' Lucy's eyes widened. 'At the place where his daughter had died only twelve months before?'

'I know. It sounds very callous, doesn't it? Ralph flatly refused, of course.'

Another thought was forming in Lucy's head. She said slowly, 'Do you think that is why Helene went there—to see the sun rise?'

'Possibly, although she had gone there with her father a few days earlier to see the sunrise at the solstice. Midsummer, or St John's Eve, is a very different celebration and nothing to do with Sir James and his druids. Bonfires are lit all along the valley, and Ralph always sends a side of beef to the village, that they may feast in style. And, of course, there are the theatricals at Adversane.'

Caroline looked up, smiling, as other guests approached and the conversation moved on.

The party broke up soon afterwards and everyone went off to change for dinner. When Lucy went up to her room she found the Long Gallery deserted and she took the opportunity to look at the portrait of Helene again. She looked very wistful, but had she really been so unhappy?

'She is very beautiful, isn't she?'

Lucy jumped. She had been so absorbed in her own thoughts that she had not heard Adam Cottingham approach. Now she looked round to find him standing at her shoulder.

'I think she looks a little sad,' she remarked.

'She was.'

'You knew her, did you not, Mr Cottingham?' Lucy hesitated. 'Was she not happy here?'

He stared at the painting.

'No, she was not,' he said at last. 'Perhaps—but I should not say this to you.'

'Oh, please,' she said earnestly, 'please tell me what you think. I would much rather things were out in the open.' She thought sadly of her father, of his absences and her mother's unexplained tears. 'One cannot deal with difficulties if they are unknown.'

'Very true, Miss Halbrook.' He looked back at the portrait. 'My cousin is not an easy man to live with. He can be… How should I put it? Tyrannical.'

'Oh, surely not,' said Lucy impulsively. 'I know he can be a little abrupt, but surely—'

'She was very fragile, you see. Far too meek and quiet to hold her own against Adversane.' His glance flickered to Lucy. 'You have the look of her.'

She blushed and disclaimed, 'It is a mere fancy, sir.'

'Perhaps.' He smiled. Lucy did not know what to say, but her silence went unnoticed for Adam continued, as if he was speaking to himself. 'Everyone loved her for her kind heart, but she was too complaisant, submissive, even. She needed to be worshipped, like a goddess. Ralph never understood that. He was impatient with her. In the end I do not think she could stand it any more.'

A sudden chill ran through Lucy.

'No. He is not a tyrant, truly.' She thought of the paint box. 'He can be very kind.'

'Kind enough, I grant you, when one adheres to his wishes.' He added quickly, 'Forgive me, I should not have said that. I have not seen Ralph for some time. He may well have changed, mellowed. Yes, of course. It must be so, if he has won your regard, Miss Halbrook.'

She did not know what to say but nothing was necessary. Adam gave a sad little smile, bowed and left her.

* * *

'I'm to dress you in the blue silk again to-night, miss, with the silver stars in your hair,' said Ruthie. 'Lord Adversane's orders.'

Kind enough, when one adheres to his wishes.

Lucy desperately wanted to put it to the test, to tell Ruthie to take the beautiful gown away and bring her another, but something held her back. Her eyes went to the paint box resting on top of the chest of drawers. By that one act of kindness Ralph had bought her loyalty, at least for a little longer.

Her maid had just put the finishing touches to Lucy's hair when there was a knock at the door. Lucy remained at her dressing table while Ruthie went to answer it. Her heart began to thud against her ribs when she heard Ralph's deep voice announcing that he had come to escort Miss Halbrook downstairs.

Lucy rose and took a last look at herself in the mirror. The sun of the past few weeks had bleached her hair, making her resemblance to Helene even more marked. Why was he doing this? Why was he putting her through this ordeal?

A simple business transaction.

The words came back to her. She had agreed to it, but had she quite understood what was involved? Resolutely, Lucy turned towards the door.

'I am ready, my lord.'

* * *

Ralph had not come into her room but was waiting for her in the passage. His figure loomed large in the narrow corridor, a shadowy form with only the snowy linen at his neck and the frills at his wrists standing out, almost glowing in the dim light. He did not move as she went out to meet him, but subjected her to a hard stare. She felt a flicker of annoyance and put up her chin.

'Well, my lord, do I look sufficiently like your dead wife?'

Nerves and unease added a sharp note to her voice, and she expected a blistering retort, but as she drew closer she was surprised to see an odd little smile playing about the corners of his mouth.

'It is strange, Miss Halbrook, but when I look at you I no longer see the resemblance.'

'Well, you may be sure your sisters saw it when I came down to dinner yesterday in this very gown.'

'You are not wearing it for their benefit.' He held out his arm. 'Come along, Miss Halbrook, or we shall be late.'

That implacable note was back in his voice. She knew it would be futile to question him further and silently accompanied him down to the drawing room. The buzz of voices she could hear through the door suggested that the other guests were already gathered. As they entered, Lucy's apprehensive gaze went immediately to Sir James and Lady Preston. Sir James merely smiled but his wife, more astute where matters of fashion were concerned, gave Lucy a long, unsmiling stare.

'Ah, here is our host.' Lord Wetherell greeted them cheerfully. 'I was just describing the very superior brandy you have in your cellars, was I not, Cottingham—Cottingham?'

'What? Oh, yes, yes.' Adam crossed the room to address Lucy. 'My wife is longing to become better acquainted with you, Miss Halbrook. Let me take you over to her.'

Lucy's fingers closed on Ralph's sleeve, as if she did not want to leave his side. Quite irrational, she told herself crossly, and hoped no one would notice. Save Ralph, of course. He could not fail to feel her clutching his arm. However, Sir James had addressed a question to him, and he merely gave her hand a pat before moving away from her. Adam led Lucy across to sit beside his wife, and he pulled up a chair to join them.

Unlike their earlier meeting, Judith Cottingham now exerted herself to be friendly. Gratified and relieved to be away from Lady Preston's disapproving presence, Lucy responded in the same vein. The conversation covered a wide range of subjects but it was interspersed with questions.

It was only natural, she thought, that they should want to know about her family and how she had met Ralph.

She answered as best she could, keeping to the history she and Ralph had agreed upon, but she could not be sorry when he interrupted them, laying one hand on her bare shoulder.

'I am sorry to carry you away, my dear, but Harry has arrived and you have yet to meet his wife.'

His touch was very light but it sent a tingle of excitement running through her, heating her blood and rousing an ache of longing deep within. Lucy quickly stifled it, reminding herself it was all a charade to convince his houseguests.

'Thank heaven for that,' she murmured as they moved away. 'I had not realised until they began asking me questions that there are so many gaps in the story we devised!'

'I thought you were looking harassed. We need to find some time alone to make sure our stories match. Slip away and join me in my study in… Let us meet on the half-hour. That will give us time to discuss the matter and be back here well before the dinner hour.'

His tone was matter-of-fact and the suggestion was most definitely a sensible one, but the sad truth was that Lucy did not feel in the least sensible when she thought of being alone with him. She might tell herself that she struggled even to be friends with Ralph, but his presence disturbed her in a way she did not understand. Once again she had to push aside her distracting thoughts as he led her across the room to make the final introduction of the evening.

Francesca Colne was as cheerful and friendly as her husband, and Lucy was soon at her ease.

'Lord Adversane says you live in London,' said Mrs Colne. 'This must be very different for you.'

'It is, but I am enjoying it very much,' replied Lucy.

'And have you settled in well, Miss Halbrook?' Harry asked her. 'You never did come to ask me all your questions about the house.'

She returned his smile. 'Lord Adversane answered most of them for me. And his sisters have been very good, too.' Her glance flickered over Ralph. 'They told me a little about you and Adversane when you were boys.'

'Then that is something you can tell me.' Francesca laughed.

'I think it is best forgotten,' Ralph growled, but the smile in his eyes gave the lie to his menacing frown.

Harry grinned.

'Dear heaven, what on earth have they been telling you, Miss Halbrook?'

'Nothing so very bad,' she admitted with a

chuckle. 'The worst I heard is that Lord Adversane broke his collarbone.'

Harry laughed. 'Yes, on Druids Rock! We were competing to see who could scale the cliff face the quickest. Ralph was in the lead but then he missed his footing and fell. However, the injury saved him from the beating that *I* received.'

'Good gracious,' exclaimed Francesca. 'And did that stop you from doing such a foolhardy thing in future?'

'Of course not. In fact, old Lord Adversane, Ralph's father, was the first to encourage us to go back and try again, but this time under supervision. We climbed the rock many times after that without mishap.' He shook his head, smiling at the memory. 'Ralph and I were a couple of tearaways when we were boys and often found ourselves in the most outrageous scrapes!'

'Oh?' Lucy cast a laughing glance at Mrs Colne. 'I am sure we should like to hear all about them.'

Ralph shook his head and after warning Harry not to sully the ladies' ears with such nonsense he went off, leaving Mr Colne to entertain them. They were soon joined by Sir Timothy, and shortly after Lucy moved away. A glance at the ormulu clock on the mantelpiece showed her that there was some time before she needed to slip away. She noted that Ralph had already disappeared and she went over to sit with his sisters, who were engaged in a lively discussion with Judith Cottingham on the benefits of education for women. When the clock's delicate chimes signalled the half-hour she excused herself and slipped out of the drawing room.

Lord Adversane's study was situated at the far side of the entrance passage, just beyond the dining room. A few words with Ralph were all that was needed to make sure he did not contradict anything she had said to Adam and Judith Cottingham. There would be no need for her to stay more than a couple of minutes. She was so engrossed in her own thoughts that it was not until she reached the study door that she heard voices from within. She recognised Harold Colne's voice, which was raised enough for his words to carry out to her with disastrous clarity.

'I cannot remain quiet any longer, Ralph. I thought at first I was mistaken but tonight, seeing her in that gown— What are you playing at, man? And what in heaven's name possessed you to offer for a girl who is the living image of Helene?'

Lucy jumped away from the door. There was no mistaking Mr Colne's disapproval. If Harry, who was Ralph's oldest friend, was uneasy about his motives, then something must surely be wrong. She retired to the Great Hall, thankful that it was for the moment deserted.

What should she do? She could pretend she

had not heard Harry's remarks, but that would not allay her own fears, which had resurfaced, stronger than ever. She put her hands to her cheeks. Had she been deceiving herself simply because she wanted to live in luxury for a few weeks, ignoring her principles because of the largess that would be hers once she had completed her contract? It was a lowering thought and crowding in close behind it came another. If Ralph had hired her merely to play his hostess then surely there was no need for her to look like Helene. She wrapped her arms about herself. Unless he was still in love with his wife's memory.

She heard a rapid footstep, and Mr Colne appeared. He was looking troubled, but the frown vanished when he saw her.

She said quickly, 'May I have a word with you, sir, before you return to the drawing room?' She rushed on, knowing if she hesitated she would lose confidence. 'Has—has Lord Adversane told you why I am here—the *real* reason I am here?'

He frowned for a moment, then came across the hall to her.

'Yes,' he said quietly. 'Ralph has taken me into his confidence.'

'Then you know we are not engaged. That I have been hired to play a role.'

'I do.'

She searched his face.

'You know him so much better than I, Mr

Colne. Tell me truthfully, do you think I should cry off now from the agreement? Adversane explained it to me, you see. He told me that he needed everyone to think he had chosen another wife, to stop them all from pestering him. I quite see that such a situation would be very uncomfortable, but is this really the solution?'

She twisted her hands together while she waited anxiously for his answer.

He said carefully, 'What does your conscience tell you?'

Lucy put her hands to her temples, saying distractedly, 'I am no longer sure! I had convinced myself there was no impropriety, but now I am here... Do you think it is very wrong, Mr Colne?'

His cheerful countenance was clouded, and he did not answer immediately.

'Miss Halbrook, Ralph has not been himself since Helene's death. He is haunted by the event. If this helps him to come to terms with it, then, no, it is not wrong.'

'Thank you, I am relieved to hear you say so.'

'But—'

'Yes, Mr Colne?'

He shook his head.

'It does not matter. Are you on your way to the drawing room? Shall I escort you?'

'Thank you, but I came out to find Lord Adversane.'

'Then I will take you to him.' He escorted her towards the study but as they neared the door he stopped. 'If you are in any doubt, Miss Halbrook, if you should wish to withdraw from this pretence at any time or if you need assistance, please remember that you can come to me.'

'Why, thank you, Mr Colne, but if, as you say, this is helping Lord—Ralph, then I am happy to continue with it.'

'If you are sure you want to continue. I would not like you to get hurt.'

'I am quite sure, sir.'

He gave her a searching look, as if to assure himself that she was sincere, then with a nod and a smile he knocked upon the study door and ushered her inside.

Ralph was waiting for her, his impassive countenance giving nothing away.

'So,' he said as the door closed upon them. 'What have you been saying to my cousin that I need to know?'

She looked at him blankly for a moment. Harry Colne's last words were still echoing in her head. Did Harry expect her to lose her heart to her employer?

This is merely a business arrangement. Nothing more. Concentrate, Lucy!

'It seems so trivial now, but Mrs Cottingham asked where *precisely* we had first met. I did not think they would be convinced if I said we had met at the house of a mutual friend.' She coloured a little. 'Our social spheres are very different.'

'So what did you tell her?'

'That we had met at Somerset House. I remembered you said you had met my father there, and I went with him sometimes, so it is perfectly reasonable to suppose our paths might have crossed.'

'An excellent answer.' He came a little closer. 'And did you tell them it was love at first sight?'

'Of course not! I, um, I hinted that I had an interest in astronomy.'

He laughed at that.

'Now that *is* dangerous ground! Your knowledge of the stars is limited to the few constellations we saw the other night.'

'I know, but I had to say *something*,' she confessed. A sudden, mischievous smile tugged at her lips. 'Thankfully Mr and Mrs Cottingham know even less, so I was quite safe.'

'Let us hope so.'

'It was not a lie,' she told him. 'I really did find the stars interesting, and Saturn was truly magnificent. I only wish we could have seen more of the planets.'

He smiled. 'Have you seen the orrery in the library? It is in the bay window at the far end, and easily missed if one is not looking for it. You should acquaint yourself with that, if you wish to see the way the planets orbit the sun.'

'Thank you. Perhaps I will.' For a moment she wondered if there was any point, since she would be leaving Adversane once the house party was over. She quickly brushed aside the depressing thought and said brightly, 'After all, the stars will be the same wherever I am, won't they?'

There was an infinitesimal pause before he replied.

'Quite.' He glanced at the clock. 'We had best be getting back to our guests. If there is nothing else?'

'No, nothing.'

'Then we shall say we met at Somerset House and after that I sought you out. Agreed?'

'Agreed, my lord.'

'Ralph.'

'Ralph.'

'Good.' He took her arm and led her out of the room. 'You had best remain vague about any other details.'

'How am I to do that if I am asked a direct question?'

'You need merely blush. You look adorable when you blush.'

He uttered the words as they crossed the Great Hall, and in such an indifferent tone that it took a few moments for Lucy to realise what he had said. By that time they were entering the drawing room, and Lucy had no idea whether she looked adorable, but she knew she was certainly blushing.

At dinner Lucy was placed between Mr Cottingham and Sir Timothy Finch. Ralph's brother-in-law enjoyed his food and Adam seemed preoccupied, so Lucy was spared too much conversation. Instead, she took the opportunity to study the other guests. It was a lively and informal occasion, although Lucy noted that Judith Cottingham, who was sitting opposite, had reverted to her quiet demeanour and said very little. Looking further along the table, Lucy observed a little stiffness between Sir James Preston and his host, but it was clear that the man was eager to bring his daughter to Ralph's attention. Lucy thought perhaps he might have been wiser not to include Charlotte so much in his conversation, since every time he did so, she responded with a giggle that only exposed her immaturity.

'So now you have had time to settle in, how do you like Adversane?'

Sir Timothy's question caught Lucy off guard.

'Lord Adversane is very, um—'

'I meant the house,' he interrupted her, laughing. 'I have no doubt you are pleased with its master, since you are going to marry him. But

you live in town, I believe. You must find life
here very different.'

She flushed a little at her error, but his friendly
manner put her at her ease and she managed to
smile back at him.

'I had many homes but all of them much closer
to London, and you are correct—they were very
different to Adversane,' she returned. 'My father
was an artist, you see.'

'Yes, Ralph told me. A case of opposites at-
tracting each other, what? Ralph being more interested in mechanical objects than art,' he added
when he observed her blank look.

'Now, Tim, do not be too hard on my brother,'
cried Margaret, overhearing. 'Ralph is interested
in many things, and has a real thirst for knowledge.'

'He wants to explain all the mysteries of the
world,' put in Sir James from across the table.
He gave a sad little shake of his head, indicating that he did not agree with this philosophy.

'Adversane merely likes to know why things
happen, rather than to accept them blindly,' said
Harry. 'Surely that is a very reasonable view.'

'Ah, but my lord will learn that not everything
can be explained by man,' replied Sir James.

Lucy glanced towards the head of the table.
Ralph was in conversation with Lady Preston
but he looked up at Sir James's final statement.

'Did I hear my name?'

'I was saying, my boy, that logic and reason cannot be applied to all life's mysteries. Take Druids Rock, for instance.'

'No mystery there,' Ralph replied. 'The latest papers on the subject are very convincing. Hutton puts forward a logical argument for the way that rocks are formed.'

'But not how they come to be piled up. That is the work of a great deity.'

Ralph shook his head. 'I fear we must be content to disagree on that, Sir James.'

'I can only hope, my boy, that age will teach you wisdom,' said Sir James.

'Why, I hope so, too, sir.'

'And *I* hope Miss Halbrook will not be discouraged by all this talk of logic and cold reason,' declared Lady Preston in repressive accents.

Ralph's eyes rested on Lucy and a faint smile played about the corners of his mouth.

'Oh, I think Miss Halbrook understands me pretty well.'

Lucy's cheeks began to burn, and she was glad when Margaret turned the subject and everyone's attention moved away from her. She was happy to let the conversation ebb and flow around her, quietly hoping to avoid drawing attention to herself. However, when the ladies retired she found Lady Preston at her side.

'I am glad to see Adversane has put off his mourning, Miss Halbrook.'

Lucy thought the matron sounded anything but glad, but she murmured a response. Lady Preston followed her to a sofa, sat down beside her and proceeded to quiz her. The interrogation was subtle, but no less thorough. Remembering Ralph's instructions, Lucy kept her answers vague where they referred to her association with him, but she saw no need to prevaricate about her family. After all, it would take very little enquiry for anyone to discover that her father had died a poor man.

'So this is a very advantageous match for you,' concluded Lady Preston. 'You are very fortunate that Adversane is happy to take you without a settlement of any kind.'

Lucy was about to make an angry retort when she heard Caroline's cheerful voice at her shoulder.

'We think it is Ralph who is the fortunate one, ma'am, to have found a woman to make him happy. Lucy, my love, do come and try out the duet again with me....'

Caroline carried her off to the piano, saying as they went, 'Pray do not mind Lady Preston.'

'I do not. It must be very hard for her to see someone in her daughter's place.'

'It is a place she wants Charlotte to fill,' retorted Caroline. 'However, the child is far too young.'

'But she is very pretty, and she will be quite beautiful in a few years.'

Caroline's shrewd look, so like her brother's, rested upon Lucy for a moment.

'Ralph has been caught once by an empty-headed beauty. He will not let that happen again. This time I believe he has found real affection and I for one am very glad of it.'

Lucy felt the warm blush of embarrassment on her cheeks and was thankful that Caro had turned her attention to the piano. She wanted to tell them that it was all a pretence, that Ralph cared not one jot for her. However, she was not free to do so, and if she was honest she did not wish the pretence to end, for when it did she would have to leave Adversane, its owner and his family and she was beginning to realise how hard that would be.

The gentlemen joined them shortly after, Sir James leading the way. He was hardly inside the door when he addressed his wife in ringing accents.

'I say, my dear, Adversane tells me the Players will be performing here on Midsummer's Eve. Is that not good news? I am particularly fond of a good play.'

Ralph glanced around the room, watching to see how the others took the news. Adam was looking particularly solemn and went to sit with his wife. Lady Preston's lips thinned.

'Life must go on, I suppose,' she muttered.

'Indeed it must, ma'am,' agreed Harry in his cheerful way. 'The Ingleston Players lost a great deal of income from last year's cancellation.'

Charlotte looked up.

'Oh, are they are paid, then, for their trouble?'

Margaret nodded.

'Yes, they are local people who give up their time and Adversane rewards them handsomely for coming here. The tradition started in our grandfather's day. The library is turned into a theatre for the first part of the evening and all our neighbours are invited to attend the play. Ralph lays on a good supper for everyone, including the Players, and then afterwards the Players go back to Ingleston to enjoy the Midsummer's Eve celebrations and the rest of us dance in the white salon until the early hours.'

'I know.' Charlotte nodded, her blue eyes sparkling. 'It is indeed the most wonderful evening. Last time I was allowed to watch the play, although I did not understand it all.'

'Thank heavens for that,' murmured Caroline to Lucy, sitting beside her at the piano. 'It was Vanbrugh's *The Provoked Wife*. Not at all suitable for a child of fifteen!'

'And this time you shall be allowed to dance

as well, my sweet,' announced Lady Preston, 'It will be good practice for your come-out next year.'

'Unless she snabbles a husband before that, eh, Adversane?'

Ralph closed his lips firmly as Sir James dug an elbow into his ribs.

Charlotte giggled.

Singing and music filled the remainder of the evening, until the arrival of the tea tray. Finding herself momentarily alone, Lucy moved to a quiet corner of the room, from where she could observe the rest of the guests.

Mr Colne followed her.

'Am I disturbing you, Miss Halbrook?'

'By no means.'

'You were looking very pensive,' he said, pulling up a chair beside her. 'I hope you are not worrying about what we said earlier.'

'Not at all. I was thinking how sorry I shall be to leave all this.'

Harry's glance followed hers to where Ralph was standing with his brothers-in-law.

He said quietly, 'If it is any comfort to you, I think your presence here has done Ralph a great deal of good. He has been looking much happier of late.'

'That is not my doing, Mr Colne. It is because he has company.'

'Perhaps. It has been a difficult two years for him. When Helene died he blamed himself. He is not one to share his feelings. Rather, he shut himself away with his grief and his pain. It is good to see him going into society again.'

'And this...' she dropped her voice '...this charade—my pretending to be Ralph's fiancée. Are you sure you do not think it is...deceitful?'

The sombre look fled from Harry's eyes and he laughed.

'You have met his sisters and seen the way Sir James thrusts Charlotte into Ralph's path at every turn. They are all determined to see him wed again. How much worse would it be if you were not here?'

'And the fact that I look like Lady Adversane?'

He regarded her for a long moment.

'Try not to let that worry you.'

She leaned a little closer.

'But it *does*, Mr Colne! You see, Ralph insists that I wear identical gowns, that my hair is dressed the same as hers. I am very much afraid that he is grieving for his lost love—'

'Ralph never loved Helene, Miss Halbrook. That is a good part of the reason he feels so guilty about her death.' He smiled, and she found herself blushing, as if Harry Colne had discovered some secret. 'You need have no worries on that head. Now if you will excuse me, my wife is looking tired. I must take her home.'

She watched him walk away. Perhaps she should not have voiced her concerns, but she guessed that Harry Colne knew Ralph better than anyone. If he did not believe Ralph had been in love with Helene, then it was very likely to be true.

And Lucy was surprised how much that mattered to her.

The warm, sunny weather continued and Lucy realised she was seeing Adversane at its best. The atmosphere in the house was relaxed, with the visitors left to amuse themselves for most of the day. Sir James and Lady Preston preferred to remain at the house with Ariadne after breakfast each morning, while the rest of the party went out riding. Ralph rarely accompanied them, attending to business during the mornings so that he could be free to spend the afternoons and evenings with his guests.

On the second day Caroline suggested they should all go for a walk. Lady Preston declined, and insisted that Charlotte should remain indoors at least until the midday sun had lost some of its heat. It was therefore late afternoon when the party set off, by which time Ralph had finished his business and was free to join them. Lucy was not surprised when Ariadne decided to remain at home and keep Lady Preston company, and Sir James also declared that he would prefer to spend the afternoon in the library with a good book. The others, however, congregated in the Great Hall, eager to be on their way.

'Which way shall we go?' asked Caroline as they stepped out of the house.

'Oh, to Ingleston, if you please,' cried Charlotte. 'We drove through it on the way here, and there were such pretty shop windows that I should dearly like to browse there.'

'So far?' said Ralph. 'It is nearly three miles. Are you sure you wish to walk such a distance?'

Margaret brushed aside his concerns.

'Pho, what is three miles? We have plenty of time to be there and back before dinner. And you may treat us all to a glass of lemonade at Mrs Frobisher's when we reach the town.'

'We could take the route across Hobart's Bridge,' suggested Charlotte, pointing to the wicket gate. 'It must be a good deal shorter.'

'Past Druids Rock?' asked Margaret. 'Are you sure you want to go there, Charlotte?'

'Oh, yes,' she said blithely. 'I have not been there since Helene died, but it holds no terrors for me.' She giggled. 'Although I confess I should not like to go there at night. It is haunted.'

'Who told you that?' asked Adam, frowning. 'It is no such thing.'

'Oh, not by Helene,' said Charlotte quickly.

'No, it is by spirits.' She looked around, her blue eyes very wide. 'The servants told me. They say that on moonlit nights you can hear the tinkle of fairy laughter at Druids Rock.'

'That would be the packhorse bells,' said Ralph prosaically. 'The jaggers often cross the moors by the light of the moon.'

'You are a spoilsport, Brother.' Caroline laughed. 'Don't you know that ladies like nothing better than to be terrified by tales of hauntings and ghosts?'

'Not when one is talking of Druids Rock,' said Adam, repressively. 'It does have very tragic associations.'

'Perhaps we should walk somewhere else,' murmured Judith Cottingham, casting an anxious look up at Adam.

'No, no, if Miss Preston would like to go there we shall do so,' said Margaret, putting up her parasol. 'Come along, then, no dawdling!'

Ralph held out his arm to Lucy, saying with a smile, 'We have our orders, it would seem.'

'Do you mind?' she asked, taking his arm.

'Not in the least.'

'I think, upon reflection that I might remain here,' said Judith Cottingham, giving the group an apologetic smile. 'It is still very hot.'

'It will be cooler under the trees,' Margaret pointed out, but Judith could not be persuaded and returned to the house.

'Well, that is very convenient,' declared Caroline, unabashed. 'Now we have an equal number of gentlemen and ladies!'

They all paired off, Ralph's sisters taking their husbands' arms while Ralph escorted Lucy and Adam looked after Charlotte Preston. The trees lining the old ride still provided some shade, and when they emerged on the far side, a gentle breeze was sufficiently cool to make walking very pleasant.

The walk downhill to the town was accomplished in good time and it was a merry party that entered Mrs Frobisher's store, where the grocer's wife had set aside a room with tables and chairs for weary shoppers to refresh themselves with tea or cups of hot chocolate in winter, and barley water or delicious lemonade during the hot summer months.

It did not take long to stroll up and down the High Street, the ladies looking in the shop windows and the gentlemen falling behind to talk amongst themselves, but by the time they set off again the afternoon was well advanced.

The old road twisted its way steeply upwards through the trees to emerge high above the valley, where the path levelled out and the going was much easier. Their route took them towards the afternoon sun and as they approached Druids Rock it towered over them, shadowed and menacing. The uphill walk had separated the little party. Margaret and Sir Timothy were marching well in advance, followed by Adam Cottingham, who had given his arm to Lucy, while Ralph followed a short distance behind with Charlotte Preston, and Caroline and Lord Wetherell straggled along at the rear. As Adam and Lucy made their way around the base of Druids Rock they heard Charlotte's youthful giggle behind them, followed quickly by Ralph's deep laugh.

Adam smothered an oath.

'How can he be so unconcerned?' he muttered in a strangled undervoice. 'I cannot—'

He broke off and Lucy turned to look at him, startled.

'Whatever is wrong, Mr Cottingham?'

'I beg your pardon, Miss Halbrook. Perhaps I should have kept silent, but it is unbearable. It is beyond anything that he should laugh here, where Lady Adversane died. How can he act so, knowing—?'

'Knowing what, Mr Cottingham?'

He pressed his lips together, but then, as if the words forced themselves out against his will, he hissed, 'Knowing that he is responsible for her death!'

'Oh, surely not!'

She glanced over her shoulder, but Ralph and Charlotte were too far behind to have overheard. Adam continued to speak in a low, angry voice.

'He was besotted with her, but she never loved

him, never! And when his demands became too much she fled here to Druids Rock to escape him.'

'Please, Mr Cottingham, I do not think you should say anything more. Especially not to me.'

Lucy withdrew her arm and began to walk on a little faster.

'But don't you see?' Adam lengthened his stride to keep pace with her. 'You are precisely the person I should speak to. You have the look of her. I noticed it immediately. Do you not see what is happening, Miss Halbrook? He is turning you into his dead wife.'

'Nonsense,' said Lucy, flushed. 'There is some slight similarity, perhaps, but—'

'And he is making you in her image,' he persisted. 'You dress your hair the way she did. And your clothes—he chose them for you, did he not?'

They had dropped down to Hobart's Bridge and were momentarily out of sight of the rest of the party. Adam grabbed her hand, forcing her to stop.

He said urgently, 'Miss Halbrook, I believe you are in danger here. You should go. Leave Adversane, before it is too late.'

'Too late for what? I do not understand you, Mr Cottingham.'

But at that moment Ralph and Charlotte came into view.

'I cannot tell you here,' he muttered.

Lucy began to walk on.

'I do not believe there is anything to tell,' she said robustly. 'Mr Cottingham, you have allowed your imagination to run away with you.'

'Perhaps you are right, madam, but I am concerned for you. I would not like you to suffer Lady Adversane's fate.'

'That will not happen, sir. I am aware that some people think she killed herself because she was so unhappy, but such an action would not be in my nature.'

'Nor was it in hers!'

They were approaching the trees, where Margaret and her husband were waiting for the rest of the party to catch up. Lucy put her hand on his arm to stop him again.

'What are you trying to say, Mr Cottingham?' she demanded.

'I think,' muttered Adam with deadly emphasis, 'that Adversane deliberately drove her to it!'

Chapter Ten

The last few yards to where Margaret and Sir Timothy waited were barely sufficient for Lucy to recover from the horror of Mr Cottingham's words. She could not believe it. Ralph would not do such a thing. But could she be sure? Her own parents had kept from her the truth about their finances and she had never guessed. Even after her father's death Mama had said nothing, until the truth could be concealed no longer. And if Mama could hide things from her, how much easier, then, for a man she had known barely three weeks? Lucy moved away from Adam Cottingham and fixed herself with Margaret, engaging her in conversation as they walked back through the old ride and the park.

Lucy thought perhaps it was her disordered thoughts that made the remainder of the journey uncomfortably hot, but as they made their way across the gardens to the house she noticed the heavy black cloud bubbling up on the horizon.

'We shall have a storm soon, I think,' opined Margaret, following her glance. 'Good thing, too. Clear the air.'

'Well, I for one am ready for my dinner,' declared Lord Wetherell as they all made their way into the house. He took out his watch. 'And, by Jove, there is barely time to bathe and change. I hope that new-fangled range of yours can cope with supplying so much hot water in one go, Adversane?'

'Of course it can.' Sir Timothy laughed, clapping his host on the shoulder. 'Next thing we know he will have found a way to pump it up to the bedrooms, ain't that so, my boy?'

'I am working on it,' replied Ralph, smiling a little.

The party dispersed, and Lucy felt a hand on her arm.

'One moment.' Ralph detained her. 'You professed an interest in the orrery. Perhaps you would like to come into the library and see it now.'

She swallowed. She would much rather not be alone with Ralph at that moment, but short of running away she had no choice. She followed him to the library.

It was not a room she was familiar with. It was such a large, lofty chamber that until the house party it had been rarely used and she had come in here only to gaze at the thousands of books on display and to choose one of the more popular novels to read. Now she noted that there was a large terrestrial globe beside the desk, and Ralph pointed out to her the odd-shaped lamps positioned on shelves and side tables around the room.

'Argand lamps,' he told her. 'They burn oil, but in a way that makes them ten times as bright as any candle. Excellent for reading in the winter.'

When I will no longer be here.

In just over a week's time, the end of the month, she would be gone. Life at Adversane would go on as it always had done but she would not be there to share it. Lucy did not know why she found the thought so depressing.

Ralph led her to the far end of the room, where the brass orrery stood in the bay window, gleaming in the light. The delicate brass arms stretched out from the circular base, each one carrying a miniature planet or an even smaller moon fashioned from ivory.

'It belonged to my father,' Ralph explained, coming to a halt before it. 'I have had it brought up to date to include Herschel's planet with its two moons, and the extra moons around Saturn. It has a fine clockwork mechanism.' He grinned. 'When my nephews are here they like nothing better than to wind it up and watch the planets spin around.'

He wound it up now, and Lucy watched, fascinated, as the various planets and moons circled the sun in a slow and stately dance.

'Why was Cottingham holding your hand at Hobart's Bridge?' Ralph asked. 'What was he saying to you?'

He was telling me that you are obsessed with your late wife and that you hounded her to her death.

Lucy kept her eyes on the spinning globes.

'Why, nothing. Our conversation became a little animated, that is all.'

He caught her wrist. 'Was he making love to you?'

'No! Nothing like that.'

'Then what?'

She should tell him what Adam had said and allow him to defend himself. She should watch his reaction and judge for herself if it was true, but suddenly Lucy was afraid. She did not want to learn the truth. She tore herself from his grasp, saying coldly, 'It was nothing that need concern you, my lord.'

'Lucy!'

She drew herself up and met his challenging gaze steadily.

'There is nothing in our contract to say I must

report to you every conversation I have, sir. That would be quite unacceptable to me.'

'Your reaction smacks of evasion.'

'And yours of jealousy,' she flashed.

His black brows drew together.

'I beg your pardon,' she said quietly. 'I am perfectly aware that it is nothing of the kind, but surely your logical mind must tell you that it is perfectly possible for a lady to engage in an innocent conversation with a gentleman?'

His scowl was put to flight and in its place she saw the gleam of humour in his eyes.

'So you would fight me with logic, would you?'

Sadness gripped her and she was suddenly close to tears. She said quietly, 'I would rather not fight you at all, my lord. Now, if you will excuse me, I must change my gown.'

Ralph watched her leave the room, curbing the urge to call her back, to demand she tell him what his cousin had said to her. He did not want to force her; he would much rather that she trusted him enough to confide everything. Yet how could he expect that when he would confide in no one?

He walked to the window, looking out across the gardens but seeing only Lucy's distressed face. He wished there was a way to carry out his plan without involving her. He admired her spirit, the dignified way she conducted herself. His sisters liked her, too; that was very clear. He could foresee a stormy time ahead, when Lucy left Adversane. His sisters had made it very plain that they considered Lucy the perfect match for him and would take it very ill when the engagement was terminated.

As would he.

The thought came as a shock. Ralph raked his hands through his hair and exhaled slowly. When had Lucy Halbrook changed from being a mere pawn in his plans and become a person? One with so much more spirit than the dead wife he had hired her to impersonate.

He had married Helene because it was expected of him, because she was beautiful and desirable, but he had known from the start that his heart was untouched. She was so complaisant that he had thought she would make him a comfortable wife, but it had not taken him long to realise the truth, that it was most uncomfortable to be in a loveless marriage, especially to a woman with whom he shared no common interests. And Helene's truly sweet nature had become a constant barb of guilt. He could give her as much spending money as she desired, but he could not love her, any more than she could care for him. He had resigned himself to the fact that once she had provided him with an heir, they would live separate lives.

Yet, although he had not loved Helene, he considered it his duty to find out the truth about her death and for that he needed Lucy Halbrook. His own desires were secondary. He frowned. What of Lucy's desires? Despite her avowed dislike of him, Ralph was convinced she was not indifferent. When he had kissed her he had ignited a fire equal to his own. He had recognised it in her response, even if she would not acknowledge it.

Ralph squared his shoulders. Perhaps, when it was over and he knew the truth, he could tell Lucy, but would she want anything to do with him once she knew how he had used her? He doubted it, but it was too late to change course now. Much too late.

Lucy had no appetite for dinner, but it was impossible for her not to attend. There were no orders as to her attire, but then, she thought despondently, whatever she wore would be styled upon one of Helene's evening gowns. Ruthie had laid out a rose silk and she put it on, not even bothering to look in the mirror before she went downstairs.

In the drawing room Lucy did her best to avoid both Ralph and Adam Cottingham and was relieved to be sitting between Lord Preston and Sir Timothy when they went into the dining room. Not that either of the gentlemen she was avoiding seemed aware of her efforts. Adam sent her no anxious looks, made no attempt to continue their tête-à-tête. Lucy wondered if he had realised the imprudence of declaring his suspicions to Ralph's fiancée. Yet if that was the case, Lucy thought he should have tried to make her an apology. As for Ralph, apart from the occasional thoughtful glance in her direction he kept his distance and in such lively company the reserve between them went unnoticed.

After dinner she waited with the other ladies for the gentlemen to join them. To retire early would attract more comment than to sit quietly in the corner. The long windows were thrown wide, but even so there was no breeze to refresh the room and all the ladies seemed a little subdued as they fanned themselves and talked in desultory tones. Lucy stepped outside, watching the sunset and enjoying the slight breeze. She was still there when at last the gentlemen came in.

As the party rearranged itself, Ralph joined Lucy on the terrace.

'You are very quiet tonight. Is anything amiss?'

She shook her head, but he saw quite clearly that she was not her usual self. The sparkle was gone from her eyes and there was a slight droop to her mouth. Ralph longed to kiss away that troubled look, but he suspected he had put it there by questioning her about Adam Cottingham. Perhaps he should not have done so, but he had felt such a worm of jealousy in his soul when he had seen them together, a feeling so much stronger than anything he had ever felt for his wife.

He was about to try and coax Lucy into a smile when he became aware of the conversation going on in the room behind them. Lady Preston was talking with Judith Cottingham but her high voice carried easily to the terrace.

'It was quite understandable that Adversane should cancel the play last year.'

'Mourning, d'you see,' explained Sir James cheerfully. 'He was besotted with Helene, of course, but I'm glad to see he's over it now and back in the world again.'

Damn the man, thought Ralph. Preston had been drinking heavily at dinner, and was now talking far too loud and free.

'Aye, he's back,' Sir James continued, his words slurring a little. 'And this year's Midsummer festivities will be an ideal opportunity for Charlotte to become accustomed to society.'

Judith murmured something which drew a laugh from Sir James.

'Oh, no,' he said cheerfully. 'We won't force her into a marriage, Mrs Cottingham. Are you worried she might make a mull of it, like her sister? No fear of that. Helene was always highly strung, of course, lived on her nerves. There's no denying Adversane handled her very ill, but

Charlotte won't be driven to such desperate measures as her sister. Made of much sterner stuff. In fact, if only she'd been a few years older she'd have made a much better bride for Adversane.'

Ralph turned, ready to put a stop to the conversation, but his sisters were before him. Margaret called for Sir James to join her at the piano for a duet and Caroline swept everyone into a discussion of what the pair should sing. Glancing back at Lucy, he saw that she was staring at him, her face as white as the trim on her gown. He was almost overwhelmed with an urge to protect her. He wanted to gather her in his arms but with everyone watching them he had to content himself with taking her hand.

'I wish you had not heard that.'

'It is not the first time, but to hear Sir James utter it, and so coolly.'

'The magistrate recorded Helene's death as an accident.'

'Naturally, in deference to your standing, but that is not what everyone believes, is it?'

'No.'

He wanted to tell her what he thought had really happened that night, but what if he was proved wrong? Would those eyes now fixed so anxiously upon him fill with disgust and loathing to think he was merely trying to exonerate himself? When she pulled her hand free he made no attempt to stop her, even though it left him feeling bereft. Caroline came to the window.

'Lucy, Ralph, do come and join us. You must sing another duet.'

She took their arms, trying to move them inside, but Lucy held back.

'Not tonight, Caroline, if you please. I—I have a headache.'

'Oh, poor love.' His sister was all concern. 'It is this thundery weather. We will all feel better once there has been a storm.'

'Yes.' Lucy's eyes flickered over him once more, their troubled look piercing his heart. 'Yes, yes, I think you are right.'

When she excused herself and left the room, Ralph wanted to follow her. He would abandon this charade, do anything to put the smile back in her eyes. Yet how could he? How could he allay her fears, offer her any happiness until he knew the truth himself? And for that he needed to go on with his plan.

The others were calling for him to join them, and he was their host, after all. He forced his thoughts away from Lucy Halbrook. He was paying her well for her part in this charade, there was no need for him to feel concerned for her welfare. But even as he joined his guests he knew that he was fooling himself. Lucy's happiness had somehow become the most important thing in his life.

* * *

Lucy passed a sleepless night, caused by the stuffiness of the room, she told herself, but she knew it had more to do with Adam's declaration as they walked back together from Ingleston. The thought that Adversane was still in love with his wife and wanted to recreate her presence made Lucy uneasy, but it was nothing to the revulsion she felt at the idea that he had deliberately caused his wife to end her own life. Lucy was convinced now that they had not been a happy couple but she could not believe Ralph had intended to be cruel. And yet...why did Helene run off to the Rock alone after the play?

She tossed and turned in her bed, Adam's accusation gnawing at her mind. After all, what did she know of Ralph? She had seen that hard, implacable look in his eyes, guessed he could be ruthless, when he chose, but at that point she sat up in bed, saying aloud to the night air, 'No. I *know* he would not do such a thing.'

Not deliberately, perhaps, but his harshness might easily overset a more gentle nature. Unfortunately that was all too easy to believe.

And as she lay down again, another thought, equally unwelcome, returned to haunt her. That he was still in love with Helene—so in love that he could not bear to let her memory go.

There was no storm that night and by the next morning the heat in the house was oppressive.

Lucy rose, heavy eyed and irritable from lack of sleep. There were no orders from Ralph so she chose a fine muslin gown worn over a gossamer-thin petticoat.

Ruthie regarded her doubtfully.

'Well,' Lucy demanded, 'what is it? Why do you look at me in that way?'

'I never saw my mistress wearing such a gown.'

'Well, thank goodness for that!'

'There *was* a muslin like it in the linen press,' Ruthie continued. 'I remember seeing it when Miss Crimplesham and I packed up all my lady's things. She took them with her when she went back to be lady's maid to Miss Charlotte.'

'Well, at least there is something that won't remind him of her,' Lucy muttered to herself as she went off to breakfast.

With the threat of thunder in the air no one wanted to ride out that morning and the guests gave themselves up to less energetic pursuits. Lucy decided to try out her new paint box. She ran upstairs for an apron to protect her gown and took her things to the empty morning room, where the light was good. Byrne brought in the old easel Lord Adversane had found for her, and after suggesting diffidently that she should avoid setting it up on the master's treasured Aubusson carpet he retreated, and she was left in peace.

The view from the window was very fine, but there was a heaviness in the air that dulled the aspect so she reached for her sketchbook to find a suitable subject. Flicking through the pages, she found herself staring at the craggy likeness of Lord Adversane.

A wry smile tugged at her mouth. No watercolour could do justice to that harsh countenance; it needed the strong lines of pen and ink, or the heavy surety of oils. She moved on and soon found a small sketch she had made of a drift of cotton grass, the delicate tufts standing white against the dark boggy ground. Her hand went to her cheek, feeling again the soft downy touch of the fronds upon her skin. That was what she would paint.

Lucy worked quickly, but painting was not engrossing enough to keep her mind from wandering. Adam Cottingham's words kept coming back to her but each time she dismissed them. She was sure Ralph could not be so ruthless, even if he no longer cared for his wife.

How can you be so certain?

The question, once posed, had to be answered. She could not ignore it. Ralph's kindness to her, his wit, their shared moments—even when they disagreed violently—had given her more pleasure than anything she had ever known.

'I love him.'

She spoke the words aloud to the empty room.

Love. What did she know of that? This was
nothing like the love she felt for her parents.
Apart from the painful grieving when Papa died,
that love had always been a comfort. There was
nothing comfortable about her feelings for Ralph
Cottingham, fifth Baron Adversane. She wanted
to rip and tear at him, whether it was a difference
of opinion or—a shiver ran through her—in the
dreams that disturbed her rest. Then she would
imagine him in her bed, her hands touching his
naked body, her mouth covering his skin with
kisses, tasting him.

She shifted restlessly. This was beyond her
experience. It could not be right to feel such vio-
lent emotion for a man she had known but a few
weeks. It was not sensible. It was not safe. The
sooner she left Adversane and its difficult, disturbing master the better.

The door opened and she looked around
quickly, expecting to see the object of her wicked
thoughts coming in. Instead, it was Lady Preston. Lucy summoned up a smile.

'If you are looking for company I am afraid
there is only me and my poor art here, ma'am.'

'It is you I wish to see, Miss Halbrook.'

Lucy put down her brush but before she could
speak Lady Preston launched into an attack.

'You think to fill my daughter's shoes in this
house, do you not, Miss Halbrook? I advise you

to think again, and reflect upon what you are doing.'

'Lady Preston, I—'

'He has chosen you because of your likeness to Helene.'

'Really?' Lucy could think of nothing else to say, since she could not deny it.

Lady Preston's lip curled. 'Oh, you may have fooled Adversane, but you do not fool me. Very clever of you to style yourself upon my daughter. How did you do that? Talked to the servants, I suppose, and to her friends. And of course now you are at Adversane there is her portrait to guide you.

'Very clever, miss, but think carefully, before it is too late.' The matron came closer. 'He does not love you, my dear. It will all end in tears. You see, Charlotte promises to be as beautiful as her sister, and in a year or two, when she has matured, she will be her equal. Then what will you do? Adversane will not want *you*, a pale imitation, when he can have the real thing.'

'Lady Preston, if Lord Adversane wishes to marry me—'

'Oh, I am sure he does, at present, because you have bewitched him. He sees Helene every time he looks at you. But how long will that last, do you think? You are nothing like the glorious creature that was my daughter. And when he does see through the charade, sees the poor little dab of a creature he has married, what then?'

Lucy began to shake. Suddenly there was no pretence. Suddenly she felt she really was Ralph's fiancée. She called upon all her resolution to speak calmly.

'Perhaps we should allow Adversane to be the judge, ma'am.'

Lady Preston snorted.

'He is so in love with Helene he cannot see beyond the superficial likeness at present, but that will change. *You* cannot replace her, however much you try to imitate her. Do you think I have not realised? But you will not catch him with such wiles and stratagems. You are not Helene. You do not have her goodness, her sweetness of temper.'

'Perhaps not, but Ralph—'

'You dare to call him by his name? What have you to offer him? It was Helene he loved. He will tire of you, Miss Halbrook, and then what will you be? His wife in name, perhaps, but rejected, ignored.' Her lip curled. 'You have only to observe poor little Judith Cottingham. Do you wish to be like her, cowed and unhappy, pitied by everyone and desperate for the slightest attention from her husband? Better to go now, miss, while you at least have your dignity.'

The venom in the woman's eyes sparkled like knife-blades. Lucy had no defence. The knowledge that she had fallen headlong in love with Ralph had left her weak and confused. There had been a spark of hope, barely acknowledged, that Ralph might come to care for her. Now that was most effectively destroyed. It had never been very strong; more a faint, distant dream tucked away in her heart, but Lady Preston's words had sliced right to her core and cut it out, leaving her so raw that she felt the tears welling up.

Without a word, she ran from the room, her last glance showing that Lady Preston was wearing a satisfied smile. Lucy hoped to reach her room without seeing anyone, but as she crossed the Great Hall, Ralph was emerging from the entrance passage. He could not fail to see her distress but she did not stop when he called to her. Instead, she flew up the stairs. When she reached the Long Gallery he was merely yards behind her. If only she could reach the safety of her room!

He caught up with her even as she opened the door. Ruthie was pottering about in the room, but a curt word from Adversane sent her scurrying away. He closed the door behind the maid and turned to look at Lucy.

'Now, you will tell me what has overset you.'

His voice was as brisk as ever, but she knew him well enough to hear his concern. It brought forth from her another bout of tears. He gave her his handkerchief and waited in silence for her to speak.

'I beg your pardon. I am being very foolish. It was L-Lady Preston. She says you only want me because I look like Helene, which I know anyway, and since this is all a charade it makes no odds...'

She trailed off, her head bowed. Distant thunder rumbled in through the open window as Ralph came closer.

'You are wrong.' He removed the handkerchief from her restless fingers and dried her cheeks. 'This is no charade. Not any longer.'

He caught her chin and gently turned her face up towards him. He kissed her eyelids, his lips drying the remaining tears before his mouth moved over hers. Lucy melted into him. It felt so right to be in his arms, as if it was her natural home.

Suddenly, it did not matter if it was all a sham, if he thought he was making love to Helene. She wanted him. She would take whatever pleasure he offered her and hold the memory to comfort her through the empty years ahead.

His kiss deepened, and her body stirred in response. The thunder rolled again, but she did not know whether it was that or desire that made the very earth tremble. Her lips parted at his insistence and his tongue was plundering her mouth, drawing out an aching longing from her very core. She could feel its tug deep in her belly and between her thighs. With something like a growl he lifted her into his arms and carried her to the bed where he lay down with her, covering her face with kisses before his lips roved down to the hollow at the base of her throat. Her body was singing as his hands explored its contours. Her breasts ached to be free of the restraining gown so that he might caress them. She could feel him, hard and aroused, pressed against her, only a few thin layers of cloth between them.

She sighed and opened her eyes. She had slept in this bed for the past few weeks but now she saw it afresh. Everything looked different, brighter, the rich hangings, the elaborately carved posts—a sudden flash of lightning flooded the room and turned the folded silk above her head a deeper blue.

As blue as the eyes in the painting of Lady Adversane.

Quickly, Lucy shut out the thought. Thunder rolled again, like the distant grumble of angry gods. Ralph was kissing her breasts where they rose plump and soft above the edge of her gown. With one hand, he had pushed aside her skirts and was caressing her thigh. Her body responded, straining towards him. He would take her, she knew it. She wanted it as much as he.

But he is making love to his wife.

Lucy told herself again it did not matter—she

was too hungry for his caresses to care. But even as her body yearned, ached for his touch, she knew it was not true. She did care. Very much. She struggled, her hands on his chest, trying to push him off.

'Ralph—no—'

Immediately he let her go and sat up.

'What is it? What is wrong?' His breathing was ragged, his eyes dark with passion. 'Tell me.'

Cold terror clutched at her heart. He would never forgive her for stopping him. She should not have let it go so far. With a sob, she scrambled off the bed and threw herself at the door. Even as the next rumble of thunder rolled through the house she was racing to the stairs.

She had to get out of the house, to get away. Lucy let herself out of the door and stepped out onto the drive. The sky was black and the first drops of rain were splashing down. A flicker of lightning illuminated the little wicket gate and she ran towards it, not stopping until she had reached the old ride, out of sight of the house.

She was crying in earnest now, for herself, for Ralph, for Helene. She had no thought other than to get away and she hurried on, walking and running by turns. The steady rain soaked her, mingling with the tears that would not stop. The very heavens seemed to be crying in sympathy.

Lucy barely saw Hobart's Bridge as she ran across it, great gasping sobs racking her body. She wanted Ralph more than she had ever wanted anything in the world before, but only if he wanted her. She would not be a substitute for his wife. The thought brought on more tears, this time for the man she had left behind. If his love for Helene was only a fraction of what she was feeling, how on earth did he bear it, day after day?

The violence of her grief could not last and when it began to abate she became conscious of her situation on the open moor, exposed to the elements. Her thin muslin gown was soaked through and the heavy rain was creating a thick grey mist that reverberated with the almost continuous roll of thunder. Lucy could see no more than a few yards in any direction and looked about her, wondering which way to go.

A solitary figure appeared out of the mist. Ralph.

Lightning flickered. She wanted to run, but what was the point? He was so close now there could be no escape. She waited for him to come up, flinching a little as the thunder crashed loudly overhead.

'The storm is getting closer,' he said urgently. 'We need to take shelter. The rocks are nearest.'

Lucy made no protest as he took her arm and hurried her towards Druids Rock. Rivulets of muddy water ran along the path and in some disconnected part of her mind she was aware that her muslin skirts were no longer cream but brown as high as the knee. Soon Ralph was leading her off the main path and up the narrow track to the rocks themselves. He pulled her through a small gap between two of the stones and into a small, dry cavity. It was too low to stand and they knelt on the earth floor, staring out at the rain.

'We should be safe enough here.' Ralph shrugged himself out of his greatcoat and put it around Lucy's shoulders. 'These rocks have stood thus for thousands of years. They won't collapse upon us.' Lightning flashed outside, followed so quickly by the thunder that Lucy jumped. Immediately, Ralph's arm was around her. He said lightly, 'I said women go to pieces in an electrical storm. Is that why you ran away from me? Were you frightened?'

She bowed her head, too numbed to dissemble.

'Not by the thunder. I could not bear it, to be in your arms, knowing all the time you were thinking of your wife.'

'That is not why I kissed you.'

She managed a sad little smile.

'No. You wanted to comfort me. That was very kind, but—'

'Kind!' He gripped her shoulders and turned

her towards him. 'By heaven, I was not being *kind*, Lucy. I have never been kind to you, more's the pity. I kissed you because I wanted to do so, because that is all I have wanted to do ever since I brought you to Adversane.'

His voice was harsh, and she peered through the gloom at him, trying to see his expression and understand what he was saying. He let her go, sitting back on his heels.

'It is true I hired you because of your resemblance to Helene, but I soon discovered that you are nothing like her. She never touched my heart as you do, Lucy. She was stunningly beautiful, yes, but there was nothing behind those blue eyes. At least, not for me.' He took one of her hands and stared down at it, saying quietly, 'I always believed I was not the kind to fall in love, but I was wrong. Since you have been in the house you have turned my world upside down. You question and challenge and stand up to me as an equal. You have invaded my head, Lucy Halbrook, but you have also touched me here.' He pulled her hand against his chest. 'That was why I want to kiss you, why I love you. Not because you are similar to Helene, but because you are *different*.'

Lucy could feel his heart thudding through the damp cloth of his waistcoat. She put her free hand on his shoulder, closed the distance between them and kissed him. She had intended

it to be a gentle kiss, full of comfort and reassurance, but when their lips met the searing
bolt that passed between them was as great as
any electrical storm. She clung to him, almost
swooning as his mouth worked over hers, his
tongue flickering, caressing, calling up the now-
familiar desire from deep in her core. There was
no grace, no delicacy—just a passionate, urgent
desire that drove them on. They began to tear
off their wet clothing between a series of hot,
breathless kisses.

Lucy's thin muslin gown was soaked through
and had to be peeled away, leaving her body
slick and wet. Ralph's greatcoat had slipped
from her shoulders and once they had dis-
carded their clothes he pulled Lucy down onto
it. A shiver of delight ran through her when she
felt his naked limbs pressed against her own
and smelled the salty dampness of his skin. He
wrapped her in his arms, covering her face and
neck with kisses. When his hand began to caress her breast, she strained towards him. His
hand slid away, and she felt his mouth on the
hard nub he had aroused, sucking and teasing
until she was moaning with the delightful tor-
ture of it. She dug her nails into his shoulders
as he continued the delicious torment and when
she pulled his head up so that she could kiss his
lips again, his fingers continued their restless
assault, moving down, stroking her thighs, ca-

ressing her so intimately that she arched, gasping against his mouth.

Ripples of delight were pulsing through her, growing ever stronger. Her body softened. She was opening like a flower, laying her soul bare to this man who could wreak such havoc with her senses. She was no longer in control; her body was responding to Ralph's demanding fingers as they stroked and circled and eased her to the very edge of ecstasy.

She cried out when he entered her, a tiny pain, followed by the slow building of pleasure again as he moved within her, slow steady strokes that had her crying out with delight. She had never felt such elation. Instinctively, she moved with him, matching his rhythm, the momentum carrying them higher and higher until at last they crested in a joyful union. The world shattered— Lucy heard Ralph shout, and she screamed, afraid that she was falling, only to feel herself held close, safely wrapped in his arms.

They lay together, bodies entwined, cocooned in a peace of their own making while the storm raged on outside. Ralph closed his eyes and breathed deeply, his body relaxed. He felt an immense satisfaction, but he was also somewhat stunned by the ferocity of their passion. Lucy had returned kiss for kiss, and if her lovemaking was a little inexpert it had been no less ardent and arousing. His sense of contentment deepened. She had much to learn, and he would enjoy teaching her. No doubt he, too, would learn a great deal in the process. She stirred and turned towards him, one arm slipping over his chest while her lips nibbled at his neck.

'Has the thunder been that loud all the time?' she murmured.

'Yes.'

'I did not notice.'

'Shall I take that as a compliment?'

She laughed softly, a low, delicious sound that stirred his desire.

'I hardly know,' she replied demurely. 'After all, I have no experience with which to compare what we have just done.'

Any remaining lethargy disappeared. He rolled over and pinned her beneath him.

'Then you should believe me when I tell you that was very good.'

'I should?' Even in the dim light he could see the mischief in her eyes. She moved slightly, and his body reacted immediately. He was tense and coiled like a spring again, ready for action. Her smile told him she was perfectly aware of the effect she was having, and she murmured provocatively, 'Perhaps you should show me again, my lord.'

Growling, Ralph stifled her laugh with a kiss. She responded eagerly, but this time there was no urgency to complete their union. He covered every part of her body with kisses. Her reactions delighted him, and she was eager to please him, too, exploring him with her hands and her mouth, learning quickly how to enslave him until he dragged her into his arms for another earth-shattering union that left them too exhausted to do anything other than sleep.

When Lucy awoke the rain had stopped. Sunlight gleamed at the entrance to their shelter and she could hear the faint song of a skylark somewhere over the moors. She stirred, and immediately Ralph's arm tightened around her.

'We must get back,' she murmured. 'We will be missed.'

Ralph rolled over and kissed her, then he eased himself up on one elbow.

'You are very beautiful,' he murmured.

She felt her whole body blushing under his gaze.

'So, too, are you.' She reached up and touched the hard contours of his chest, pushing her fingers through the smattering of crisp black hair. 'I have never seen a man's body before, save in paintings or sculpture. I think I would like to stay here and look at it for ever.'

'I would dearly like to indulge you, my love, but unfortunately you are right, we will be missed. I must get you back to Adversane. But don't worry.' He caught her hand and raised it to his lips. 'There will be plenty of opportunities for us to study each other in future.'

The thought made her shiver with pleasure. She sat up and reached for her clothes.

'They are so wet it will not be easy to dress,' she remarked. 'Will you help me?'

Putting the cold, wet material onto her body was neither easy nor pleasant, but at last she was dressed and while Ralph threw on his own clothes she tried vainly to tidy her hair. Then it was time to crawl out of their shelter.

The sun was blessedly hot and Lucy shook out the mud-splattered skirts, saying with dismay, 'I fear this gown is quite ruined. What will everyone think?'

'That we were caught in a thunderstorm,' said Ralph. 'They may of course guess at what occurred while we were sheltering, but if they do they will not think much about it. We are betrothed after all.' He took her hand. 'There can be no question of calling off the engagement now, Lucy.'

'Do you *want* to marry me, Ralph?'

His smile banished her doubts. He pulled her close and kissed her.

'Yes, I do. Very much.'

Another kiss set her heart singing. She clung to him for a moment, wondering how it was possible to be so happy.

* * *

With a reluctant sigh, Ralph lifted his head, trying to ignore the temptation of those soft lips and the green eyes that positively smouldered with passion. Not that she was trying to be seductive. He found her very innocence intoxicating. But it was a responsibility, too. He would take care of her.

Better than the care you took of Helene.

The thought was like a hammer blow to his conscience. Was he wrong to marry again? After Helene's death he had vowed never to do so, but his resolution had wavered and died when Lucy Halbrook swept into Adversane, turning his life upside down. But was she strong enough to stand up to him, or would he see her spirit crushed by his impatience? Dear heaven, he prayed he was not making a mistake!

Some of the pain it caused must have been displayed in his face, for he saw Lucy's look change to one of concern. Banishing his darker thoughts, he said with a smile, 'Let us get back before they send out a search party. Are you cold in those wet clothes? Would you like to wear my greatcoat?'

'Thank you, but, no. I am quite warm now and the sun will dry me a little as we walk.'

'Come along, then.'

He took her hand and with his greatcoat over his free arm they set off. When they reached the spot where he had come upon her she asked him how he had known where to find her.

'You left the wicket gate open. I saw it as soon as I looked outside. I would have found you sooner, only I thought you would be hiding somewhere in the house.' His frantic search of the dark, storm-filled house now seemed like part of another life. 'I did not think you would be so foolish as to go out of doors.'

'I wanted to get away from you and everyone. I thought you would be so angry that…that I had stopped you…'

The unease in her voice tore at his heart.

'Not so much angry as bemused,' he said, remembering that when she had pushed him away he had hoped—prayed—it had been the storm that had frightened her and not his passion. 'Then, when I realised you were heading for the moors I was afraid for you. Electrical storms can be very dangerous.'

'So you came after me.'

'Yes, although I had not planned to ravish you.' He squeezed her fingers. 'Do you regret it?'

She shook her head.

'Not at all.' She stopped. 'Unless you do— Ralph, you will tell me, won't you, if you decide you do not want to marry me?'

Looking down into her upturned face, he knew how much he wanted to marry her, but should he do so? Could he be a good husband?

That little worm of doubt still gnawed at his conscience. He thrust the thought aside and pulled her close, giving in to the temptation to take just one more kiss.

'That will never happen,' he said. 'You are mine now, Lucy Halbrook, and I shall never let you go.'

Lucy's heart soared. She accompanied Ralph back through the old ride, her heart singing. However, when they reached the house grounds she found her apprehension growing.

'Ralph, is there a way we can slip into the house unnoticed? That door in the wall perhaps…'

'That leads to the kitchen gardens and unfortunately there will be servants everywhere at this time of the day. To creep in like a couple of thieves would give rise to the very worst sort of conjecture. No, my love, we must brave it out.'

My love.

The words gave her courage as he led her towards the main entrance.

Chapter Eleven

Byrne was waiting for them, his countenance even more wooden than usual.

'I have taken the liberty of sending water up to the rooms, my lord.'

Ralph resisted the temptation to put his hand up to his neck cloth as he saw the butler's eyes slide up to it, then on to Lucy's dishevelled appearance. He was relieved when Ariadne came bustling over.

'Oh, my heavens, I saw you coming across the lawn. Lucy, my dear, your gown—!'

'We were caught out in the storm,' Ralph explained. 'We took shelter at Druids Rock, but not before Miss Halbrook suffered a drenching. Perhaps, Cousin, you would be good enough to take her to her room?'

'Yes, yes, of course. Come along, my love.'

He said, as he accompanied them across the hall, 'Did anyone else observe our return?'

'No, I do not think so. Everyone is in the library or the drawing room. I had gone upstairs to fetch my book and saw you from the staircase landing.'

Lucy put a hand up to her wet hair.

'I must look quite frightful.'

Her voice shook a little and Ralph wanted to gather her in his arms again, but Ariadne was bustling around her like a mother hen.

'You will feel much better once we have found you some dry clothes.' She took Lucy's arm as they began to mount the stairs, sparing no more than an impatient look for Ralph.

'There is no need for you to tarry here, Adversane, I will look after Lucy. You should run on to your own room. The sooner you have changed the sooner you can look after your guests.'

Lucy watched him take the stairs two at a time. His short, dark hair was already dry. A change of clothes and no one would know he had been caught in the rain. For herself, she knew she would be going down to dinner with her curls still damp.

Mrs Dean accompanied her into the dressing room, where Ruthie was overseeing the filling of a hip-bath.

'We should put a little elderflower oil in the water. It is very good for aches and chills. I have some in my room.'

'Oh, would you fetch it, please, Ariadne? I am sure it will help.' Lucy gave the widow a tiny smile. 'Ruthie will look after me now.'

Having sent the widow bustling away, Lucy went back to her bedroom to undress. She assured Ruthie she could manage quite well on her own and ordered the maid to make sure the servants did not spill the bathwater.

'There, Miss, you looks quite respectable again.'

There was no guile in the maid's open countenance; she thought merely that her mistress had been caught in the heavy rainstorm which had quite ruined her gown. The thin muslin was muddy and too badly damaged to repair. It had been thrown away, bundled up with the undergarments that bore the tell-tale signs of Lucy's lost virginity. She was now ready to go down to dinner, dressed in green silk and the only evidence of her soaking was her damp hair.

She was a little apprehensive about entering the drawing room, and Caroline's cheerful greeting informed her that her escapade had not gone unnoticed.

'So, Lucy, my brother had to rescue you from the storm.'

Ariadne shook her head and murmured, 'So foolhardy to go out at all in such weather.'

'Miss Halbrook is not used to the sudden violence of our northern weather.' Ralph was holding out his hand to her and smiling. 'I hope her experience today will not give her a dislike of Adversane.'

Lucy read the message in his eyes and tried desperately not to blush. She risked sending him a message of her own.

'Quite the contrary, my lord.'

'Ralph,' he reminded her. He pulled her hand onto his arm and led her across to Ariadne. 'But you see, Cousin, she is looking even more radiant, so there's no harm done.'

'I sincerely hope not.'

The words were uttered so quietly that only Lucy heard them as she sat down beside Mrs Dean.

'But why did you go out at all?' asked Charlotte. 'Mama said you were painting in the morning room, only you were not there when I went to find you to tell you that we were going to play charades.'

'I wanted a little air,' Lucy replied. 'I did not realise I had wandered so far…'

Margaret chuckled. 'Giving Ralph the opportunity to play Sir Galahad.'

'And you took shelter at Druids Rock,' stated Adam.

'Yes.' Lucy knew he was watching her closely and hoped she sounded nonchalant.

'Remarkable place, Druids Rock,' added Sir

James. 'I am glad the storm has passed, for I want to go there to see the dawn tomorrow.' He looked around, beaming. 'Summer solstice, you know. Perhaps some of you would like to join me?'

'With Midsummer's Eve looming?' Judith Cottingham shook her head. 'I for one will be resting and building up my strength for that.'

There was a general murmur of agreement and Ralph said, 'You are welcome to go, of course, Preston, but I doubt you will find anyone to accompany you.'

'Of course I would not expect *you* to go there, Adversane, but I am not unhopeful... Charlotte, my dear, what about you?'

His daughter wrinkled her pretty nose. 'Not I, Papa! I am not like Helene, slipping off to Druids Rock whenever she could get away. She must truly have thought it had magic powers, since she was always going there.'

Lucy felt the change immediately. There was a tension in the air and everyone was looking uncomfortable. Ralph was frowning and Lady Preston hissed at her daughter, who merely shrugged her shoulders.

'Why must I not mention her? After two years we should be able to talk of my sister without so much constraint. I thought that was why Lord Adversane had invited us here.'

'You are quite right, Miss Preston,' replied

Ralph. 'The past is done, but I am afraid it still haunts some of us.'

Byrne came in to announce that dinner was ready and Lucy was aware of a definite feeling of relief as they all made their way to the dining room. With only three days to go until Midsummer's Eve, the play was the natural topic of conversation once everyone was seated.

'What are they performing this year?' asked Caroline.

Ralph helped himself from a dish of chicken before him and did not look up as he answered.

'The Provoked Wife.'

'But that's—'

Sir Timothy's exclamation was cut short, Lucy suspected by a kick under the table from Caroline, who was sitting beside him.

'Yes,' said Ralph carefully. 'It is the same play they performed two years ago.'

'So everything is to be as it was before,' murmured Judith Cottingham.

'With one exception,' put in Lady Preston. She fixed her pale eyes upon Lucy. 'You have no Lady Adversane.'

'True, but I do have a fiancée,' Ralph replied coolly. 'I shall use the occasion to announce our formal betrothal.'

Ariadne's fork clattered onto her plate.

'That is not what was planned, Cousin.'

'Plans change.' Ralph was looking at Lucy,

a little smile playing about the corners of his mouth. 'Well, my love? Would you object to it?'

Before she could reply, Adam brought his hand crashing down upon the table.

'Dash it all, Adversane, this is not the time or the place to ask such a question. You put Miss Halbrook in a most awkward position. If she has any objections do you think she would voice them here, in front of everyone?'

Lucy shook her head. 'Truly, I—'

Ralph put up his hand to silence her, his eyes solemn.

'Adam is quite right, my dear. You should consider well before giving me your answer.'

Lucy did not want to consider. She knew what she wanted, but Ralph's announcement had caused so much consternation that she dare not say so. Instead, she kept her peace and Lord Wetherell adroitly changed the subject.

No more was said of the engagement during dinner, but afterwards it seemed everyone had an opinion to share with Lucy. As the ladies made their way across to the drawing room, Lady Preston came alongside her.

'I advise you to think very carefully before you commit yourself to Lord Adversane's proposal, Miss Halbrook. Once the betrothal is made public there can be no going back.'

'I am aware of that, ma'am.'

'Are you?' Lady Preston put her hand on her arm and gave her a pitying smile. 'Are you truly ready to tie yourself to a man who can never love you?'

Lucy put up her chin. 'You are mistaken.'

Had Ralph not proved this very day how much he loved her? As if she were reading her thoughts, Lady Preston curled her lip.

'You are very young, my dear, and do not yet know the difference between a man's lust and true, lasting affection.'

Lucy responded with nothing more than a shake of her head as they entered the drawing room, but no sooner had she moved away from Lady Preston than Margaret and Caroline came up to her.

'Has her ladyship been trying to dissuade you, Lucy? Pay her no heed. She wants Adversane for her daughter.'

'I know that, Caro, but—'

Margaret patted her arm. 'If Ralph wants you, he will have you.'

'Meg's right,' added Caroline. 'Do you not yet know that my brother is not to be gainsaid?'

Their words did not give the reassurance Lucy wanted. She declined their invitation to join them at the piano, preferring to sit a little way apart and collect her thoughts. She was not allowed to do so for long.

'You are looking a little fatigued, Miss Halbrook.' Judith Cottingham sat down beside her. 'I am not at all surprised. I find Caroline and Margaret's company quite as exhausting as their brother's. They must always be on the go, always doing something. And so strong-willed, too.' She gave a little laugh. 'My husband says they have none of them any concern for anyone's feelings but their own.'

'I have not found that to be so,' said Lucy.

'Perhaps that is because you are naturally complaisant.'

'I do not think—'

Judith caught her arm, saying in an urgent under-voice, 'Have a care what you are about, Miss Halbrook. This is not a happy house. It is full of shadows and secrets.'

'Mayhap I can make it happier.'

'No. You look too much like Helene.'

'A little, perhaps, but—'

The grip on her arm became almost painful.

'You should not stay here,' Judith hissed. 'You should leave before he destroys you, too.'

Lucy drew back, startled. Mrs Cottingham put up her hand and shook her head, a frightened look on her face. 'Forgive me. Please, I beg you, forget that I said anything.'

She hurried away, leaving Lucy to stare after her. She had thought Judith Cottingham a meek, colourless little woman, so her sudden outburst had been all the more alarming. What did she mean? Was she warning her against Ralph? She looked around. If only he would come in. She needed the reassurance of his presence, but a glance at the clock told her not to expect the gentlemen for another half-hour at least.

Restlessly, she went over to the windows, throwing them open so that she could stroll out onto the terrace, but even there she was not alone for long.

'Such a lovely evening now, after the earlier rain.' Ariadne came to stand beside Lucy, looking out over the gardens. 'Ralph's decision to announce your engagement—does it have anything to do with your being caught out in the storm together today? My dear, I do not mean to pry, but I am anxious for you. This is a very long way from his original plan.'

Lucy hesitated, collecting her thoughts.

'I am aware how it must look to you, ma'am, but since I have been here, since I have become acquainted with Lord Adversane—'

'You have fallen in love with him?'

Lucy gave her a grateful smile. 'I have. I cannot tell you how much I—'

'Then pray do not,' exclaimed Ariadne, consternation shadowing her kind face. 'Oh, my dear Lucy, I would like nothing better, but…' She took her hands. 'Are you sure Ralph returns your affection? But of course you are. How could I doubt it?'

'You are not happy about it.'

'I cannot deny I am concerned, Lucy. You have known my cousin for such a short time, and you are so very young—'

'I am four-and-twenty, Ariadne.'

'Very well, you are not a child, but all the same, this is so very sudden. Would it not be better to wait a little longer, just to be sure?'

Lucy pulled her hands free and gave a little cry of frustration.

'Oh, why is everyone so concerned that I do not know my own heart?'

She turned away, blinking back the hot tears that threatened to fall. After a moment Ariadne squeezed her arm.

'Oh, my dear, it is not *your* heart that I doubt.'

Lucy heard the older woman's sigh and then she was alone. The joy and happiness she had felt earlier had quite disappeared. Was everyone against her marrying Ralph? No, Caroline and Margaret were pleased for her, weren't they? What was it Margaret had said?

If Ralph wants you, he will have you.

There was nothing lover-like about that— it was more a statement of possession. As the threat of tears subsided, Lucy gazed out across the gardens, watching the shadows lengthen. This was Adversane land, as far as one could see. Ralph was offering to make her mistress of all this and more, but she knew it was not enough. She wanted none of it if she could not have his love, as well.

'So here you are.'

That deep, dear voice had her spinning round, reaching out for him. Without hesitating, Ralph took her in his arms. He kissed her, melting her doubts like snow in the sunlight.

'I would like to carry you upstairs right now.' He murmured the words against her skin as his lips nibbled her ear, making her shiver with delight. 'Yet I suppose we must be circumspect, at least while we have visitors at Adversane. It will not be easy for me to keep away from you.'

She put her hands against his chest and looked up at him.

'Do you truly wish to marry me, Ralph?'

His brows went up.

'What is this? What have my family been saying to you?

She dropped her eyes to his neck cloth, but the precision of those intricate folds only reminded her of how she had struggled to tear it off earlier. The thought brought the hot blood surging through her once more. He pulled her close again, murmuring between kisses.

'They all think we have been betrothed for the past year. Surely they cannot think it is too soon?'

'No, but Ariadne knows the truth and she is most concerned.'

'She will come round when she sees how I love you.'

'Do you, Ralph? Do you truly love me?'

He met her glance with a glinting smile. 'Can you doubt it?'

She shook her head. When he was so close, holding her like this, she did not doubt it at all.

'Then unless you have any objections we will announce our betrothal after the play, and then in a week or so I shall take you to London to inform your family. Would you wish to be married there, or shall we give my tenants the privilege of seeing you become my bride at the parish church in Adversane? It is your choice, although Hopkins will be most disappointed if he is not to perform the ceremony—'

'Stop, stop.' Laughing, she put a hand up to his lips. 'This is all too much, my—Ralph. We can decide upon such details later.'

He kissed her fingers. 'You are right. One thing at a time.' He raised his head, listening. 'And if I am not mistaken, Byrne has brought in the tea tray. I suppose we must go and join the others.'

After another swift kiss he took her inside. She knew her eyes were shining with pleasure and her happiness was not in the least dimmed by the arctic glare Lady Preston cast in her direction, nor by Judith Cottingham's frowning look.

She helped Mrs Dean to serve the tea, then

took her own cup to a quiet corner, content to be alone with her own thoughts. However, she was soon joined by Adam Cottingham. She managed to greet him with a smile.

'You are to be congratulated,' he remarked, sitting down beside her. 'I do not know when I last saw Adversane so happy.'

Lucy looked across the room to where Ralph was talking with his brothers-in-law.

'Do you think that is because of me, Mr Cottingham?'

'Undoubtedly.'

'Then I, too, am content.'

Adam put his cup down, frowning. 'You should not be.' He directed a solemn look at her. 'I would beg you to have a care, Miss Halbrook.'

'You have said as much before, sir, but I believe you are mistaken.'

'You do not understand. I cannot speak here. Meet me at nine o'clock tomorrow morning. In the shrubbery, where we will not be overheard.'

She sat up very straight.

'I do not think that is wise, sir. I beg you will say what you have to here, now.'

He gave a quick shake of his head.

'I cannot, Adversane is watching us. But believe me when I say that you need to know this.' He rose. 'Tomorrow morning, Miss Halbrook.'

She watched him walk away and half expected Ralph to ask her what they had been talking of, but the party was breaking up. Adam collected his wife and retired, followed shortly by Caroline and Lord Wetherell. Lady Preston declared loudly that Charlotte needed to rest.

'The next few days are important if you are to look your best for Midsummer's Eve.' She turned to her husband. 'And you, sir, you will need some sleep if you are to walk to Druids Rock to see the sunrise.'

Sir James chuckled. 'Well, I did think I might sit in the library and read by the light of one of Adversane's new-fangled lamps. After all, it is hardly worth going to bed—the nights are so short.'

'By all means, if that is what you wish,' said Ralph mildly.

Lady Preston was adamant, however, and carried both her daughter and husband away.

Sir Timothy grinned.

'We know who rules the roost in that household! If you do not object, Adversane, I shall step out onto the terrace to smoke a cigar before I retire.' He held out his hand to his wife. 'Are you coming, Meg?'

She went willingly, leaving only Lucy, Ralph and Ariadne in the drawing room. Mrs Dean rose, smothering a yawn.

'I shall go to bed, too,' she said. 'Shall you come with me, Lucy?'

Lucy began to follow her to the door, until Ralph detained her.

'You go on up, Cousin. I will escort Lucy upstairs in a moment.' Ralph added, when she hesitated. 'It is customary to allow engaged couples a little time alone.'

Ariadne's eyes narrowed.

'And that is a crow I meant to pick with you, Adversane. About your betrothal. When did—?'

'Yes, yes, but not tonight, it is far too late to explain it all.' Ralph shepherded his cousin to the door. 'Goodnight, Ariadne.'

When at last she had retired, he closed the door and stood for a moment with his back to it, regarding Lucy.

'I thought I should never get you to myself.'

He took her hand and pulled her down beside him on one of the sofas. Lucy made a half-hearted protest, reminding him that Sir Timothy and Lady Finch were still on the terrace.

'What of it?' he muttered. 'They will not come in for a while yet.'

He began nibbling her ear, causing such pleasurable sensations to course through her body that she forgot everything but the sheer pleasure of being in his arms. Her bones were liquefying, even before he moved his attention to her mouth. She returned his kiss, running her hands through his hair and turning her body into his, pressing against him as the familiar longing raged through her blood.

'Enough,' he muttered at last. 'Enough, or I shall have to take you all over again.'

Reluctantly, she let him pull her to her feet.

'I fear I must be sadly wanton,' she said, sighing, 'for there is nothing I would like more.'

'Not until I have made an honest woman of you.' He drew her into his arms, and they shared another long, lingering kiss. 'But, by heaven, I am tempted to purchase a special licence to do it!'

A gurgle of laughter escaped her as she relished her power over him. They went out of the drawing room and up the grand staircase hand in hand.

'I have business in Halifax tomorrow morning with Colne. Come with us,' he urged her. 'It should not take long, and the scenery is magnificent. You might bring your sketchpad.'

'I should love to come with you, but Mrs Sutton is bringing the scarlet gown.' She stopped. 'I could send her word not to come.'

Even in the dim light she saw the shadow cross his face.

'No, you need the gown for Midsummer's Eve, so you must see Mrs Sutton tomorrow. I shall take you to Halifax another time.'

They were on the stairs, and she stepped up onto the next tread so that her eyes were level with his.

'But why, Ralph? I have more than enough dresses—'

'But that is the one to wear for the play. There is something I must know.'

'If you are still in love with Helene, perhaps?'

The hard, distant look left him then. He cupped her face in his hands.

'No, I promise you it is not that.' Gently, he kissed her lips. 'I must ask you to trust me, just a little longer. Will you do that?'

'But I do not understand, Ralph. Why—?'

'I will explain everything on Midsummer's Day, I promise you.' He gazed deep into her eyes. 'Can you do that, Lucy? Can you trust me for just a little longer?'

'Of course, but—'

He put his fingers against her lips.

'No buts, my love. Trust me.'

He loves me, I am sure of it.

Lucy repeated the words to herself as Ruthie undressed her, but when she had blown out the candle and lay alone in the darkness, she questioned why, if she was to trust Ralph, he would not trust her with his reasons.

Unbidden, a memory came back to her. She was standing beside Mama on the pavement while the landlord piled their belongings around them.

'I don't understand, Mama. Why didn't you tell me?'

It was only then, while they waited for Uncle Edgeworth to send his carriage to collect them, that Mama had told her the truth. Only then that she had trusted her daughter enough to share the pain that she had endured during those final years, shielding Lucy, telling her Papa was away painting while in fact he was gambling and drinking himself into a pauper's grave.

Lucy turned her face to the pillow. Was it always to be thus, that those she loved most would not trust her?

The problem still nagged at her when she awoke the next day. She had arranged to go out with Caroline and Margaret after breakfast, and Ruthie had laid out her riding habit in readiness. As Lucy made her way downstairs she saw that it wanted but a few minutes to nine, the time Adam had suggested she meet him in the shrubbery. She had fully intended to stay away, certain that she did not want to hear what he had to say, but now instead of going to breakfast she made her way out to the gardens. Adam was Ralph's cousin; he had known him all his life. Perhaps talking to him might help her to understand why Ralph would not confide in her.

She found Adam waiting for her at the entrance to the shrubbery. As she approached, he held his arm out to her.

'Good morning, Miss Halbrook. It is such a lovely day no one will wonder at us strolling here, if we should be seen.'

After the briefest hesitation she stepped up beside him, placing her fingers on his sleeve.

'Sir James will have witnessed a beautiful sunrise this morning.'

It was all she could think of to say. Now she was here she could not bring herself to ask him about Ralph. That would be too disloyal.

'I am surprised he can go there, knowing it is where his daughter...where his daughter ended her life.'

Lucy said gently, 'But I understand it was also one of her favourite places.'

'Oh, yes.'

Adam said no more, and she looked at him. He was frowning, lost in his own thoughts, and she felt a flicker of impatience.

'Mr Cottingham, I—'

'You will be wondering what it is I wanted to say to you.' He interrupted her. 'I warned you to be on your guard, Miss Halbrook. My cousin is a passionate man.'

Lucy flushed.

'That is not a crime.'

'No, when it is under regulation. But...Adversane's temper is ungovernable.'

'I have seen no sign of it.'

'But how long have you known him? I mean *really* known him, not merely meeting him in company.'

She put up her chin.

'I think I know him quite well. He is a strong character, of course, but—'

'Strong! Oh, yes,' he said bitterly. 'Adversane must have his way in all things!' He fell silent, as if fighting with himself. At last he spoke again, his voice unsteady with suppressed anger. 'It was always thus. As heir to Adversane he was denied nothing—imagine what that did for a temper that was naturally autocratic. He grew up demanding that everyone bend to his will.'

'I do not believe that.'

'Oh, he hides it well, dressing up his demands as requests, but he will allow nothing to stand in his way.'

If Ralph wants you, he will have you.

Lucy tried to shut out Margaret's words.

'But he is well respected. I hear nothing but praise for him when I go out—'

'Hah! Money and power will buy you many friends, Miss Halbrook.'

'No, it is genuine, I am sure—'

But he was not listening to her.

'Ralph and Helene should never have married,' he said, scowling. 'She was an angel. Everyone says so. Everyone loved her. She was too good, too kind for that monster—'

Lucy pulled her arm away.

'Enough,' she said angrily. 'I will not have you talk of Adversane like that!'

She began to hurry away from him, but he followed her.

'He took Helene for his wife, frightened her with his passion and his harsh words, so much so that in the end she was desperate to get away from him. *That* is why she ran to Druids Rock on the night of the ball.'

'You cannot blame Ralph for her accident.'

'It was no accident.' Lucy stopped and he continued in a low voice, 'She went to Druids Rock to end everything, and it was because of my cousin.'

She shook her head and said again, 'You cannot blame Ralph.'

'Who else should I blame? He was her husband. He should have cherished her, loved her.'

'I am sure he did, in his way.' She looked up suddenly. 'But how do you know so much of this?'

'I?' he said, startled. 'Why, I am Adversane's cousin. I spent a great deal of time here. I observed him and his wife. Perhaps I saw too much.'

'I am not sure you should be telling me this, Mr Cottingham.'

'But I am concerned for you.'

'Thank you, but I can look after myself.' They had reached the entrance to the shrubbery, but as she went to leave he caught her arm.

'I am sure you can, ma'am, but you know he is trying to change you.' He came closer. 'She was beautiful, but when she did not live up to his ideal he drove her to her death. Now he is trying to mould you into her image!'

'No!' Lucy shook him off. 'Good day to you, Mr Cottingham.'

It was preposterous. Outrageous. She would not believe it. She had been a fool to listen to him. Lucy hurried into the house, glad that Adam did not follow her. Margaret and Caroline were already at breakfast with their husbands and they all looked up as she entered.

Margaret paused, her coffee cup halfway to her mouth.

'My dear, you are looking very pale. Are you unwell?'

Lucy stopped just inside the door.

'I hardly know.' She felt a little dazed.

'Missing Ralph, no doubt.'

Margaret frowned at her sister. 'Be quiet, Caro. Lucy, you do not look at all well. Let me take you to your room.'

Lucy waved her back into her seat.

'No, thank you, I can manage. But I will go and lie down.'

'Good idea,' agreed Sir Timothy. 'I think it is too hot for riding. In fact, I am trying to persuade the ladies not to go.'

'Pho, as if we should listen to you, Timothy! Meg and I will not melt because of a little sunshine…'

Lucy left them to their banter. She would stay quietly in her room for a while until she could organise her chaotic thoughts. Not that she believed a word that Adam Cottingham had said, but meeting with him had not helped her at all. It was her own fault, of course. She had encouraged him to be open with her and now she could hardly blame him for voicing his opinions. She entered her bedchamber and was surprised to see the dressing room door was open. Someone was moving around inside. Ruthie should have gone downstairs to her own breakfast by now. Lucy crossed the room, intent upon sending the maid away.

'Oh.' She stopped, frowning, when she found herself confronting not her maid, but a complete stranger.

Before her stood a thin, grey-haired woman, soberly dressed as befitted an upper servant. Lucy's brow cleared.

'Miss Crimplesham, isn't it?'

'Yes, ma'am.' The woman dipped a reluctant curtsey but made no attempt to leave. Her face was blotched, as if she had been crying.

Lucy said gently, 'I have no doubt you are very familiar with these rooms, but you are Miss Preston's dresser now, and she is in the guest wing.'

'It's all the same.'

Lucy frowned. 'I beg your pardon?'

'Nothing's changed.' Miss Crimplesham turned back to the gowns hanging on the pegs along one wall. She began to pull out the skirts, one after the other. 'All these dresses, all identical to those worn by my lady. The quality is not the same, of course—my lady always had her gowns made by the best modistes in Harrogate and London. And they are bigger, too. Slender as a reed was Miss Helene. You've the look of her, but you're not as beautiful as my mistress. Lord Adversane always said she was the most beautiful woman he had ever known. She could have been so happy, if it hadn't been for that man.'

Lucy drew herself up.

'That is quite enough, Crimplesham. I think you should go now.'

She injected as much quiet firmness into her voice as she could, and was relieved when the dresser swept past her and out of the room. Alone at last, Lucy sank down upon her dressing stool. She was trembling and she wrapped her arms about herself. What did it all mean? Was there some sort of plot to turn her against Ralph?

She shook her head, putting her hands to her

temples. No, she did not believe Miss Crimple-sham was party to any conspiracy. The poor woman was merely disturbed by grief, but coming so soon after her encounter with Adam Cottingham, Lucy found herself wondering if she was wise to trust Ralph.

Perhaps he, too, was so grief-stricken that he wanted to recreate his lost love. That would explain why he had chosen her, why he insisted she wear gowns identical to those worn by his wife. Lucy did not want to believe it, but what other reason could there be?

'There must be another reason,' she told herself. 'There has to be.'

But no matter how much she thought about it, no other explanation presented itself.

Chapter Twelve

'Ooh, Miss, you look a picture!'

It did not need Ruthie's hushed exclamation to tell Lucy that she looked very well. She was standing before her mirror in the scarlet gown. The colour accentuated the creamy tones of her skin and set off her hair, which had been lightened to honey-blond by the recent sunshine.

'Indeed, madam, I do not think I have ever made a finer gown.' Mrs Sutton stood to one side, smiling with satisfaction as she regarded her handiwork. 'And it fits perfectly. No alterations are required, save to put up the hem.'

Lucy stared at herself in the long glass. If only she had not gone out to meet Adam that morning—and if she had not come back to find Miss Crimplesham in her room—she might have been able to overcome her doubts, but now the thought of wearing the gown filled her with unease.

She said suddenly, 'Would you mind waiting a moment? I would like to slip outside.'

Holding up her skirts, she went out to the Long Gallery and stood before the portrait of Helene. She was being foolish, she knew, but she was hoping there was some mistake, that the gown was not a perfect replica, but when she studied the painting it was clear the gown was exact to the last detail. Only the wearer was different, she thought sadly. A pale imitation of perfection.

'Helene!'

The tortured whisper made her swing around. Adam Cottingham was staring at her. After a moment he gave a start.

'Miss Halbrook, is that you? For a moment I—' He came closer, frowning. 'That gown, why––no, don't tell me,' he added bitterly. 'Adversane ordered it.'

'Yes.'

'He cannot make you wear it.' His face contorted with disgust. 'It is too monstrous! Tell me you will put it away.'

'I cannot do that, sir,' she said gently. 'I have agreed to wear it on Midsummer's Eve—'

'No, you cannot, you must not!' He grabbed her hand, saying urgently, 'Promise me you will wear something else. It is too dangerous!'

'Dangerous?'

She frowned, but he was already shaking

his head and saying in an agitated voice, 'Forgive me, it is no business of mine.' He raised her hand to his lips. 'Seeing you there, suddenly I thought...' He cupped her face with his free hand and gazed at her, the sadness of the world in his eyes.

'Mr Cottingham,' she began, unnerved. 'Adam—'

'Forgive me,' he said again, before shaking his head and rushing away.

'Very touching.'

Ralph's voice, cold as ice, made her jump. He was standing at the far end of the gallery, and she guessed he had just come in. He was dressed for riding and still carried his crop in one gloved hand.

'Would you mind telling what you were doing here with Cottingham?' His tone was cutting, and the end of the riding crop tapped an angry tattoo against the side of one dusty top boot.

'Not at all,' she retorted. 'If you would ask me in a civilised manner!'

Ralph's jealous anger receded as quickly as it had come. By heaven, she looked magnificent, standing there in that red gown, her green eyes sparkling like fiery emeralds.

'I beg your pardon. I have this moment returned from Halifax. I was...surprised to see you here.' His eyes slid over her gown. He thought she had never looked better.

'Mrs Sutton is waiting in my chamber to finish the hem,' she explained. 'I just wanted to compare it to...' She tailed off, waving one hand vaguely in the direction of the portrait.

'And my cousin found you thus.'

'Yes. It was all very innocent.'

The image of Adam cupping her face flashed into his mind. He said curtly, 'For you, perhaps.'

'And what do you mean by that?'

'Ariadne tells me you were walking in the gardens with him this morning.'

'Yes, I took a walk before breakf—'

'I would rather you did not allow him to be alone with you.'

'Oh? Why?'

Ralph hesitated. Why indeed? Some instinct, a gut feeling, said Adam was a threat, but cold logic told him that could not be. After all, he had already ascertained that Adam was with his wife the night Helene died.

'Well, my lord?'

He was goaded into a retort.

'I should have thought that was obvious.'

Her brows went up.

'Can it be that you are jealous, my lord?'

Was that it? Was that the threat he feared, that Lucy might prefer his cousin? His mouth twisted into a wry smile.

'I think I am.'

He watched the stormy light in her eyes die away and a becoming blush mantled her cheeks. It was as much as he could do not to sweep her up and carry her off to his room. Instead, he contented himself with picking up her hand and placing a light kiss on her fingers. They trembled slightly beneath his touch.

'Ralph?' She was looking up at him, a faint question in her eyes. 'May I not wear another gown on Midsummer's Eve?'

'But you look truly lovely in that one, my dear.'

And perfect for his plans.

'But why is it so important to you that I wear this one?'

Tell her the truth, man!

He gripped his riding crop even tighter. The Adversane name, the family honour was at stake. Pride would not allow him to voice his suspicions without more proof.

'Please, Ralph, I would be happier in something else.'

How he wanted to please her, but he was so close now. She had to wear that gown if he was ever to know the truth. When it was all over he would tell her, even if it meant admitting he was wrong. But not yet. Not now.

'I need you to wear it,' he said at last. 'I need to prove something.'

'But you will not tell me what it is.'

'No.'

'Ralph—'

'By God, madam, must you question me at every turn? I cannot tell you. Not yet.' He dropped her hand. 'It was so much easier when you were merely an employee.'

Pain flickered in her eyes as his words lashed her, and he immediately regretted his rash utterance. She pulled herself up, almost trembling with a proud, stubborn anger that matched his own.

'Then that is what I shall be. I will wear this gown, since you insist upon it, but if you will not tell me why, if you cannot trust me, then I cannot marry you. I will fulfil the contract and then I will leave, as we originally agreed.'

Ralph stared at her, recognising a kindred spirit. She took his breath away. He was standing on the edge of a precipice and she was cutting the ground from beneath his feet. He needed to respond but could not find the words. Lucy met his hard gaze steadily. He only had to speak, to tell her. The moments crept by in a long, painful silence while he tried to formulate a sentence, a phrase, but nothing would come. At last, keeping her head high, she turned and walked away.

Lucy went back to her chamber. She fought back the tears, determined not to cry in front of Ruthie or Mrs Sutton and her assistant. She stood silently while they fussed around her, all of them too intent upon the beautiful robe to notice her wooden countenance or the brevity of her responses.

She had just stepped out of the gown when Adversane walked in unannounced. Ruthie gave a small shriek and quickly threw Lucy's wrap around her bare shoulders.

'Leave us,' he barked. 'I wish to talk to Miss Halbrook alone.'

Lucy gave him a haughty look.

'Mrs Sutton has yet to sew up the hem.'

'Then she may do so elsewhere. Go. Now!'

The dressmaker and her assistant snatched up their things and almost ran from the room, but the maid hovered beside Lucy, frightened but determined not to abandon her mistress.

Lucy touched her arm. 'It is all right, Ruthie, you may go. I will ring when I need you.' As the maid scuttled from the room, Lucy turned back to Ralph, saying coldly, 'What now, my lord, do you have some new demand for your employee?'

'You are angry with me, and rightly so. I have come to explain.'

There was no softening of his countenance or his tone, but Lucy did not expect that. The fact that he was here at all was more than she had dared to hope for.

'Very well.'

She glanced about her before perching herself on the dressing stool. The only other seat in the room was the small sofa at the end of the bed and she would not risk him sitting beside her. For a long time he stood in silence, looking down at her.

'I do not see her,' he said at last. 'When I look at you, I do not see Helene.'

'But I look like her.' Lucy shivered as she thought of Lady Preston's words. 'A pale imitation.'

'There is nothing pale about you. Harry saw it from the beginning. He said you had fire in you.'

'Mr Colne knows your plan?'

He nodded. 'I told him of it the night he brought Francesca to dinner. He had guessed something was amiss when he saw you in that blue gown and came to my study to challenge me.'

'I know.' Lucy nodded. 'I heard him.'

He sat down on the little sofa.

'Are you angry, that I told Harry the truth and not you?'

'He is your best friend. You should have told him from the outset.' Despite the weight on her spirits she felt a wry smile tugging at her mouth. 'I suspect you were too obstinate.'

'Too obstinate and too proud. It has taken an equally stubborn woman to make me see that I was wrong to keep all this to myself. Helene's character was frail, weak. Yours is much stronger. Where she was cold and fearful, you are warm and brave.' A faint smile lightened his countenance. 'Helene was a beautiful ninnyhammer. You are intelligent, and beautiful in a different way.'

'But you loved her.'

'No. I was dazzled at first, perhaps, and happy to have such a beautiful wife, but love? No. I never loved her, any more than she loved me.'

'That is very sad.'

'It is the way of most arranged marriages. I had resigned myself to it. I thought she had, too.'

Lucy gripped her hands tightly in her lap to stop herself from reaching out to comfort him. It was too soon.

'Perhaps you should tell me everything.'

'Perhaps I should.'

He sat forward and rested his elbows on his knees, hands clasped together and his eyes fixed upon the floor. Lucy forced herself to remain silent, waiting for him to begin.

'Three years ago I went to Harrogate looking for a wife. Helene Preston seemed an ideal choice. By birth she was a good match, her nature was sweet and of course she was stunningly beautiful. By the autumn we were married.

'It was not a love match, we both knew that, but her parents were eager for the alliance and Helene herself was not averse to it. And I—desired her. I thought that love would come later. If not love, then at least affection. I thought we could be comfortable together, despite the differences in our natures that very soon became apparent. We hid those differences well. To the outside world we were the perfect couple. We had separate interests, of course. Helene's were centred upon society. She wanted to see and be seen. Oh, she was accomplished—she had read the most fashionable authors, she could paint and draw and play the piano, but it was all done by rote, with little understanding.

'My interests bored her, as did the running of the estate and living at Adversane. I was equally bored by the life she wanted, the one we led for the first few months of our marriage, which was one long round of visits and house parties. Helene's beauty and impeccable manners made her universally admired. Everyone agreed I was a very fortunate man.'

'Everyone save you?'

'It was my choice. What right had I to complain? By the following spring, after a winter spent here, I realised how ill-suited we were. Helene's nature was timid. She disliked hunting, was terrified of the dogs and frightened of my horses—she was even frightened of me.' She saw his jaw clenching as he struggled with the memories. 'I hoped that would change, in time. I did my best to treat her gently. Sir James had told me she was highly strung, but it was more than that. She was unstable, like a skittish colt, shying away from my advances. I tried to be patient with her, I curbed my temper, never raised my voice, gave in to her every whim. By heaven, I showed her a good deal more tolerance than I have done anyone else.' He glanced up to look at Lucy. 'Certainly I treated her with more kindness than I have shown you! I thought we needed time to get to know one another, so I held back. I never forced my attentions upon her. We had our separate rooms and I allowed her to go her own way.' He added, as if to himself, 'Perhaps that was my mistake.'

With a hiss of exasperation, Ralph jumped to his feet, saying roughly, 'This is an unedifying tale. I should not be sullying your ears with it—'

She was at his side in an instant, catching his arm as he made for the door.

'No, please, do not go.'

'It was madness to involve you in my harebrained scheme. The more I think of it the more nonsensical it seems to me now.' He took her hands, saying urgently, "You should leave now, Lucy. I can never make you happy. It was wrong of me to think I could. Do not worry about the money—I shall pay you everything I promised, and more. You need never want for anything.'

Some part of her wanted to rip up at him, to

accuse him of trying to buy her off, but she knew that wasn't the case. He was trying to protect her.

She said simply, 'But I do not want to leave.'

'You must. If I find I have destroyed one woman, I will not risk doing the same thing to you.'

'I do not believe you destroyed Helene.'

'That is because you do not know the whole—'

'Then tell me,' she said. 'Tell me and let me decide for myself.'

'You may hate me when you know everything.'

'That is a risk, certainly, but if you send me away now my imagination will conjure up something far worse.' Lucy took a breath, desperate to make him understand. 'All my life the people I have loved have tried to…to *protect* me by keeping unpalatable truths hidden from me. If you care for me at all, then pray do me the honour of trusting me with the truth. I am not so feeble that it will break me.'

His mouth quirked at one side as if a smile was being forced out of him.

'No, I think in some ways you are stronger than all of us.'

He returned to the sofa, and she sat down beside him, saying quietly, 'It does not seem to me that your marriage was a very happy one.'

'As happy as many another couple, but I began

to suspect that Helene had a lover. Men had always clustered about her, attracted by her beauty, but she never showed the slightest preference for any of them. However, that last spring at Adversane, she changed. She was more nervous and on edge than ever, and she began avoiding my company. Her manner was agitated and she would burst into tears even more often than before. She had always gone to Druids Rock with her father when he visited Adversane, but now she began to walk there almost daily.'

'You never went with her?'

'Occasionally, but it was very clear she did not want my company. She often waited until I was occupied with estate business to go off.' He paused. 'She always took Crimplesham and despite my suspicions I never followed her, never questioned her maid or had her watched. I did not wish for her to think of me as her gaoler.'

'And you never spoke to her about your suspicions?'

'Only once, on the morning of Midsummer's Eve.' He exhaled slowly. 'Helene had been pampered and cossetted all her life. Everyone adored her and it was rare indeed that she incurred anyone's disapproval, but her gentle nature could not withstand the least hint of criticism. However, I knew I could not let the situation go on.' His lips thinned to a bloodless line. 'I have told you, soft words are not my style. I tried, but I had to explain to her that I could not accept another man's bastard as my heir. She ran off in tears, whether from guilt, or remorse, or because she was innocent—to this day I have no idea, because by morning she was dead.'

Lucy bit her lip to prevent any exclamation of horror and after a few moments' silence Ralph continued.

'The matter was not mentioned again. Helene appeared happy enough at the play that night, but then, her serene smile never gave anything away. I hoped, foolishly, that she had resigned herself to life with me. After supper there was the usual dancing. I watched Helene closely but could see no sign of her favouring any one of her partners over the others. As soon as the guests had gone she retired. I offered to go with her, but she refused, saying she had a headache.' He shrugged. 'I had grown quite used to that. She did not want my company and I would not force it upon her. It was only the next morning I found out she had not gone to bed, when the maid Ruthie raised the alarm.'

He ran a hand across his eyes.

'I am haunted by the thought that I might be maligning Helene, that she was innocent and killed herself because of what I said to her. I know it is what my family think. Yet there is another explanation, although I have no proof.

'I cannot rid myself of the suspicion that she went off after the dancing to meet her lover.'

Lucy's hand crept to her mouth.

'Oh, good heavens.'

'I cannot prove it,' he said again. 'After we found her body I made endless enquiries of those who had been present, to see if any of them remembered Helene saying or doing anything that might explain why she went to Druids Rock, but no one could help me. I questioned Crimplesham, but she insisted her mistress was innocent and was outraged that I should even think such a thing. Yet still the suspicion remained and I determined to know the truth.' Ralph straightened. 'You see, it has been proven that recreating a scene or an event can spark a memory, so that was my plan. I took a small portrait of Helene to Mrs Killinghurst and asked her to find me someone who bore a resemblance to my wife. She found you.

'I brought you here, dressed you in the styles and colours my wife favoured and waited to see what happened. Adam's reaction convinced me that my plan would work. I thought if you appeared at the play dressed as Helene had been on that last fateful night, her lover would not be able to hide his reaction. And I should be watching.' His lip curled. 'Foolish, perhaps, but better to think she was meeting a lover at Druids

Rock than that she went there to kill herself because of me.

'I told no one. I wanted no hint of scandal attached to Helene if my suspicions were unfounded. I had no wish to sully her good name or cause her family more distress. I wrote to Ariadne and asked her to come here as chaperone, telling her the same tale I told you.'

He sat back and raked his fingers through his hair. 'But why should you believe me? It sounds too fantastical, as if I am trying merely to shuffle off the blame for what happened.'

'But I do,' she said slowly. 'I do believe you.'

He shook his head.

'You want to believe me innocent, because you cannot bear to think that my temper caused the death of such a sweet, gentle creature.'

'No. I believe it because I know—I was informed—that Lady Adversane was going to leave you.'

Chapter Thirteen

A heavy silence followed Lucy's words and she said quickly, 'Ruthie told me. She is a chatter-box, but she has given me her word that she kept the secret until now. She said she was appointed as lady's maid when your wife's dresser broke her arm.'

'Yes. That was why I assigned her to you, because I knew she could dress your hair in the same fashion.'

'I guessed as much, but it is not important now. Ruthie said Lady Adversane let it slip that she was planning to leave you. She then made Ruthie promise not to say a word about it.'

'Did she say why Helene was going?'

'Because…' Lucy faltered. 'Because she was so unhappy here.'

'So it comes back to me,' said Ralph bitterly.

'No! She would hardly have thrown herself from Druids Rock if she was planning to run away. It does not make sense.' She frowned, trying to recall her maid's exact words. 'Lady Adversane told Ruthie that when Crimplesham learned of the proposed flight she insisted on accompanying her. Don't you see, Ralph? Helene had already decided to run away before she even told her dresser. From all I have learned of your late wife I do not think she would contemplate going off alone.'

'She wouldn't!'

'No, it seems to me much more likely that someone had persuaded her, and that she went to Druids Rock that night to meet them.' She hesitated. 'Are you certain it would have been a guest?'

His lip curled. 'My wife was too conscious of her worth to dally with anyone beneath her own station. I questioned all my house guests, including my brothers-in-law. Logic told me I must eliminate everyone, however innocent I might think them. At one stage I seriously considered Helene might be in love with my cousin, for she was certainly on very good terms with him. You have seen for yourself that Cottingham has the happy knack of being able to put ladies at their ease. He flirts effortlessly, whereas I— Such frivolity is not a part of my nature.'

'That is no loss, to my mind,' she said softly.

He caught her hand and kissed it. 'Bless you for that.' He held it very tightly while he continued. 'But Adam cannot have been the one she was going to meet. Judith confirmed they were together all night, and in any case I saw them myself, going up to their room once the dancing had ended. The only other men I suspected are all neighbours—local gentlemen.' His mouth twisted. 'Everyone was asked if they could throw any light upon the matter, but by heaven, I have known all these men for years. I could scarcely accuse any one of them of being Helene's lover without very strong evidence.'

'Of course not. But you think, if I wear the gown, it will provide that evidence?'

'It might just stir up a memory or two that will lead me to the truth. Who knows, it might even reveal her lover, if there is one.'

'And if she *did* have a lover, do you think…?' She bit her lip. 'Do you think he killed her?'

'I don't know. All I am sure of is that I cannot bear the thought that I caused her death.'

'Then I will wear the gown.'

'No, Lucy, I cannot ask it of you. It is time I was honest with myself. I have been clutching at straws. Perhaps her death should be laid at my door. She was miserable living here at Adversane. She thought me hard and domineering.'

Lucy gripped his arm. 'No, no. You can be brusque, I admit, but I also know you are very kind. I will not believe you did anything to drive her to suicide.'

'I married her.'

'That was an arrangement between you and the Prestons,' said Lucy practically. 'You said yourself Helene was in favour of the marriage.'

'Yes, because she did not know then how difficult I can be.' He took her hand and laced his fingers through hers. 'Lucy, if I am wrong, if there is no lover, then I must face the fact that I killed my wife. If that is the case then you must leave here, and we must never see each other again. I will not risk ruining your life.'

'Ralph—'

'No.' He put a finger on her lips to silence her. 'My conscience would never allow it.'

She straightened, saying crisply, 'And my conscience will not allow you to punish yourself in this way, so we must do what we can to discover what really happened that night.'

Lucy lay in her bed, listening to the early morning birdsong flowing in through the open window. Midsummer's Eve, and there was still much to be done. She had thrown herself into the arrangements for the forthcoming festivities with an added zeal, following Ralph's disclosures. So much rested on the forthcoming event, her whole happiness was at stake. The library had been rearranged in readiness for the play, and dancing was to take place in the white salon, a large, richly decorated room on the ground floor.

Lucy had happily donned one of her old gowns and worked alongside the servants to transform the salon into a ballroom. She worked hard, as eager as Ralph to discover the truth, knowing that if he thought himself to blame for Helene's death he would send her away and she would never see him again.

Ralph had been adamant about that, saying it would be a mistake, that he would not risk making her unhappy. Lucy had argued but he would not be moved. She could not help wondering if guilt was the only reason he had decided they should not be wed. Perhaps he had realised that he didn't love her. He had said he never loved Helene, but wouldn't any man say that to his future bride?

Her doubts would not quite go away, and they were enhanced by Adam Cottingham's behaviour. Since their encounter in the Long Gallery she had on several occasions found him watching her with an almost mournful intensity. From everything Ralph had told her, she knew Adam could not be Helene's lover, so he must truly believe that Ralph was in some way responsible for her death. She *had* to believe that he was wrong, just as Lady Preston was wrong when she thought Ralph was still in love with her daughter.

Lucy stirred restlessly. If only she could tell them why Ralph had brought her here, why she had agreed to wear the scarlet gown, but he had sworn her to secrecy. How she hated secrets!

She sat up and tugged at the bell-pull. She might as well get up now and attend to the last-minute preparations. If all went well, they could soon know why Helene had gone to Druids Rock that fateful night. One way or another Lucy was determined to lay the ghost, so that she and Ralph could move on, free of the spectre of his dead wife.

An air of expectancy hung over the house. They had dined early so that they might all go off to change afterwards, in readiness for the forthcoming entertainment. When Ralph came to Lucy's door to escort her downstairs she rose quickly from her dressing stool to meet him as he entered her room.

Ralph was staring at her, a look she could not quite interpret in his eyes. When he did not speak she dismissed her maid before saying awkwardly, 'Well, my lord. Will I do?' She shook out the scarlet skirts. 'Ruthie has dressed my hair in an identical style to that of the portrait. The sun has made it much lighter, so I think the resemblance is now most striking.'

'It is indeed,' he muttered. 'No one could fail to see the likeness. Are you sure you wish to go through with this, Lucy? It will be an ordeal for you. There will be talk—'

She put up her chin.

'Let them talk. It may well jog a few memories.'

'I hope so.' He held out a small leather box. 'You will need these.' As he opened the lid she saw the flash and sparkle of precious stones. 'The Adversane diamonds.' He handed her the earrings, and when she had put them on he clipped the bracelet around her wrist. 'Now for the necklace.'

Ralph indicated that she should turn around, and she stood, head bowed a little, as he fastened the diamonds around her throat. His fingers were warm on her skin, and then she felt the unmistakable touch of his lips on the nape of her neck.

'My brave girl,' he murmured, putting his arms about her. 'Whatever happens tonight, I want you to know how much I love you.'

She turned to him, gripping his coat.

'If that is so, Ralph, then don't send me away. Whatever happens tonight, say you will marry me and let me help you to forget.'

His jaw hardened.

'No, we must wait and see. But heaven only knows how I will live without you.'

'You do not have to live without me, Ralph.' She reached up and cupped his face with her hands, drawing him down until she could kiss his lips. 'I believe in you, my darling. Whatever Helene did you cannot be held entirely responsible.'

'Not entirely, perhaps, but enough to make me blame myself for the rest of my life. I could not ask you to live with that.'

He drew her close and she leaned against him, closing her eyes. He would not change his mind, and she could only pray that they would learn something to ease the pain she knew he was suffering. But that could only happen if their plan worked. She stirred, and immediately he released her. Summoning up a smile, she took his arm.

'We must go downstairs, Ralph. Ruthie tells me the Ingleston Players are already setting up in the library and your guests will be arriving soon.'

'You are sure you wish to go through with this? They will all be agog to meet you, thinking you are my future bride.'

'And if your plan works that is exactly what I shall be.'

'But if it proves nothing—'

'Then I would still marry you,' she said with quiet vehemence. 'I would risk everything to be your wife!'

He stopped for one final, bruising kiss before he escorted her out of the room.

Lucy glided down the stairs beside Ralph, the scarlet gown billowing in a whisper of silken skirts. She could hear the faint echo of voices from the Great Hall, where everyone was gathering to greet the guests when they arrived.

Pulling Lucy's hand more firmly onto his arm, Ralph led her into the hall. The chatter and laughter stopped almost instantly. He heard Judith Cottingham's little moan of dismay and the gasps of surprise from his sisters. Lady Preston's countenance was impassive, save for a narrowing of her eyes. The gentlemen raised their quizzing glasses to regard Lucy and he even heard Sir Timothy mutter, 'Good Lord!' before giving a very unconvincing cough. Only Ariadne showed no surprise, but then, she had been present at the dressmaker's visits and knew what to expect.

Little Charlotte Preston was goggling at Lucy and she cried artlessly, 'Oh, my goodness, Mama, she looks exactly like Helene!'

'Nonsense,' snapped Lady Preston. Her eyes raked over Lucy and she leaned towards her daughter as if to speak confidentially, but her words still carried to everyone present. 'It is a similar gown, I grant you, but Miss Halbrook does not have Helene's figure, nor her elegance.' She turned away as if to demonstrate that Lucy was not worthy of her attention. Ralph felt his anger rising at this studied insult, but Ariadne was already drawing Lucy away from him, saying in her calm, unruffled way, 'Well, well, Lucy, you look delightful, my dear. And Adversane has given you the diamonds to wear. How charming.'

The rest of the party had regained their composure, and Ralph watched as they crowded around Lucy, eager to compliment her and make up for Lady Preston's lack of manners. Lord Wetherell broke away and strolled over.

'For God's sake, Adversane,' he murmured. 'What hellish game are you playing here?'

Ralph gave the tiniest shake of his head.

'I'll tell you later. When my guests arrive, take note of how they react to Miss Halbrook, would you?'

'They may well be struck dumb, as Cottingham appears to be.'

Ralph's eyes shifted to his cousin and he frowned. Adam was staring at Lucy, a muscle working in his cheek. With a word to his brother-in-law, Ralph moved towards Adam until he was close enough to ask him what he thought of Miss Halbrook.

'Miss—?' Adam tore his eyes away from Lucy. He was very pale, but he recovered himself and gave a little laugh. 'By Gad, Cousin, for a moment I thought I was seeing a ghost. What in heaven's name are you trying to do, Ralph? Why have you dressed her thus?'

Ralph wondered if he should confide in his cousin, but after another, frowning look at

Adam he decided against it. He said lightly, 'Scarlet is a favourite colour of mine.'

He glanced at Lucy. She looked nervous, and his heart ached for her. She was so brave, so determined to do this for him. She would be his saviour, he knew it.

I would risk everything to be your wife.

Her final words to him wrapped themselves around his heart, warming him, giving him hope. Suddenly he wanted to reach out to her, to show her how much he loved her. He raised his voice so that it would carry across the hall.

'Perhaps it would be a good time to tell you all that I shall be making Miss Halbrook my wife, just as soon as the banns can be called.' He saw Lucy's startled glance, then the tremulous smile and flush of pleasure that brightened her eyes. He held out his hand to her. 'I cannot begin to tell you how happy she makes me.'

Lucy approached, shaking her head at him.

'Why this change of heart?' she murmured as he pulled her close and kissed her fingers.

'My heart has not changed, only my head. If you are willing to take a chance with me, then I would be a fool to turn you away. I could not resist making the announcement. It was imperative that you know how I feel about you.' He added, as if to convince himself, 'It will not affect my plans. I have already ascertained that if Helene *did* have a lover the fellow is not anyone here.'

Ariadne came bustling up.

'The guests are arriving,' she declared, waving everyone into line. 'To your places, please. Lucy, you must stand with me. Come along, dear.'

Adam was scowling, and Ralph touched his arm.

'You are looking very grim, Cousin. Perhaps you had come to think of Adversane as yours?'

'What? Oh, no, no, nothing like that, I—'

The flush on Adam's cheeks gave the lie to his words, and Ralph regarded him with disdain. Adam had been his pensioner for years and had never made any attempt to rectify the situation.

'You need not worry,' murmured Ralph, as he moved away to greet the first of his guests. 'I shall not stop your allowance, even when I remarry.'

The guests were pouring in now. Ralph glanced at Lucy standing next to Ariadne. She looked adorable, the scarlet gown highlighting her flawless skin and dainty figure. There was a slight flush on her cheek and he knew she was nervous, steeling herself for the coming ordeal. He watched her as the guests moved along the line. She smiled and said everything that was necessary. As each gentleman was introduced to her Ralph registered their astonished looks, saw more than one frowning stare bent upon her, but could discern nothing more than a very natural surprise in anyone's reaction.

At last the introductions were over and everyone began to make their way into the library for the forthcoming entertainment. Ralph saw Lucy going in with Ariadne. He wished he could be at her side, but that was not possible, not yet.

'A quiet start to your evening,' murmured Harry, pausing beside him. 'No revelations as yet.'

'No, nothing. But perhaps the play will provoke a reaction,' agreed Ralph. 'I'd be obliged if you would watch for anyone taking more than a little interest in Lucy.'

'Of course. Francesca would prefer to sit at the back, in any case. In her present condition she might well have to slip away.' He hesitated. 'I hope you do not object—I told her of your plans for tonight. She knows it is in strictest confidence, of course, but I have always shared everything with my wife.'

Ralph was silent for a moment, thinking of the relief he had felt after he had told Lucy of his suspicions. He gripped Harry's arm and grinned.

'No, I do not object at all, my friend.'

Having ushered everyone into the library, Ralph took his seat at the front beside Lucy. He reached for her hand.

'Are you ready, my dear?'

'I am.' She smiled at him. 'I am quite looking forward to it. I have never seen *The Provoked Wife* before, although I believe it was very popular when Mr Garrick performed it.'

Ralph grimaced. 'In my opinion it is an unedifying piece, but it was the play they performed two years ago and I wanted everything to be as exact as possible.'

A drum roll announced the start of the performance, and silence enveloped the audience. Lucy watched the play unfold with growing disquiet. The portrayal of Sir John Brute as the drunken, buffoonish husband was nothing like Ralph, yet Lucy could imagine Helene's overwrought mind making the connection. She felt sick to her heart. Perhaps there had been no lover. Perhaps Helene had been driven to despair by her loveless marriage.

Lucy struggled through the first three acts and it was with relief that an interval was announced, and everyone repaired to the white salon for refreshments. She wanted to cling to Ralph's arm, but she knew he needed to circulate amongst his guests and he would want her to do the same, to try to stir their memories. She moved amongst the crowd, concealing her nerves behind a cheerful countenance, but her smile became genuine when she saw Mrs Dean approaching.

'Ariadne, pray stay with me a little while. I feel quite bereft of friends.'

'No, why should that be? I assure you every-one is delighted that Adversane has decided to marry again!' Ariadne patted her hand. 'I admit I was quite put out when Ralph set it about that you were his fiancée. I was not at all in favour of spreading such a tale, since there was no truth in it, but now, of course, everything has changed. I am so happy for you both. I have no doubt that you will make Adversane a perfect wife.'

Heartened, Lucy said fervently, 'I do hope you are right, ma'am.'

With her spirits somewhat restored, Lucy moved on, but still the play haunted her. Had Helene's imagination turned Ralph into the mon-ster Adam branded him? What if they proved nothing tonight, beyond the fact that Helene had taken her own life?

The thought was very daunting, because if that was so she knew Ralph would never forgive himself and she would not be able to help him. She felt the tension building into a headache and put a hand to her temple, moving towards the open windows, where the air was a little fresher.

'You look as if you might enjoy a little re-freshment, Miss Halbrook.' She swung round to find Adam Cottingham beside her. 'I do not think you have yet sampled the famous Adversane punch, have you?' He held out one of the two glasses he was holding. 'Here you are. Do try it. It is made from a secret recipe that the family has used for generations.'

Lucy realised that she was indeed thirsty and she sipped gratefully at the dark liquid. It was a mixture of wine, brandy and herbs, although there was a faintly bitter after-taste that made her wrinkle her nose. Adam laughed.

'Do not worry, one grows accustomed to it. Drink it up, now, Lucy. It is just the thing to revive you for the remainder of the evening.'

She tried to laugh.

'With two more acts of *The Provoked Wife* to endure I think I shall need it.'

'Are you not enjoying the play?'

'The performances are very good,' she replied cautiously, 'but I do not find the subject matter—boorish husbands and unfaithful wives—entertaining.'

'Do you not? Helene did not like it, either. It was too much like her own situation.'

Lucy's heart sank. So she was right—it had precipitated the poor woman's flight. She put down her glass.

'If you will excuse me, I think I should find Ariadne. The heat and noise here are making me a little dizzy.'

'No need to bother Mrs Dean,' he said. 'Let me take you onto the terrace for a moment.'

Lucy glanced out through the open doors. It *would* be cooler, but it was almost dark now, just a glimmer of light showing on the western horizon. When she hesitated Adam took her arm.

'Come, there can be no harm in it. We need only step outside the door...'

Ralph was dog-tired. Sitting through that damned play was more harrowing than he had anticipated. He hoped it would be worth it. He glanced around the noisy, crowded room. Lucy should be easy to spot in that scarlet gown, but she was nowhere to be seen. He made his way back to the Great Hall where some of his guests had congregated. He spotted Judith Cottingham moving between the chattering groups. She was such a mouse-like, unsmiling little creature and he had never really warmed to her, but now, despite his preoccupation, he felt a twinge of sympathy. He doubted if her marriage to Adam was a happy one. There was an anxious crease on her brow and he reached out to touch her arm as she passed him.

'Is anything amiss, Cousin?'

She started.

'I was looking for Adam, my lord.'

Probably flirting with another man's wife.

He was shrugging off the bitter thought when

he heard a giggle behind him and Charlotte Preston's childish voice assailed his ears.

'I certainly understand the play much better this year, Mama, but I cannot see what it is about it that made Helene cry so.'

His lips thinning, he was about to move Judith away when Lady Preston's response stopped him in his tracks.

'It wasn't the play, you silly girl,' she snapped. 'It was the scold I gave her beforehand. By heavens, I was never nearer to boxing her ears than that night!'

Ralph turned. Lady Preston had not seen him and would have walked on if he had not stepped into her path. She started, and he could tell by the dull flush on her cheeks that she had not meant him to hear her comment.

'And may I ask why you were scolding my wife, Lady Preston?'

Her cold eyes glittered angrily but her lips remained firmly shut.

'Oh, was that why you sent for Helene, Mama?' said Charlotte artlessly. 'We had all gone upstairs to change our gowns, do you remember, and I went to ask Crimplesham if she would put up my hair, only she could not because she said you had asked her to bring Helene to your room and Helene looked so guilty that I knew something must be wrong—'

Lady Preston waved a dismissive hand.

'Yes, yes, there is no need to go on!'

'Oh, I think there is every need to go on, Lady Preston,' said Ralph grimly, 'But not here.'

He took her arm and escorted her briskly out of the hall and into his study. He heard footsteps behind him and guessed Charlotte was following. Well, let her come. He was determined to get the truth from Lady Preston as soon as possible.

'Now, madam, you will explain, if you please, why you thought it necessary to admonish my wife.'

'I was saving your marriage!' When he said nothing she gave a huff of impatience. 'She was playing you false, Adversane. I am surprised you did not see it. I knew something was amiss the moment we arrived but Helene denied it. However, on Midsummer's Eve Crimplesham confessed the whole and I had her bring Helene to me. The foolish child was planning to leave you. She told me she had fallen in love and was going to run away. I soon put an end to that nonsense.'

'You never mentioned this after Helene's death,' said Ralph.

'There was no point. It could not change anything.'

'It might explain why she went out.'

'And would you want such a reason made public?' demanded Lady Preston.

'Why not?'

'She was meeting her *lover*, Adversane.

She had been meeting him at Druid's Rock
for months, although she assured me Crimplesham was always with her, and they had shared
nothing more than a few stolen kisses. You
will imagine my outrage, that any daughter of
mine should—' She broke off, breathing deeply
to control her anger. 'I convinced her that she
must remain here and do her duty as your wife.
She told me she had arranged to meet her lover
later that night but I ordered her not to go. Let
him cool his heels at Druids Rock.' She stopped
again, her eyes snapping. 'She disobeyed me.
That is what comes of your being too soft with
her, Adversane. She would never have dared to
do so before she was married. Crimplesham told
me the next morning that Helene had come crying to her, saying she was determined to see him,
to tell him it was over.'

'And who was this lover?'

'That is not important.' Lady Preston waved
one hand dismissively and began to stalk back
and forth across the room.

Ralph looked at her in disbelief.

'Not important, when you say she had fallen
in love with this man?

'Love, hah! She told me how he had courted
her, pursued her with his kind words and false
promises. She said he would take her to London
or Brighton, where there was an abundance of
good company. It was I who pointed out to her

that she would not be received by polite society in either of those places. She would be obliged to live abroad, an exile. But he had anticipated that, too, for she told me he would take her abroad, where the climate would suit her very well.

'By heaven, her infatuation was such that I believe she had lost the little wit she was born with! I scolded her mightily, I can tell you, and reminded her of her duty. Duty is all, my lord. She had a duty to you, as your wife. I told her that, since you do not appear to have done so.'

'And what of your duty to Helene? Did it not matter to you that by keeping quiet you might be shielding her murderer?'

'Not at all, as long as there was no breath of impropriety. To name him would result in the whole sorry business being dragged into the open and Helene's name besmirched.'

'And your good name means that much to you?'

'Of course it does. Think how poor Charlotte would suffer if her sister's *affaire* was known. And I was protecting your name, too, Adversane. I was determined to save us all from the scandal.'

'I would rather have had the scandal than your daughter's death, madam.'

She curled her lip.

'You may say that, but you would be singing

a different tune if she had left you, and for your own cousin, too.'

'Cottingham!' Ralph's eyes narrowed. He said slowly, 'No, you are wrong. Adam was with his wife all night.'

There was a soft whimper and he looked around, surprised to see that it was not Charlotte standing behind him, but Judith Cottingham, her face ashen in the candlelight.

'Adam escorted you upstairs,' he said to her. 'I saw him. I remember saying goodnight to you both.'

Judith was shaking.

'He...he did not stay,' she whispered. 'He made me say he had been with me all night, but it was not true. No sooner had we reached our room than he slipped out again through the side hall.' She folded her arms across her narrow chest. 'I d-did not see him again until dawn.'

He turned back to Lady Preston, observing the defiance in her eyes.

'You knew,' he said slowly. 'You knew she was meeting him that night yet you said nothing?'

'She was dead,' she retorted. 'How she died was not important.' She had the grace to look a little embarrassed. 'Besides—it may well have been an accident.'

'It was.' An anguished whisper came from Judith. 'It *must* have been an accident.'

A cold hand was clutching at Ralph's chest as he made for the door.

'Let us hope for all our sakes you are right, madam.'

The play was about to recommence and the hall was emptying rapidly. Ralph saw Harry and beckoned him over. 'Have you seen Lucy?'

'She went into the white salon, but she's not there now.' Harry glanced into the library. 'And she has not returned to her seat.'

'We must find her,' Ralph told him urgently. 'Be a good fellow and look for her.' He caught Harry's arm. 'Discreetly, of course.'

Ralph's meaningful look was not lost upon his friend.

'Of course, leave it with me. She is probably in the cloakroom gossiping with your sisters.'

'Most likely,' replied Ralph, but without conviction. He added grimly, 'I need to find Cottingham, too.'

He saw the alarm in Colne's eyes.

'You think—'

'I don't know,' Ralph ground out.

Harry nodded.

'I'll check the house,' he said shortly. 'You had best see if anyone has driven off recently.'

Ralph left him and slipped out to the stables. The whole area was packed with horses and carriages belonging to his guests. He spotted his groom amongst a noisy group of stable hands gathered in one corner of the yard.

'All our horses are accounted for, my lord,' said Greg, in answer to Ralph's enquiry. 'And none of our carriages missing. Of course with so many people here tonight there's no knowing if any of them have gone out.'

The cold band around his heart squeezed harder. Ralph issued a few terse instructions before returning to the house. He found Harry waiting for him in the hall.

'Neither of them are in the house, Ralph, I am sure of that. Nor are they in the gardens.'

'Greg is even now checking with the man we posted at the main gate to see if any carriage has left that way.'

'Perhaps we should enlist Wetherell's help, and Sir Timothy—'

'No, not yet. I need to be sure I am not merely being fanciful.' He saw the butler crossing the hall and stopped him. 'Something has come up, Byrne, but I do not wish to spoil everyone's enjoyment. Tell the players to go on without us, will you?'

With a small bow Byrne moved off, and Ralph hurried to the door, saying over his shoulder, 'Come on, Harry, we'll go to the stables and wait for Greg to return.'

They had just reached the entrance to the stable yard when the groom came running up.

'No one has left by way of the gate, my lord.'

'Then where can they be?' muttered Harry. 'Surely they would have been seen if they had crossed the open park.'

Ralph frowned and slammed one clenched fist into his palm.

Think logically, man!

No, logic would not help him here. Cottingham would not be thinking reasonably...

'He has gone to Druids Rock!' Ralph grabbed Harry's arm. 'Adam could have taken Lucy out through the gardens and to the old ride with very little chance of being observed.' He began to run. 'Harry, inform my brothers-in-law of what has happened and ask them to cover our absence. Then you and Greg follow me!'

He dashed into the stable, issuing orders as he went. As soon as the bridle was fastened on Jupiter, Ralph did not wait for a saddle but hurled himself onto the horse's back and clattered out of the yard.

'Adam, we should go back.'

Lucy stumbled through the darkness. Her head was spinning, and she could not keep her balance. Adam had one hand around her waist, and although she knew she should protest she was afraid that she would collapse if he did not support her. Her head ached too much for her to think clearly, but surely they should not be quite so far from the house?

It seemed such a long time since she had stepped outside. Adam had suggested they walk around the gardens, assuring her that the fresh air and exercise would soon drive away her un-accustomed dizziness. She must be inebriated. The punch had been very strong and she was glad she had only drunk a little. In any case she could not go back indoors in such a state. Adam was right—she must walk it off.

She was dimly aware that they had strayed a long way from the formal gardens and the ter-race. In the gathering gloom she did not rec-ognise this area at all. Then Adam pulled her through a door set into a high brick wall and she could see the palings and the black shapes of trees in the distance.

'Why have we left the gardens?' She tried to tug herself out of his grasp. 'Adam, no more. Take me back now.'

The arm about her waist tightened and pulled her along.

'It is not much farther.'

She stumbled on beside him, but when they reached the old ride a sense of danger broke through the fog in her brain.

'No!' She clung to the gate. 'No. Let me go.' Adam prised her fingers from the wood and dragged her roughly away. 'Help me! Some-one, help!'

'There is no point in shouting,' he said. 'No one can hear you at this distance from the house.'

It was impossible to resist him. She felt so tired, all she wanted to do was to lie down and sleep, yet Adam would not let her rest. She struggled to put one foot before the other as he pulled her on through the evening twilight. However, by the time they reached Hobart's Bridge the exertion had cleared her mind a little.

'You drugged me,' she accused him. 'There was something in the punch.'

'It was necessary.'

His breathing was laboured. The heaviness was easing from her limbs, but she decided it would be safer if Adam did not know this, so she continued to sag against him.

'Why is it necessary?' she asked him. 'Why are you doing this?'

He gave a sob, but did not slacken his pace as he responded.

'You cannot live. You cannot be allowed to take her place.'

'Do you mean Lady Adversane?'

'Of course, who else? I cannot allow you to marry my cousin. I am very sorry. Ralph does not deserve you.'

She dug in her heels and tried to resist him.

'But he did not kill Helene.'

He whipped about.

'Yes, he did! He d-drove her to it.'

'No. He told me what happened—'

'And do you think he would tell you the truth? He wants you to take her place. She never loved him, she loved me. *Me!* And I loved her, worshipped her.'

A chill of uncertainty made her shiver, but she pushed it aside, saying urgently, 'But this won't bring her back. Let me go, Adam. You do not really want to hurt me, do you?'

'No, of course not, but you are his punishment. I see that now. Adversane thinks he can find happiness with you, but why should he? If I cannot have Helene, then he cannot have *you.*'

Fear and the cool night air were combining to clear Lucy's mind. She realised they were heading for Druids Rock. A glance at Adam's contorted face made her shiver, for there could be no reasoning with him. She held back, making it necessary for him to half carry, half drag her along. It was slowing them down, and Lucy could only pray that it was using up his strength, too. Night was closing in but the rising moon was already giving off a faint light. If she ran away from him now there was no cover, nowhere to hide, but she must look for an opportunity to escape.

Ralph set Jupiter racing through the old ride at a gallop, but when the great horse stumbled he steadied the pace. He was riding bareback, and it would not help Lucy if he broke his neck getting to her. They crossed Hobart's Bridge and cantered on along the old track. He sat up, straining his eyes against the near darkness. The rising moon gave a little light, enough to show him the moors stretching away in every direction, desolate and empty. What if he was wrong? What if they had not come this way? He pushed aside his doubts and dug his heels into Jupiter's flanks, cantering around the ridge until Druids Rock was in sight, looming black against the night sky. There was movement on the rock's sloping incline. He could see the outline of two figures struggling. Ralph slid to the ground and ran closer, crouching in the hope that they would not see him. Adam was slowly pulling Lucy up to the top but she was resisting him, talking, arguing. The steady wind was blowing his way, so they did not hear his approach. He dropped lower into the grass and moved a little closer, concealing himself behind the thick mounds of heather that grew all around. Lucy's voice floated to him on the breeze, calm, reasoning, no hint of panic.

'Adam, please. Helene would not want you to do this.'

'Adversane never loved her as I did. I wanted to make her happy—he only ever wanted to possess her, like some beautiful trophy. He never knew the real pain of her death. And now he wants to put you in her place. He thinks you can be another Helene, but I won't allow that. And this time he will feel it. When he sees your body smashed and broken he will suffer, just as I did two years ago.'

Ralph gritted his teeth. It was as much as he could do not to break from cover and race towards them, but the risk was too great. Adam was walking backwards up the slope and pulling Lucy after him. The moon was climbing higher now, and he would have a good view of anyone approaching. Ralph calculated the distance to the highest ridge. If Adam swept Lucy up in his arms he could be at the edge before Ralph could reach them. There was only one way to approach Adam without being seen: he must climb the steep face of Druids Rock. Ralph glanced again towards the couple. Lucy was still arguing, holding back, delaying the inevitable by precious moments. It might just work.

Keeping low, Ralph turned and hurried around to the far side of the crag. Tearing off his coat, he looked up. The black rock towered over him, rising almost vertical to the sky. He had done this dozens of times as a boy, but not so much as a man, and never in the dark. The thought of Lucy being dragged inexorably closer to the precipitous drop sharpened his resolve. He put his hands against the rough stone and began to climb.

* * *

Lucy resisted with all her might, bracing her feet against each tiny ridge, but Adam forced her upwards inch by inch, stopping only when he had to reply to one of her questions. She kept asking them, using everything she could think of to slow him down. Far below in the valley she could see tiny pinpoints of red light in the darkness. The people of Ingleston were celebrating Midsummer with bonfires. She could even smell the wood smoke carried to her on the night air. In the town and at Adversane life was carrying on, and no one was aware of her plight. Ralph might not even have missed her yet. The thought made her feel terribly alone.

Concentrate, Lucy. Keep him talking.

'Tell me what you think occurred that night, Adam. Why do you hold Ralph responsible for Helene's death? He was not even here when it happened.'

'No, but he drove her to it. He wanted to possess her, and she would do anything to get away from him.'

Even through her fear, Lucy felt the stab of jealousy. Helene had been so beautiful, how could Ralph not love her, whatever he might say? Adam continued, unprompted.

'She knew it was a mistake soon after they were married. She was such an innocent. Her parents persuaded her to marry him for his money, you know. She thought he would take her to London, that they would live in society, but instead he brought her here, where he could have her all to himself. Oh, there are a few families in the neighbourhood, but Helene wanted parties and concerts every night. She needed to be admired, you see. She craved approbation. I could give her that. Ralph couldn't, it is not his way. He is too impatient, abrupt. I could see she was a delicate creature who needed to be nurtured. And I promised to take her abroad. The Italians would go wild for her fair beauty. I promised to love her and cherish her for the rest of her days.'

'But, Adam, you have a wife. What about Judith?'

He gave a wild, scornful laugh.

'An arranged marriage to a drab female no one else wanted. With Helene on my arm it would be different. Every man would envy me. And why not? Why should Cousin Ralph have everything? Let him keep Adversane and his fortune, but Helene—I wanted her. I *loved* her.'

His heart-wrenching cry tore into the night.

'I understand how you must feel—'

He interrupted her with a snarl.

'You understand nothing! She is dead, *dead*! And you are going to follow her.'

'No.'

Lucy struggled but to no avail. There was nothing she could do to prevent Adam dragging her the last few yards towards the brink and that sheer drop to certain death.

'Let her go, Adam.'

Lucy thought the deep, calm voice was in her imagination until Adam stopped. She looked past him and saw Ralph standing at the very edge of the rock, feet apart, the white sleeves of his shirt fluttering gently. Like wings, she thought dizzily. Her guardian angel.

'Never.' Adam's voice rose hysterically. 'Devil take you, Adversane. She will die, as Helene died.'

'No. I won't let you do this.'

Lucy forced herself to keep still. Adam might yet make a run for the edge, killing them both, perhaps even taking Ralph with them.

'I will stop you,' said Ralph. 'Look behind you. Colne and Greg are here, too. You cannot fight all three of us.'

Lucy glanced back. She had not heard the horses come up, but now she saw them quietly cropping the grass not far away while the two men stood at the edge of the slope, Harry Colne with a pistol in his hand. Ralph took a step nearer.

'It is over, Adam,' he said quietly. 'Let her go.'

'No!' Adam dragged Lucy hard against him. 'Why should you have everything? You think she will make you happy, another Helene to grace your house and your bed.'

Ralph was coming closer.

'Lucy is not Helene, Adam. I would not want her to be.'

'Helene is dead because of you—'

Even as Adam spat out the words Lucy felt his grip slacken a little and she wrenched herself free. Ralph reached out for her, drawing her close as Harry and Greg hurled themselves at Adam. He struggled against them, cursing, but he could not shake them off. He glared at Lucy, standing silent and trembling within the circle of Ralph's arms.

'Don't you see? He has turned you into the image of Helene. He is possessed, so much so he must replace her, even though he drove her to her death—'

The terrible logic of his words stabbed into Lucy like a dagger, making her sob. It made sense that Ralph was still in love with his wife, despite everything he had told her. She pushed her hands against his chest and stared up into his hard face, aghast. He met her eyes and gave the slightest shake of his head.

'Trust me, love. I have no secrets from you now.' His arms tightened about her and he said over her head, 'I did not love Helene, Adam, and I did not kill her. *You* did. You met her here on Midsummer's Eve. Judith has told us everything. Helene's walks here were nothing to do with nature or the druids, were they? It was not even to escape me. She came to meet you.'

'We had to meet somewhere. She could not take a carriage—the servants would have informed you, and she would not ride out alone. When I was staying at Adversane we only needed to slip out separately and meet up here. And when I was at Delphenden I would ride over and leave my horse in the woods, out of sight, while I walked up here. If anyone saw me it was easy enough to say I had business in Ingleston.' He laughed. 'We fooled you all. No one knew of our meetings.'

'Save your wife.'

Adam gave a dismissive shrug.

'Judith did not dare to speak out against me. She knew Helene was the love of my life, that nothing must come between us.'

'Oh, that is so cruel,' exclaimed Lucy.

'Judith does not need your pity. She was happy enough with the house and the children. Besides, what could she offer me, compared to my darling? Helene was too good, too kind, she did not want to hurt anyone, but at last I persuaded her that we could be happy abroad. They understand these arrangements on the Continent. But in the end she could not do it.' Adam raised his ravaged face to Ralph again. 'You tricked her, you warped her mind, hid your true nature behind a mask of kindness so that she believed she should stay with you.'

Lucy heard the barely controlled anger in Ralph's voice when he spoke again.

'So when she came to meet you, to tell you it was over, you killed her.'

'No, no. It was an accident. She slipped. It had been raining, do you remember, Cousin? The rock was wet. She came to tell me she would not leave you, that she would do her duty as your wife. Your wife!' His gaze shifted to Lucy and he said savagely, 'After all I did for her, the chances I took to meet her, to court her, I thought she loved me. I slipped away and came here to wait for her, but when she arrived it was to tell me she wouldn't leave. Adversane was a good man, she said. He was trying to make her happy, so she wanted to do her duty by him. Don't you see, Lucy? If he hadn't persuaded her to stay with him she wouldn't have refused me, we would not have quarrelled and she would not have slipped over the edge!'

Adam dropped his head in his hands as his tortured confession continued.

'I tried to reason with her, but she said she was going back. She refused to meet me again, save as your wife, Adversane. Even though it would break my heart. I tried to stop her, tried to kiss her, but she pushed me away, only she was standing too close to the edge, and lost her footing…' He fell to his knees and began to sob. 'I loved her. I have never loved anyone else. There isn't a day goes by that I don't wish I had died with her!'

Ralph stared down at him, his anger giving way to pity as he regarded the wretched figure crouched on the ground.

Harry pulled Adam to his feet.

'Come along, Cottingham,' he said. 'Let's get you back to the house.'

He and Greg began to lead Adam away. He walked quietly between them, his shoulders drooping, all resistance gone.

Ralph felt Lucy sag against him, and his arm around her tightened.

'What's this?' he muttered. 'You are not going to faint on me now?'

Her brave chuckle tore at his heart.

'No, indeed, but I am still feeling a little dizzy. He drugged me, you see, by putting something in the punch. Thankfully I did not drink it all.'

'My poor darling. Would you like to ride back? Jupiter has no saddle but there is Greg's horse, or Colne's.'

'No, thank you. I think I would be better walking it off, if you will help me.'

Lucy was grateful for Ralph's arm about her as they followed the others back to Adversane.

As they walked Ralph recounted his meeting with Lady Preston.

'So you were in no way to blame,' said Lucy when he had finished.

'Except that my warning, coupled with her mother's scolding, drove Helene to tell Cottingham she would not run away with him.'

'From what Adam said it was your forbearance that persuaded her, Ralph. Helene recognised that you were trying to be kind to her.'

'She did.' He let out a long breath. 'We were not suited and I regret what happened, but I no longer hold myself responsible for her death. I shall try to do better by my next wife, I promise you.'

She stopped and turned to throw her arms about his neck.

'Oh, my darling, I know you will.'

He kissed her then, swift and hard, and her heart sang for the love conveyed in that one embrace.

The house was in sight, and they walked on in silence, following the others around to the side hall, where it was agreed they could more easily slip in unobserved. As they neared the house, Lucy was surprised to hear the scrape of fiddles coming from the open windows of the white salon.

'I thought the dancing would be ended by now,' she murmured.

Ralph took out his watch. 'No, we have not been away that long. Supper is over, but the dancing will continue for an hour or so yet.'

'Heavens,' she replied faintly. 'I thought it must be nearly dawn.'

'It will be by the time everyone departs.'

A figure ran across from the stables and Lucy recognised Robin. He tugged his forelock.

'Mr Greg said I was to keep an eye out for you,' he said, his astonished gaze fixed on Adam, standing passively between the groom and Harry Colne.

'Aye, well, take the horses back to the stable and keep your mouth shut,' ordered Greg.

The stable lad had just led the horses away when the side door opened and Judith Cottingham appeared.

'I was looking out for you.' She stepped back for them to enter, and Lucy noted how grey and drawn she was. She stared at her husband, then raised her anxious eyes to Ralph's face. 'Is it over?'

'Yes.' He nodded. 'He has told us what happened. It was an accident, as you thought. Helene slipped and fell.'

Judith sighed and closed her eyes for a moment, then she stepped up and took Adam's arm. He was gazing before him, his eyes not seeing anything. Lucy thought she had never seen such a broken man.

'Let me take him to our room,' said Judith. 'I will look after him now.'

'If you would rather not—' Ralph began, but she stopped him with a shake of her head.

'He is my husband,' she said simply.

She led him away, and Ralph turned to Greg.

'Find someone to help you stand guard on Cottingham's door. Make sure he does not leave his room again tonight, and assure Mrs Cottingham that she may call upon you should she require assistance.'

'Should we inform the magistrate?' asked Harry, as Greg went off.

Ralph looked at Lucy, who shook her head.

'Not on my account,' she said.

Ralph agreed. 'I shall make arrangements for him in the morning, but now we know the truth I do not think he is any longer a threat. However, I would like to keep tonight's little escapade quiet, if we can.'

'Then we must go back to join your guests,' declared Lucy.

'No,' Ralph objected, frowning. 'You should rest now.'

'I do not want to rest, and my continued absence might well give rise to conjecture.'

'Then I shall make some excuse for you—'

She put a hand against his mouth, saying with

a smile, 'This is my adventure as much as yours, my lord. You shall not deny me my part in it.'

'We wouldn't dream of it, Miss Halbrook,' put in Harry before Ralph could respond. 'If Wetherell and Sir Timothy have done their work well, then it is possible we have not been missed.'

Ralph's eyes narrowed.

'Outmanoeuvred, by heaven!'

Harry laughed.

'Indeed, Adversane! I should admit defeat graciously if I were you. And *I* had best find Francesca and let her know that all is well.'

Ralph nodded. 'Very well, you go and do that now, Harry. Tell Wetherell and Finch that we are back, too, but pray keep this from my sisters if you can. I do not want them quizzing us about it just yet.'

As Harry went off, Ralph glanced down at Lucy's gown. The scarlet silk was torn and dirty from her ordeal.

'You cannot go into the ballroom like that, and if you change your gown people are bound to notice.'

She shrugged. 'They will, of course, but I shall tell them I spilled a glass of punch.' She added with a glimmer of a smile, 'Ruthie will help me and I am sure I can rely on her discretion. She has the makings of a very good lady's maid.' She saw the concern in his eyes and took his hands between her own, saying urgently, 'I want to do this, Ralph. For you. For us.'

She met his eyes steadily, trying to convey all that she felt for him. Gradually, she saw his hard glance soften to something much warmer.

'Very well.' He lifted her hand to his lips. 'Go, then. I will meet you in the ballroom.'

Chapter Fourteen

Twenty minutes later Lucy walked into the white salon, the scarlet gown replaced by midnight-blue. Ruthie had re-dressed her hair and even managed to fix the silver stars amongst her curls and they winked and sparkled in the candlelight. She looked magnificent.

Ralph felt a sudden tightness in his chest as she walked towards him. She was smiling, and he marvelled that she should look so calm and serene after all that had occurred. If anything, her green eyes glittered with an added brilliance. She positively glowed with happiness. Had there ever been a time when he had not loved her, this brave, intelligent girl who challenged him at every turn?

He took her hand and led her onto the dance floor, aware that those around them were smiling and nodding their approval. By this time formality had disappeared from the ballroom and the final dance was noisy and energetic. He watched Lucy closely, determined to whisk her away at the first signs of fatigue, but she skipped and twirled and smiled as if it was the first dance of the evening rather than the last. Ralph wanted to tell her, but whenever they came together he found himself merely smiling at her like a mooncalf.

At last the music ended, everyone applauded the small orchestra and the ballroom began to empty.

'I must take my leave of my guests,' he murmured to Lucy, reluctant to let her go. 'Come with me.'

'If you wish.'

Her smile lifted his heart. Caroline and Margaret were standing with their husbands by the door, and as he took Lucy past them Caroline put her hand on his arm.

'A pity you did not announce your betrothal to everyone after the play tonight, Brother. Meg and I were most disappointed.'

'I think Adversane had other things on his mind,' remarked Lord Wetherell.

'I cannot think what that might be,' she replied saucily, 'especially when the two of them have been smelling of April and May all evening. Why, when they were dancing they could not take their eyes off one another!'

With a laugh Ralph carried Lucy away. He

sent a footman running for her shawl and draped it carefully about her shoulders before allowing her to stand by the open door to say goodbye as their guests filed out.

A rosy dawn was already lighting the eastern sky by the time the last guests took their leave. Lucy managed to stifle her yawn until the last carriage rolled away. Ralph put his arm around her.

'Tired, love?'

'A little,' she admitted.

'Too tired to walk with me? Ariadne and the family are waiting for us in the drawing room, but I want you to myself for a little while.'

'Oh, yes, and your brothers-in-law will have told them everything by now! By all means let us stroll around the lawn. I would rather do that than answer their questions just yet.' She put her hand on his chest. 'But you must be exhausted. How *did* you manage to climb that cliff—and in the dark, too?'

He stopped and pulled her closer. 'It was easy, knowing you were waiting for me at the top.'

She closed her eyes as he kissed her, melting into him. When he stopped, she sighed and leaned her head against his chest. 'Oh, Ralph, it is quite horrible to think that Adam and Helene—'

'Then do not think of it. The Cottinghams

will leave Adversane in the morning and it will be a very long time before they are allowed back again, I promise you.'

She raised her head, peering through the darkness to search his face. 'Are your ghosts laid to rest now?'

He nodded. 'Quite gone, my love.'

'Adam's revelations were very dreadful.'

'But not as bad as I feared.'

'Do you believe him, then? That it was an accident?'

Ralph nodded slowly. 'I do. I only wish he had confessed it all at the time.'

'Then we might never have met.'

'Oh, I think the Fates would have found a way.'

She smiled up at him

'Fates, my lord? I thought you only believed in reason and logic.'

With something like a growl, he pulled her closer.

'You have changed that, darling Lucy. Now I believe in love, too.'

* * * * *

A sneaky peek at next month…

HISTORICAL

AWAKEN THE ROMANCE OF THE PAST…

My wish list for next month's titles…

In stores from 1st August 2014:

☐ Beguiled by Her Betrayer — Louise Allen

☐ The Rake's Ruined Lady — Mary Brendan

☐ The Viscount's Frozen Heart — Elizabeth Beacon

☐ Mary and the Marquis — Janice Preston

☐ Templar Knight, Forbidden Bride — Lynna Banning

☐ Salvation in the Rancher's Arms — Kelly Boyce

Available at WHSmith, Tesco, Asda, Eason, Amazon and Apple

Just can't wait?

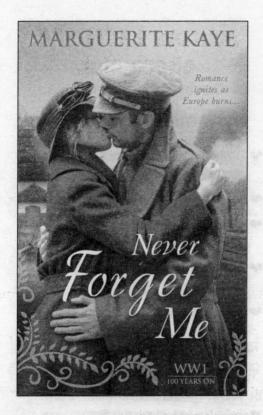

Aa a war blazes across Europe, three couples find a love
that is powerful enough to overcome all the odds.
Travel with the characters on their journey of
passion and drama during World War I.

**Three wonderful books in one from top
historical author Marguerite Kaye.**

**Get your copy today at:
www.millsandboon.co.uk**

5

Discover more romance at

www.millsandboon.co.uk

- ♥ WIN great prizes in our exclusive competitions

- ♥ BUY new titles before they hit the shops

- ♥ BROWSE new books and REVIEW your favourites

- ♥ SAVE on new books with the Mills & Boon® Bookclub™

- ♥ DISCOVER new authors

PLUS, to chat about your favourite reads, get the latest news and find special offers:

- ⓕ Find us on facebook.com/millsandboon
- 🐦 Follow us on twitter.com/millsandboonuk
- ♥ Sign up to our newsletter at millsandboon.co.uk